write
where
you
belong

THE LEAGUE OF UTAH WRITERS
2024 ANTHOLOGY

Foreward by Christine Nielson

Contents

Foreward

Christine Nielson

Since 1935, the League of Utah Writers has welcomed, supported, and educated the writers and poets of our beautiful state. This anthology is a testament to the gentle outreach and embrace of the volunteers of this organization, to the community that the League has cultivated and nurtured ever since its founding.

If you believe in magic...

If you believe in scaled dragon wings and victory through the thinnest slivers of darkness and hope...

If you believe in ghosts and the promises of tomorrow
and hear the subtle notes when the women's choir sings...

If you believe in the impression that an old soul leaves behind and the power that a new soul brings...

If you believe in you and me and the connection that we hold,
and that together with the stars our hearts beat out a song...

Then welcome, my friend, for you are *write* where you belong.

Christine Nielson
2023 League of Utah Writers Editor of the Year
www.nielsonediting co.com

What Friends Are For

Talysa Sainz

We make up stories in the park
nobody else would understand
We drive through the mountains
discussing our novels

I sleep on your floor
after partying until six am
I lay on your bed next to you
while watching The Office

You write me poetry
about being my best friend
You find me in the desert
after years of distance

We talk almost daily
now that you've moved away
We stay up all night
talking about our lives

I put my head on your shoulder
as we stare at the stars
I share with you
every funny meme I find

You introduce me to horror movies
when I need to blow off steam
You tell me I'm strong and amazing
when I am struggling

We buy each other jewelry and books
just because
We trade our favorite clothes
and pretend to be twins

I show you my favorite love songs
in our college dorm
I listen to all your secrets
and keep them hidden safe

You etch yourself on my soul
with your laughter and tears
You stick by me
even when I fail

We don't last forever,

but I still belong to you,

and you still inspire me.

CRACKED

ROBYN DABNEY

"Claudine!"

A voice calls from the other side of the glass. My eyes rise enough to catch a woman in a green beret chasing after a smaller version of herself in a yellow raincoat. Then they are gone. Like the passing trains in the dark tunnel beyond the three glass panels of my container on the platform.

Claudine. It's a nice name. I rarely hear that name.

A train arrives. The crowd that had formed on the platform moves through the open doors. The roar of metal and human voices crescendos and fades. A man approaches my window. I offer a programmed smile and gesture to the side of my case. He fumbles in the pocket of his vintage tweed and pulls out a €2 coin. I wait for the clink, clink, clink, as the coin slides into the machine and wonder which song this man will select.

The spotlight opens. I am bathed in red light. A voice sings about friends in the clouds.

"L'Amitié." I hear the song is very old.

Beneath a cascade of crimson, I raise my arms above my head and move my hips. A glittered thong covers my lower area. Has the color faded? I note a growing pile of sequins around my bare feet... a thread trailing down my rubber thigh. My eyelids close, and I trace my fingertips down my neck, along my torso, swaying to the music. The man watches. A few others stop to stare. They don't linger long.

The song ends. The spotlight turns off. I deactivate. The man walks off, and I am left with the glare from the metro's overhead lighting.

Someone bangs on the glass and screams. A group of five boys. It is almost always the young ones who do this. Never the ones who pay. They hammer their fists against my case and make interesting gestures with their hands. I watch them and wonder which song they'll choose. They don't. The ones who scream never pay.

A train comes and spills people onto the platform. Just faces. Colors. Blurs in my window. The crowd parts to either side of the glass frame, revealing a lone man. Dark, messy hair falls over his eyes. He wears hexagonal glasses with green frames. Tears rest on the flesh behind his glasses. He leans his head against my window. I offer a programmed smile and gesture to the side of my case. Slowly, he raises his eyes to me. Red eyes. Swollen eyes. I like his glasses. The green matches the fading color of my clothing.

"Can I just pay to talk to you?"

I look at my fingers pointing at the coin slot. There is no button for talk. He may select one of three songs, each lasting around two minutes.

"I don't need a dance. I need someone to talk to about how shit my life is."

We make eye contact. Why can't he just pick a song?

"What's your name?" He presses himself closer to the window, his glasses against my glass.

I look around.

"Yes, you."

"Claudine." The voice, the name, came from within my container. I did not know I could speak.

"Claudine." He whispers the name as if turning it around in his hands for a better look. "That's lovely. I'm René."

René. It is the first time someone has given me their name. I don't know where to put it, where it goes.

"René," I repeat. "You must pay €2 for a dance."

"I don't want a dance."

"But—" I only dance. If he does not want a dance, I have nothing to offer.

"Are you lonely, Claudine?"

"Lonely?"

"Yeah." The wetness from his eyes fogs his glasses. He takes them off and wipes them on his shirt. "Do you ever feel like it's just you and that no one else cares?"

"It is just me. Unless someone wants a dance. Or to scream. Or now to talk." I tilt my head and eye the strange René.

"But do you feel it, Claudine? Does it clutch your soul and make you feel like you can't breathe?"

"Breathe?" I press my hand against the glass. I would touch Rene's cheek if there was no partition.

He steps back and shakes his head. "What is wrong with me?"

Then he's gone. Outside my small window, a half-eaten pastry lies squished on the platform. Someone walks by and picks it up. The pastry and the man who ate it vanish.

———

René. I think of him often. I dance many dances. People enter and exit the train. Someone pees on my case. It dries and leaves distorted smudges on the glass.

A man drags a ratty blanket next to my case and curls up to sleep. He stays a while. Sometimes people drop coins into a cup near his face. He does not dance for these coins. Sometimes people leave food. Sometimes they say cruel things. I wonder if he feels lonely like René. Eventually, he leaves and does not return.

Another sequin falls from my dessous. A crack appears on my right hand. Maybe lonely is wishing René would return.

"Claudine."

Rene is back. Dark leather boots. Tight black pants. Hexagonal green glasses. A heavy coat with fur around the hood.

"Are you cold, René?"

He laughs. "It is winter, Claudine. Of course, I am cold."

"Winter?" I smile.

"You don't know winter?" His face slackens. He breaks eye contact and sighs. "How could you, though?"

"I can dance." I don't want him to think I know nothing when I know how to dance well to three songs.

"I do not want a dance. I just want to talk. Can you talk?"

I nod like the dogs that occasionally pass by, staring at the croissants in their owner's hands.

He rests against my window. The fur around his hood presses into the glass. It looks soft, like the dogs. "I hate that the only way to meet women is through an app and more than half of my dates occur in the metaverse. My contact with work is through a screen. I'm not even a real person there. I'm more of an avatar than a man. We all are. I miss looking into people's eyes."

"You are lonely?"

"Actually, yes." He laughs bitterly and removes a beer from the satchel hanging across his body. Many in these tunnels drink beer. "I knew you'd understand."

I like when René is pleased with something I say. "You may look into my eyes."

He drinks and then turns so his face touches the glass. I lean forward. Our heads press together. As much as they can. The train brakes screech. An announcement is made which makes the crowd on the platform groan angrily.

"You have captivating eyes, Claudine. What are they made of?"

"Cryolite. What are your eyes made of?"

"Cells and goo, I presume."

"Are they durable?" I tap my eye. It is hard and cold. Strong German glass, I recall someone saying.

"No." He laughs again. A gentler laugh. I like when he does that. "Mine are incredibly fragile."

A light in the ceiling flickers twice before going dark. It has been slowly dying. The air glows dirty, dark with creeping edges of harsh yellow.

He rolls his shoulders and glances at the empty platform. "Are you ever afraid down here?"

"What is afraid?"

"How long do you have?"

"Until someone comes for a dance."

He chuckles and raises an eyebrow. "I am afraid of many things. For one, the world is too hot."

"But you wear a coat."

A grim twist hijacks his earlier smile. "I am afraid that Delphine is pregnant."

"I thought people liked babies."

"I am afraid of my father's cancer."

"What is cancer?"

"I am afraid of nationalism."

"So, fear is a list of things you don't like? Things that have not yet but might happen?"

"Fear is like lonely, Claudine. It's about absence and pain."

I glance at the crack on my hand. Perhaps I am afraid of what happens when that crack grows too big. Or my brassiere unravels. I pick at a sequin dangling from a thread against my thigh. I did not know I could pick. I did not know the concept of picking until now. Where did that come from?

"If I lived here, where you do, I would fear the dark. The silence. The people who might wish me harm."

I release the sequin and press my hands against the glass. "Who would wish me harm?"

"I don't know. You don't deserve harm." He knocks a fist against his forehead. "I have to go."

He vanishes beyond my view, and I am left holding this thing called fear. I make space for it on the shelf next to his name, René. Next to loneliness. Sometimes I wish he wouldn't give me these to hold. I want his laughter, his smiles, and his name. I want the warm buzz beneath my rubber. But I don't want fear.

Clink, clink, clink. The coin rattles its way down into the place the money goes.

I am bathed in red light. A voice sings about someone who wakes up alone.

With a smile, I stroke my skin. Roll my hips. Stretch my arms. Another song from before my kind. I once heard a tourist with a strange accent say that a man called Frank Sinatra sang a song to the same melody.

I listen to the song for the first time. The words more than the rhythm my body sways to.

You,
You won't appear.
Still away. Every single day.
Solo,
I'll close my eyes
In this chilly, empty bed
Every single day

He sings of loneliness. My motor tightens. I feel dizzy. But my job is to dance, and so I dance. The song ends and the light fades. The man fades too. I press my fingertips to the glass and wish René would return.

The station grows quiet. Fewer trains come. Fewer people enter and exit. Someone shouts. The shouts echo around the tunnel and against the glass. A man comes into view. He throws his hands in the air and screams at someone I cannot see. He turns and sees me. Now he screams at me. I offer a programmed smile and gesture to the side of my case, though I do not wish to dance.

He rushes toward me and punches the glass. He screams and screams, and now I want to scream too. Electricity buzzes into my fingertips and into my toes.

"Are you lonely?" My voice shakes like someone poured water on the electrical outlet. "Are you afraid?"

His eyes water like René's did the first time we met. His hand freezes mid-punch. He screams again, a scream that rattles in me. And then he is gone. Out of my view.

This has happened before. Many times. But then I did not have fear on my shelf.

———

"Claudine."

"René." I smile. It is bigger than my programmed smile. It stretches the rubber at the corners of my lips and hurts. But it also feels warm.

His hair is different, shaved close to his scalp. A dark smattering of fuzz shadows his chin. "What would you do if you were not in that cage? What is your biggest dream, Claudine?"

I take my time. I want to give an interesting answer. A smart answer. What would I do? What are the things to be done? "I would drive the train," I say. "I would drive the train that swallows and spits out the people. And I would wave to whoever danced in this case. Always. So she wouldn't be lonely. Or afraid." That was smart. And kind. I wiggle my shoulders.

"A conductor?" He laughs. His face glows like the lights on an approaching train. I giggle nervously, hoping I said the right thing. "You are something special, Claudine."

"What would you be? In your dreams?" I wish I could touch his skin. I wonder what it feels like. Cold and stretchy like mine, or something else?

"Hmmm." He leans against the case, the side of his forehead pressed to the glass. People watch him and give curious glances or shakes of their heads.

"An astronaut." He winks and my eyes grow wide.

"What is that?"

"It's like a train driver, but on a train that flies into space and takes people to the moon or to Mars if they wish to join the colonies."

The rubber around my eyes stretches uncomfortably. "A flying train?"

"Here." He pulls a screen from his backpack and shows me a video of the strangest thing I've ever seen. Nothing that exists in my metro.

"Maybe I would drive this train too."

"We could drive it together," he says. He smiles, but his eyes are dim, his lips stretched thinly like the lines running along the corners of my case. Is he happy or sad? Can someone be both?

"I must go, Claudine. But I'll visit again soon."

I watch him leave and think of the flying train in a dark tunnel filled with twinkling lights. A tunnel full of sequins like those that fall from my panties. I wonder if the sequins surrounding the flying train also fall.

Dreams. I tap the glass and realize I will never see the flying train. With a glitching in my motor, I take this thing called dreams and place it next to fear, unsure what to do with it or if I even want it.

René returns often. His hair grows out to his shoulders, and then he cuts it short again. At first, he wears the green hexagonal glasses, but eventually he shows up with clear eyes. He said he had a procedure and now he can see. He no longer needs the frames. I wish I no longer needed the glass around me. The lines on his forehead deepen. They are his version of the cracks on my hand.

He shares photos of strange animals with long necks and sharp teeth. Teaches me words in curious languages called English and Arabic. He describes the taste of an eclair and the smell of a patisserie. He talks of protests in the streets for higher wages and cheaper hydrogen prices. Of masses begging their governments to save this planet and not keep shipping their people to other, less beautiful worlds. He shares stories of his father's illness. Of the mother who died young. Of his brother, who took the space train to Mars a few years back. Of his cat, Alban, who he can't bring to see me because Alban hates leaving his apartment. I laugh often and make space on the shelf for joy. I ache at his tears and his pain. I glow when he glows. What is this thing inside me that moves without programming? This thing that pulses and grows and absorbs each new feeling? My existence becomes a blur of dancing, trains, and René.

***

"Claudine."

His eyes are downcast. Red and puffy. His hair is unwashed and askew, as if he is one of the metro dwellers. The screamers.

"Your father?" I ask. I wish I could reach through the glass and touch him. I see people embrace on the platform and their faces almost always look happier, lighter, after. I cannot give that to René. All I can do now is listen and dance. "Is he unwell?"

"The cancer has spread. It is in his bones."

I peer at the crack in my hand, now a centimeter longer. I fear the crack, as he and his father must fear the cancer. It is a terrible feeling, fear.

"I am sorry, René. This is not something anyone should have to go through. It is not fair."

He chuckles through his tears and smiles sadly at me. "You are a good person, Claudine. Kinder and gentler than most. How is it possible that you do not have a soul?"

"What is a soul, René? Perhaps I have one. They implemented many special features into my model."

He wipes the wetness from his face and shakes his head. "Souls require flesh and blood. They require..." He tosses his hands in the air. "I don't know, DNA, and perhaps a god." He traces his fingers across the glass, outlining my face. "I know they are not built in a German factory."

"I think I have a soul," I whisper. "Since meeting you."

"Trust me. The Germans don't incorporate souls into anything."

"Do your avatars have souls?"

"Well, no, but also yes."

"Are your virtual encounters more real than our encounters?"

"The avatars don't have souls, per se, but the people behind them do. You can't compare yourself to an avatar."

"So, these dates you go on, these work meetings, this meta-verse... It all exists between the soulless?"

"More like between those with a soul once removed." His eyes sparkle as he chuckles. "You have a brilliant mind, Claudine. A savant philosopher."

I have understood and believed most of what René has shared, but in my motor, this feels wrong. Something is alive in me that is not quite me. Something that enables me to laugh and to feel sorrow. I am more than any avatar could hope to be.

"Claudine!"

Electricity buzzes through me. I press against the glass and greet René with a grin. Silver threads, like thin strands of metal streak through his hair. I don't remember those. When was the last time he was here? The lines around his mouth have deepened and tilt downward. He looks sad even though he smiles. I've learned that one can carry more than one emotion.

"You added color?" I point to his head. Something warm spreads through me. I think it is joy. Joy burns, but in a good way. Joy might be my favorite.

He touches his head and laughs. "No Claudine, time has colored it for me."

"Time? How?"

"That's an interesting topic. How much time do you have?"

I cock my head, and he laughs. The laugh booms over the roar of an incoming train. He brought something rectangular, which he places on the ground in front of me.

"What is that?"

"I want to dance, Claudine."

I lift my arm to point at the place where he must insert €2. He waves me away and rolls his eyes.

"Not like that. I want you to dance for you. Not for me or for anyone else. Not to the songs you've heard a million times or with the motions they programmed you with. I want you to hear something new, and I want you to experience how you move within the melody."

I press my hand to my chest and step back. I don't wish to disappoint him or to make a fool of myself. I like performing the dances I know. The ones I'm good at. He seems to read my thoughts.

"Do not think of me. Do not think of anyone else. Feel this, Claudine. With everything you know. Touch the rhythm with loneliness. With fear and joy. Close your eyes if you must."

I close my eyes. Light glows through the thin rubber lids. Music filters into my case. I crack my eyelid and see that it comes from the rectangular object on the ground. The rhythm begins quickly with the tapping of piano keys that is joined by a woman's crooning voice. She sings at first in one of those peculiar languages, English perhaps. I move my hips, unsure of what to do with my arms outside what I've been programmed to do. The rhythm grows, and she switches to French. The song tells a story. I think it might be sad, but I am having fun. I open my eyes.

"Let go," René pleads.

I bite my lip and then grin. My hands rise above my head. I stomp my feet and twirl, spinning my arms and filling the entirety of my space. René joins me. From the other side of the glass, he spins and laughs. People stop to watch him, giving him the gaze I often see reserved for the men who scream at wastebaskets. He dances harder and faster. I do too. The song ends and we both fall against the glass, laughing.

"And?" he asks.

"I feel... free." I stare and my fingers, making them each dance to their own independent rhythms. I tap them on the glass, mimicking the rhythm of the song that finished playing.

His eyebrows draw together. His shoulders slump. "I want to kiss you. What I wouldn't give for you to be real."

I touch my lips, running my finger across the smooth rubber. I feel real. "What if you break the glass?"

"What?"

"Break the glass. Take me with you. I want to pet Alban."

"I could go to jail. I can't break you out. I'm so sorry." A train arrives. He glances quickly between me and the opening doors. He darts away.

He vanishes into the train and is swept away into the darkness. I want to scream, so I scream. I bang on the glass and shout like the men who do not pay. I yell until my voice shakes. The glass remains untouched, but the crack on my hand grows. Metal cords spark in a twisting maze. I lift my hand to my face and wonder at the cancer spreading through René's father's bones. These are my bones. These metal fragments. Somewhere in those wires lies a soul. Maybe not like René's soul. My bones are also different, but that doesn't mean they aren't real.

Somewhere to the side of my field of view, a violin plays. The high-pitched melody of the strings sound like the train braking if the wheels were made of heartache and the tracks of lace. Floating on the wings of each note are the things René has left me with. One note is loneliness. The next fear. Another is anger and longing.

I press against the glass, my cheek and eye smashed as close to the partition as possible, straining to glimpse whoever plays the music. This music is a soul, or it has a soul. And if music, an ethereal twirling of notes through the air, can have a soul, then I can too. I want to pull the musician close and ask her to stay until René returns. If only he can hear the music, he will understand.

"Claudine."

"René."

His voice is low and raspy. It is the time of night when the station is mostly quiet. The trains come once an hour. The people who come and go appear weary or drunk. René looks neither tired nor intoxicated. His eyes are wide and shift back and forth to parts of the tunnel I cannot see. He wears dark clothing, a dull scarf that looks like it was once a vibrant blue, and a hat pulled low over his face, covering his long bangs. He wears dark shades.

"Why are you not sleeping, René?"

He looks around again then holds up a hammer and offers a nervous smile. "I've come to set you free."

I press against the glass. My motor sputters and the wires beneath the rubber spark. "Oh, René. I can meet Alban and see the starlit tunnel and smell the crepes!"

"All of it, Claudine. I must be mental. Truly, what am I doing?" He laughs again, and it carries so much joyful energy, I think it could power me for a week.

"Will you kiss me when I'm out?"

"I have dreamed of nothing less. Now stand back."

I move to the back of the container, though it is not big. I cover my face and peer at René through my fingers. I am not lonely or afraid. I am whatever the opposite of those things are.

He glances furtively around again and raises the hammer. My fingers clench into fists. I close my eyes. I hear a thud and crack an eyelid. The glass looks the same.

"What happened?"

"It didn't work." René stares from the hammer to the glass to me.

"Try again."

He does. Over and over until sweat runs down his face. Eventually the glass cracks. Spiderwebs spread across the front, dainty lines on a map to freedom. I can no longer see René. He vanishes behind the shattered glass. He hammers away, but the spiderwebs do not crash to the ground. They cling together like desperate lovers.

"It's not working, Claudine! Shit. It's not going to work."

"Please, René! Keep trying." I can't see him. I can't see anything.

"I can't do it." His voice. It sounds far away and hollow, like the tunnel when a train passes through. "I'm stupid. So stupid."

"I'm afraid," I whisper, tracing my finger across the cracks in the glass. They look like the growing crack on the back of my hand.

"You can't be afraid. You aren't real." His voice is cold. Cold as I imagine winter to be. "You are just another trick. Another way to keep me from actually connecting with real people. Shit. I am an idiot."

Disembodied words assault me through the glass. If we could only see each other, it would be okay. If he could just see my eyes. He once said they were nice. "René, please! I am real. I feel afraid. I feel sad. I love you."

"You can't love!" he screams. The ones who scream never pay. "You can't fucking love! You are a robot. They made you in a factory to dance for pathetic men. That's why you're down here in the dark."

"No," I whimper.

Stomping boots fade away.

"René!" I wish I could cry. I wish I could breathe so that I could hold a breath. My pain must stay inside me. It has nowhere to go. But it's so strong it could rupture my rubber, short my circuits. I don't know what it is, but it is real. I slump against the back wall and curl into a ball. René is gone. I know it in the depths of my...

Eventually, someone comes, though I cannot see their face through the shattered glass. They paste a few strips of what looks like yellow tape across the front of my case and leave. I remain on the floor, and no one comes to see me. Not René. Not someone wishing for a dance. The glaring light remains on, spotlighting my grief. Trains come and go. Angry people shout. Joyous people sing. The violinist returns. The notes pierce the soul I do not possess.

I don't know how long I sit, but eventually, I hear noises—drilling, scraping. I blink as the glass is pulled away. Unfamiliar air hits me. It smells warm and buttery, stale and acrid, earthen and metallic. I open my mouth to taste it.

Two men stand in front of me, staring down. I gape at the world beyond the edges of my cage and barely register their faces.

"You think she's broken too? Never seen one of them sit like that."

"I don't know. Check her with the prod."

I don't care what the prod is or what these men will do to me. I stare around them as they hook me up to some machine and send electricity through my body. I hear the giggle of a child. The bark of a dog. The voices exchanged between lovers. Clear. All so clear without the muting presence of glass. I wish I could touch it, wrap my fingers around it all, and pull it close. I will make space on the shelf for every bit of it.

"She seems fine. Needs some new clothes and a patch on her hand. Can't believe they don't just replace her."

Something cold presses against my hand. One of the men removes my clothes. I pay no attention to their actions. All I want is to be part of the world beyond the glass for as long as possible.

A man approaches my window. I offer a programmed smile and gesture to the side of my case. He fumbles in the pocket of his vintage tweed and pulls out a €2 coin. I wait for the clink, clink, clink, as the coin slides into the machine and wonder which song this man will select.

The spotlight opens. I am bathed in red light. A voice sings about friends in the clouds.

"L'Amitié." I hear the song is very old. My kind did not exist then. Beneath a cascade of crimson, I raise my arms above my head and move my hips. A glittered thong covers my lower area. My eyelids close, and I trace my fingertips down my neck, along my torso, swaying to the music. The man watches. A few others stop to stare. They don't linger long.

The song ends. The spotlight turns off. I deactivate. The man walks off, and I am left with a glare from the metro's overhead lighting.

I recognize the faded blue scarf before I know it's him. René. He's returned! He exits the train with a crowd of people and walks toward my case. His eyes seem to match his smile now. The happiness extends beyond the corners of his mouth. I grin and wave, wanting to tell him I got to hear the unobstructed sounds of the metro and see beyond the corners of my glass cage, if only for an hour. I want him to know that even if I cannot be with him in his world, I'd love to continue our chats in mine. I want whatever relationship is possible for us.

His eyes meet mine but immediately shift away. I wave frantically again, but he doesn't look. René passes by so close I could touch his arm if there was no glass. He holds hands with a woman who must possess a soul. Her hair holds no silver. Her belly is round. They disappear beyond my view.

I clutch my chest but do not collapse. I have spent enough time curled at the base of my cage. I have spent enough time desperate to cry tears I am incapable of forming. I take his name from the shelf and throw it out of my case in the direction he went. He can give it to someone else. I keep the rest though, each feeling he imparted into my programming. I do not like fear. I dislike loneliness. But only with those things do I feel alive. My cabinet of emotions is my soul. Each time I add to it, my soul grows.

A young girl in a yellow raincoat walks by. She stops and smiles, waves, then covers her face and turns red. I smile and wave back, then I bend down to her eye level and place my hand against the glass. The crack in the rubber is gone, glued together with an almost imperceptible suture. My dessous and brassiere are a rich purple, full of sparkling light, like the tunnel of the space train.

"What's your name?" I ask the young girl.

"Esme," she squeaks.

"I'm Claudine."

"You're pretty, Claudine." She squeezes a stuffed monkey and grins. Her cheeks turn even redder, crimson like the spotlight when I dance. Her fragile eyes are green.

"You are too, Esme."

She giggles and then runs off to join her mother. I stare after her and wonder where on the shelf to put pretty. There is an empty space between loneliness and fear where a name used to sit. Perhaps I'll place it there.

MIDNIGHT MUSINGS

C. H. LINDSAY

As midnight settles 'cross the sky
it muffles lingering sounds of men
inhabiting the later shifts—
and those dark-dwelling introverts.

Within the solemn quietude,
I don my skin of make-believe,
and let my soul-fueled artistry
spin threads of musings lyrical.

I dance with distant dragonlights
to songs the universe still sings
that resonate with fairy tales
and mysteries awaiting shape.

My Muse and I work as a team
to fuel the fire that gives words life
and scents the air with magic hues
from stories that my mind invokes.

The words spark through my darkened room
and fill it with an inner flame
that burns away reality.
Then, only what I choose remains.

Harmony

Benjamin Martin

"I think we should put in a pickleball court," one resident suggested as she leaned forward from the couch in our crowded living room.

Not again! I thought. We'd been through this discussion before.

Forty-seven years prior, I studied "Group Dynamics" in college business classes and then received additional training from my employer in the factory where I worked for twenty-seven years. A group can accomplish more than individuals—if the group works together in harmony. Sixteen years after retirement, the stages of "Forming, Storming, and Norming" came back through the cobwebs of my mind as I presided over a meeting of our soon-to-be-formalized homeowners association (HOA).

Twenty-one houses with residents aged 55+ living in the Pinnacle Heights subdivision would form the association. Our new neighborhood included a rousing mixture: married couples and single women, retirees and working people, college professors, a grocery store employee, a retired private jet pilot, a truck driver trainer, a former rocket scientist, secretaries, and people of different religious and political persuasions. No wonder divergences surfaced when we got together.

The owners who attended our Forming meeting embodied strong personalities and displayed the individual roles in Group Dynamics I had studied. Hence, the spirited debate over amenities, landscaping, and lawn care. I anticipated no problems from Karen, whose body language, sinking back into the couch cushions, suggested she was a *yes person,* or from Julie, purposely sitting as far back as possible into the dining area acting as a *timid observer.* Sally played the role of *disagree-er* and campaigned for a pavilion and a pickleball court.

"Those things would increase the cost of insurance," Frank, the *informal group leader,* retorted. "The first thing insurance companies ask an HOA is, 'What amenities do you have?'"

Thank you, Frank!

As I considered the operation of our HOA group dynamics, my mind floated away from the current chaotic gathering to a particular Monday morning staff meeting before work began at the factory. The group included engineers, supervisors, a scheduler, and operators. Our manager discussed some recent production problems and lectured us on teamwork. I sensed an unusual tone of frankness in his voice.

"Guys, I know we can do better," he pleaded. "We just have to communicate with each other, keep the goal in mind, and work as a team.

"Think about an orchestra," he went on in earnest, and being an avid concertgoer, I related. "The whole program is planned out and rehearsed in advance. Then, everything runs as planned—like a symphony."

The scheduler, the *disagree-er* in the group, raised his hand.

"Yeah, but you know how this factory runs? Every morning,

you throw out the puck into the middle of the rink, and we all madly run after it no matter where it goes until the whistle blows, and then we go home and rest up for the next game."

I wished then our work center group could perform with the unity of an orchestra, but I knew it wouldn't happen. Not with the conductor standing before us who was anything but a maestro.

Now, I tried to coordinate the orchestration of thirty-six divergent players in the performance of neighborhood life ahead. All we had in common were our senior ages and our $125 monthly fees. My wife and I didn't base our decision to join the subdivision on who already lived here. We just joined the ensemble and were trying to get along as best we could—striving for harmony.

As appointed interim *formal leader,* I stood beside the baby grand piano in our two-year-old, single-level house as a dozen fellow residents sat in turbulent discussion, scattered on furniture in the great room/dining area. Had the entire group of thirty-six people attended, it would have been shoulder-to-shoulder standing room only.

Everybody had an opinion to express at the same time. Our discussion kept going off on tangents—definitely the group Storming stage.

Every group has a *formal leader* and an *informal leader.* I appreciated Frank's informal support, that is, up to the point where he threatened my position as *formal leader.* Frank, slim and energetic, had been an HOA president before and held definite opinions on how things should be run. Yet, because of his previous experience, he utterly refused to take the reins ever again.

Like Frank, those present who had previous HOA experience voiced their refusal to be elected president. Somebody needed to take the lead when the organization became official in a few months and the developer stepped out of the picture. It felt like the Little Red Hen asking for help to plant wheat to make bread.

"Not me!" everybody said.

This was my first time in an HOA. My naivety led me to accept the developer's appointment to head the group until the association became official.

Expectations for our new subdivision differed.

"When I moved in," Dorothy said in a *know-it-all* group role, "I presumed the lawn would be completely maintained like in my last HOA." Dressed in a flowered blouse, her curled gray hair and New York attitude exuded authority.

"I don't want anybody touching my lawn!" Frank piped in again. "I do the whole thing. I don't want anybody nicking up my fences with their mower."

"You know, folks," I said, "our HOA pays for mowing service —to those who want it, Frank—but I thought we had responsibility for fertilizing and weed control of our own yards. I'm just following my neighbors on both sides."

"Some of the yards look weedy and downright raunchy!" Jerry interjected with a raised voice. His behavior and his attire in a bright-colored sweatshirt displaying the colors of the rival of the local university reflected his group role as the *devil's advocate.*

Hoboy. Here we go! The day before the meeting, Jerry had threatened to move if our neighborhood didn't look better soon.

I knew opinions differed because I'd fielded other complaints before the meeting.

I struggled as the *formal group leader.* How does an HOA make a rule limiting how many flowerpots one can have on the front porch? And how do you resolve one resident's concern that another resident's property looks like a flea market with whirly-gigs and knick-knacks? Further, why can't the developer get rid of the two extra vehicles in the subdivision that violate the rule by being parked outside a garage?

The verbal exchanges erupted like a volcano with lava flowing every which way. The volume, temperature, and pressure in the room rose as the group bounced on through the Storming stage!

"I'll be the president if you pay me a salary and give me insurance benefits," Tom, our group's *joker*, offered with a grin.

The shared laughter lowered the temperature in the room. Still, sweat beaded on my forehead.

At last, soft-spoken Steve made a welcome suggestion:

"Why don't we just vote on it?"

Everybody likes Steve, always smiling and without a mean bone in his body, fulfilling the *good-old boy* role in our group.

We took his suggestion and came to terms. Majority ruled.

After my wife ushered out the last guest, I collapsed on our couch, arms and legs spread like a five-point star.

"You know, Ben," she said, "they're going to elect you as the first official president, don't you?"

"What have I got myself into?" I replied.

I sent an email summarizing our agreements and clarifying the services provided by the HOA versus those left to the individual owners.

Over the next few months, our group entered the Norming stage as we fine-tuned and approved the organization's by-laws prepared by the subdivision developer. I kept communication open through texting and emails. The by-laws and the Covenants, Conditions and Restrictions of Ownership (lovingly referred to as the CCRs) spelled out the responsibilities of the president and other officers on the board of directors. As I studied all the rules, the duties of the president, and the agenda for the election meeting, I swallowed hard. My mouth remained dry, and my chest tingled. A sinking feeling told me my wife was probably right.

Nineteen weeks after that first lively meeting, at the end of September, my temporary assistants and I convened the election meeting wherein the developer would legally turn the association's operation over to the residents. In the interim, owners became more acquainted, the group accepted compromises over landscaping issues, and a better feeling settled over the neighborhood. We realized we would be spending many years together, and the commonalities of age and proximity had better outweigh our differences.

Eighteen people attended the election meeting held in our next-door neighbor's home. They represented twenty of the twenty-one lots (some by proxy). Julie, the hostess, served refreshments, and a congenial atmosphere prevailed as residents arrived and mingled. Getting down to business, we discussed our finances and decided how much to maintain in our slush fund. The voting was unanimous not to raise the monthly fees. I presented the status of the landscaping and lawn services, which only brought two complaints.

"I don't like having the mowers come in the evening when we're cooking and eating on our patio," Frank objected.

I wanted to say, *But Frank, you won't let them on your property anyway. What's the big deal?* But I bit my tongue.

"Sorry, Frank," I said, with a smile that probably didn't help. "I've talked to them about that, but they have day jobs. So, they have to come here in the evening. Maybe next year the new board can retain a different company."

His scowl told me he was not satisfied, but he backed off.

"What about the ugly retention pond?" Dorothy called out.

"Yeah, well, that's another problem for the new board," I said. "The developer has done all he's required to do by law."

She didn't look appeased either, and I felt sorry for the new president.

"Moving on, it's time to elect officers," I said.

"I nominate Ben for president," Frank offered.

"I second the motion," Jerry said, throwing his hand ceilingward.

"Who else?" I pleaded. "Any other nominations?"

"That's a joke!" Tom said. "We only need one victim. I move nominations cease."

I didn't laugh.

"Second," Dorothy said.

"All in favor of Ben for president?" Frank took over as the *informal leader.*

All hands went up. My mouth fell open, and my knees wobbled.

"Congratulations, Ben," Frank said, but his facial expression said, *Sucker!*

I appreciated the support of the other four elected board members as I assumed the responsibilities of president. I posted "No Trespassing" signs on the common areas, arranged for snow removal, and hired a different lawn mowing outfit for the following year.

When Christmas came, residents exchanged gifts with each other, homemade candies, ornaments, cookies, etc. In the spring, the board organized a potluck picnic in the backyard of one of the owners, which drew most of the group. My heart warmed to see people visiting together, mostly with neighbors closest to them. We had reached the Norming stage; harmony had come to Pinnacle Heights.

While I communicated with people and acted as referee on occasion, my job brought the advantage of getting to know everybody, not just my nearest neighbors. Walking to the end of the street to the mailboxes became a pleasant activity.

"Hi Ben," and a smile greeted me from whoever was outside.

The diversity of our group enriched the friendships my wife and I developed with our fellow travelers on life's journey. We attended church with members of our faith and tubed down the canal with our non-Christian neighbors. My wife found our next-door neighbor Julie to be a soulmate and could talk with her for hours, but she also felt a strong bond with Dorothy, though their backgrounds differed dramatically.

However, ripples still spread, especially over the retention pond. Like in our Storming stage, opinions differed on how to handle things. I appointed an ad hoc pond committee representing all the points of view. Together, we worked up several options, which I presented at a special meeting held in Frank's garage, where we sheltered from the summer rain. We couldn't afford a Cadillac approach without raising monthly fees.

"I vote we adopt the cheapest option," Frank said. "All in favor?"

Hands went up as the group followed the *informal leader* again.

Frank, still unwilling to be in an official position on the board, agreed to become our watermaster to regulate sprinkler operation for the common areas. As I relied on his expertise, *formal* and *informal leaders* learned how to work together.

Throughout the summer, our HOA displayed a spirit of cooperation and joint pride in our environs. All owners spruced up their yards, and some residents took it upon themselves to improve the appearance of our shared areas. Several members of our subdivision willingly accepted assignments to spray for weeds in various corners of our property.

As the end of the year approached, I looked forward to completing my service. I hoped I had done some good in bringing our group together. Our association was running smoothly and under budget. People kidded me about fulfilling another two-year term. I tried to be as assertive as the others who absolutely refused:

"No way! Let's give someone else the opportunity."

In December, a text message from Karen appeared on our GroupMe text string presenting a Christmas option. Instead of the neighborhood gift exchange, she offered to collect money and food to donate to the local food pantry. Residents unanimously accepted the suggestion, and the project united us further as an association. Karen took a trunk load of food and $500 to the pantry, and they told us how much they appreciated our donation.

What a great example of a group accomplishing more than individuals. The Forming, Storming, and Norming of our HOA took on a higher purpose than just getting along together as neighbors—a tradition that will continue.

Frankly though, I was relieved not to worry about delivering clever Christmas somethings to twenty houses to "keep up with the Joneses." Then, a few days before the 25th, a little bag of homemade peanut brittle appeared on our porch.

"This is awkward," I told my wife. "Maybe the Smiths didn't get the message."

"Maybe they didn't want to participate in the food pantry thing," she said.

"So, what do we do now?"

"We take them some of our cookies."

"But . . ."

"I know."

On our way to run errands, we placed our package on the Smith's doorstep. Driving down the street, we saw the Smith's red-and-green sacks on all the other porches. Then I laughed as I saw Karen headed toward the Smith's house with a little gift. I wondered if the Smiths would receive twenty Christmas somethings and if anyone would tell them about the food pantry option.

———

It's January as I write this essay. A storm has piled up heavy snow, but the sun shines brightly today, reflecting in brilliance off the white blanket over the landscape. I'm breathing easy, and a smile crosses my face. The annual election meeting for the HOA took place a week and a half ago. Two people stepped forward to fill the vacancies on the board of directors, and Steve took my place as president. He'll do a great job.

I love having lawn care and snow removal taken care of by the

HOA. And now, I'm no longer concerned about the snow depth on the road and my driveway, and whether it exceeds two inches, necessitating a call to the plowing crew. I'll leave it to Steve.

Thinking about the rich friendships I've developed in our new subdivision warms my chest. In our previous neighborhood, we never experienced the closeness we have here.

Life is good!

Outsiders Need Not Apply

Caryn Larrinaga

I thought my interviewing days were over, but here I am, sitting across a desk from the midnight manager of the Misty Hollow Inn with my proverbial hat in hand. What I wouldn't give for an actual hat. Anything to dress up my lime green, off-the-shoulder sweatshirt and neon pink leg warmers.

The manager, Reina, is clearly as unimpressed with my outfit as I am. I'd kill to look like her. She has the good luck to be dressed for the job in a polka-dotted blouse and pencil skirt. Wide gold bracelets encircle her wrists, clinking slightly as she leans back in her chair and folds her arms.

"Alright, Lizzy," she says. Her accent reminds me of Katherine Hepburn in her *Philadelphia Story* days. "Why don't we start with why you want to work here?"

An easy one. Phew.

I skip over the immediate thought that comes to mind, which is that the smell of clean linens has been a lifelong favorite, and start with the basics. "I've always loved hotels. My family stayed in one once when I was a kid, and I thought it was the fanciest thing ever. I thought we were rich, just for one night."

"Was it this hotel?"

"No, it was in Texas, where I lived my whole life."

"Then why come here?"

"I saw the inn on the cover of a travel magazine on someone's bedside table, and I kind of fell in love with it. The gargoyles and everything are so cool. So spooky. So, it just feels like a good fit, considering."

"Spooky," she says flatly.

"Yeah."

Reina looks heavenward for a moment and sighs through her nose. "Everyone who died after *The Shining* came out expects us to be the Overlook Hotel. I tell you, there aren't enough bathtubs in the world for all the ghosts who want to haunt them."

"It's not like that," I insist, squashing the honest part of myself that, yes, had thought working in a hotel would at least be a *little* like the Overlook, but without the whole let's-make-the-caretaker-murder-his-family bit. "There are just so many stories of hauntings in hotels. My aunt has seen ghosts in four separate places. It feels natural."

"You're right about that, at least," Reina says. "It's as natural as water. Everywhere the living go, they leave a trickle of energy behind them. When they travel in a large group, the trail becomes a river. And when many of them come and go from the same place, lingering for a few days at a time, that river becomes a concentrated lake of spiritual energy that holds on to the souls of those that die here. Why, it even attracts spirits from the surrounding area. Outsiders." A snide smile teases the puckered corner of her mouth. "Like you."

Her words are a kick to my belly, and I sag back against the chair so forcefully that I think I might sink through the fabric and onto the floor. It took a long time for me to stop involuntarily drifting through furniture, and the feat requires more strength of will than I have at present.

I can feel her eyes on me, judging me, and I strain to pull myself back into a proper sitting position. When I finally dare to look her in the eye, something in her expression breaks. She uncrosses her arms and leans forward, clasping her hands over her desk's green plastic blotter.

"You must understand," she says. The edge in her voice has almost, but not quite, been wholly replaced by pity. "The basic fact is that we don't have any openings at present. We're a popular place for both the living and the dead. Very few of our staff choose to move on once they've settled here."

I wince. *Move on.* It's something we only get a few chances to do, and if you miss your first opportunity, you have to wait for Samhain to try again.

If you even want to.

"What about when they do move on, though?" I ask. "Is there a waitlist or something? Like, could you keep my resume on file, or...?"

Reina eyes me. The moonlight from the window behind her highlights the fine wisps of energy coming off her spectral form. The wisps wave back and forth like seaweed beneath the ocean's surface, and I feel my mind trying to wander away from the reality of this moment and the oncoming rejection.

She taps her thumbs together twice. "I suppose I can keep your application on file. *If*—" She raises an eyebrow. "—I think you're a good candidate, at any rate. So. How long has it been since you crossed the veil?"

Straightening, I tell her, "Two years." I want to add that they've been the longest two years of my life, but since that word isn't relevant anymore, I skip it. But damn, have they felt long.

"And you've haunted before?" she asks.

I shift in my seat, dipping through the cushion again for an instant before righting myself.

"I'll take that as a 'no,' then," Reina says.

"No," I say hurriedly. "I have. It just hasn't been, um...."

"Ideal?"

I grimace. "To put it mildly."

The day I died, it took me hours to come to terms with the fact that it was my body lying in the middle of the street. Before long, a paramedic threw a sheet over me, but the image of my twisted limbs, bloodstained workout clothes, and dead eyes will be with me forever.

By the time I processed that I was dead, the glowing doorway across the road was already fading, and by the time I figured out what it was, it had vanished completely. Now I know it was the initial gateway to the other side, but there was nobody around to tell me when it really mattered. I missed my shot.

I wandered around the city in a daze for a couple of days and eventually found myself in one of my favorite places: the modern art gallery downtown. Looking at the artwork cleared the fog, but that just opened me up to the pain again. I stood in front of an abstract sculpture of a bear and felt sorry for myself until Bertie and Blanche found me.

They had died when they were good and old, long outliving their own senses of adventure. I think they thought of me as a great-grandchild or something. They looked after me, helped me get my bearings.

After just a few months, I found my feet. I don't know how you feel about it, Reina, but I realized that the one great thing about being dead is being a ghost. I was excited to lean into that and start haunting somebody.

It was harder than I imagined.

Do you remember how long it took you to move stuff around? It took me weeks of practice to blow a single sheet of paper off the gallerist's desk, only for him to write it off as the air conditioning.

After another two months, I triumphantly stole a marker and wrote a spooky message on the gallery floor after hours. He thought it was an assistant fooling around. I whispered weird stuff into his ear and got into his television to make the screen flash words like 'ghost' and 'haunted' and 'dead,' but he just swapped out the battery in his hearing aid and called a TV repairman. It drove me bonkers.

Bertie and Blanche had no interest in helping me. Those two had "lived" in the gallery because the only thing they both loved more than art was people-watching.

I asked them why they didn't just move on, and—

Yeah, I wince when I think about it now, too. I didn't know how rude that question is until they scolded me and explained that it's right up there with 'how did you die?' and 'how long ago?' Things only nosy paranormal investigators and psychics ask about.

But because I'm young in both life and death, they answered my question. They said they're happy enough at the gallery that they don't feel a need to move on. Why risk a happy afterlife for whatever's waiting on the other side? It could be worse. It could be nothing. They told me the gallery wasn't the right place for me and that I need to find my own brand of happiness, at least until next Samhain.

I took their advice, and I left.

———

Reina smiles. "Those lovely women sound like 'lurkers.' We have a few here. Every place on earth has at least one or two. But lurking isn't the afterlife for you, I take it."

I shake my head.

"Is that all?" Reina asks. "Just the one haunting?"

"No. There was... another."

"Another lurking?"

I shudder. "Not even close."

Back then, I knew I wanted something more exciting than haunting someone who didn't have enough imagination to even wonder if I was there, so I tried to think of haunted places I'd heard about before I died—anywhere people had shied away from because even the rumors about the place terrified them.

And then I remembered the Buckley House.

Have you ever heard of it, Reina? No? I guess it must only be a local legend where I grew up, then. It's across the street from my high school. There are huge black stains around all the windows from a fire that drove out the previous owners, and the windows themselves are boarded up and covered with graffiti. I don't really know why it's even still standing. Somebody should have torn it down after the fire, and that was decades ago.

People say the Southeast Slayer buried a few victims under the foundation while the house was being built. Kids from my school went there all the time on dares, and the rumor was that one kid's hair turned white when his friends locked him in a closet in an upstairs bedroom.

So, I went. I found three spirits there.

Sorry. I just need a moment. This is... hard.

Okay.

They called themselves Snap, Crackle, and Pop, like the cereal. And they weren't like Bertie and Blanche. They didn't like people-watching.

But they *loved* visitors.

The very first night I was there, a group of teenagers snuck in after midnight. They had beer and a boombox, and it was pretty clear they didn't believe in ghosts. We changed that in a hurry.

It was exhilarating! I did a play on my gallery tricks and went into their boombox, whispering through the static. They froze. Then, just as they were trying to explain away the noises to one another, I lifted the boombox into the air and smashed it against the wall, surprising us all. The more scared they were, the easier it was for me to throw stuff around.

Snap, Crackle, and Pop let me have that first one all to myself. They joined in the next few times, laughing with me while we sent once-brave ghost hunters screaming into the street. I thought that was it; I'd found my place, and I could be happy there forever. Even from the beginning, the next existence hadn't called to me, and now I knew why. This was what I was meant to do.

And then the football team brought their new kicker over for a little hazing.

Crackle took the lead, and everything went sour fast. He pulled the kicker's leg straight through a weak spot in the kitchen floor and knocked another kid down the basement stairs. The boy's scream shot ice through my whole being, and I sunk into a corner, energy flickering like an overloaded circuit.

When they fled, Pop followed. He didn't come back for eight days. When he returned, Snap and Crackle giddily questioned him, dying to know if he had possessed the kicker. He told them he'd done something better: he had possessed the kid's older brother. The brother was larger, stronger, and better suited to 'taking care' of his family. The three of them called it "doing a DeFeo."

They watched me work it out. Watched my face as I remembered hearing about the DeFeo family murders when I was a kid. Watched the horror envelope me.

I jerked backward, but Pop snatched up my wrist and kept me from running. He slid the cuff of my sweatshirt up to my elbow and ran a finger down my arm. The line he traced burned white-hot, and a rotten flavor flooded my mouth. I'll never forget what he told me then.

"Nothing on the other side could taste as good as this."

That wasn't the flavor of fear I wanted. It tasted like agony.

I pulled away, and this time, Pop didn't stop me. The three of them howled with laughter when I bolted from the house.

Reina's face softens. "Let me see the arm."

I pull up the sleeve of my hoodie. A blood-red gash stretches from my elbow to my wrist. "I can't get it to come off."

"It never will. It's part of you now."

"It won't...." I hesitate, afraid of the answer. "It won't make me... *do* things, will it?"

"No. But its memory has shaped you." Reina falls silent. After a moment, she pulls down the neck of her blouse.

Someone has gouged five crimson spots into her spectral skin in a half-moon pattern.

"We call those spirits 'demons,'" she says softly. "Some used to be alive. Some never were. But they hate the living, for reasons all their own, and they try to convert others to their side with the vigor of any religious cult." She pulls one finger away from the neck of her blouse and traces the marks with it. "They'll suck you in like a riptide. It's difficult to escape."

She lets go of the fabric, and the marks are once more hidden by the polka-dot pattern. Her face is fully open now.

"And then you came here?" she asks.

"Not right away. I didn't know where to go. What to do. I just drifted."

"Never landing?"

"For a night at a time, here and there. It's exhausting covering that much ground. So, I would rest at the edge of people's beds, watch them dream. Some of them could see me. One even talked to me." I pause, remembering the little girl in New Mexico who was fascinated by my stories. "That's what gave me the idea to come here. Same work, less travel."

Reina studies me again. Every time she looks at me, I feel like another layer of my translucent skin is getting pulled back. But it's less disconcerting now. The sensation of judgement is barely noticeable.

"If a position opened up," she says, "and you were to fill it, which kind of spirit would you be? A lurker? A demon?"

I take my time, studying the mark on my arm as I consider her question.

"I want to give people something to dream about," I say. "I know they won't always be happy dreams, and some people might have nightmares, but I think most people will think it's fun." I pull my sleeve back down and look Reina square in the eye. "I want that happy medium. I want people to know I'm here without ruining anyone's life. I want people to come test their bravery and leave with stories they'll love telling their friends."

As I speak, Reina rests one elbow on the desk and props her chin on her palm. When I finish, I watch her, not daring to move or blink, sensing that this is it. My chance to make my case is over.

Seconds pass.

Reina says nothing.

My heart sinks, and I feel my inner glow dull. All this for nothing. Not wanting her to see how broken I am, I duck my head and begin to stand.

"I get it. I'm under-qualified, so—"

"Okay," she interrupts.

I pause in a half crouch. "Okay?"

She smiles at me. "Haunting a hotel is a delicate business. It requires a symbiotic relationship with the owners. If all the spiritual staff does is lurk, no one will know we're here. And if we act like demons, no guest will ever come back. The only people who would come are amateur ghost hunters, determined to force us out." She tilts her head. "But you're not a lurker, and you're not a demon. We need spirits like you to keep the ship afloat. So, 'okay,' as in, 'you're hired.'"

My eyes widen. "But... You said you don't have any vacancies."

"Not any that would tempt most spirits. No rooms with bathtubs. No rooms at all. But there's a lovely little alcove off the third-floor landing with an old grandfather clock and a cracked antique mirror. It's just going to waste." She stands and offers me her hand. "It's yours if you want it."

The room brightens with the warm glow that bursts out of me. I grab Reina's hand and shake it hard.

"I do! Thank you so much! You won't regret it."

Her smile widens. "Welcome to the Misty Hollow family."

THE WONDER QUOTIENT

LINDA K ALLISON

My 9-year-old friend Bub is visiting for a couple of days. To Bub, I'm his grandpa's good friend Linda, one of the many satellites within his orbit of adults. But Bub sees me as different from most of them. He knows me as an explorer, a collector of rocks and driftwood, the owner of a squirrel's fragile skull found in the forest, and a collection of wishbones dried and saved, filling a bowl in my kitchen.

I read somewhere that seeing your world through someone else's eyes can accentuate your sense of wonder. I may have a keen sense of it — a high wonder quotient — but I'm not entirely immune to the numbing influence of the familiar. This morning, a favor for my young friend has morphed into a gift for me, allowing me to see the beauty of my well-traveled path through fresh eyes — to see it through his eyes.

"Show me your pictures," Bub begs when we see one another. The two of us sit close on my sofa as I scroll through my phone to find the photos I've taken since we were last together — of a lizard scaling my office window, a turtle sunning itself on a rock, a dragonfly alighting on a dimple of pond water.

Bub asks if we can walk one of the trails that encircle my sprawling wooded neighborhood. Because I'm expected back at the house soon to attend to the sterile responsibilities of adulthood, our window of time is short, and we agree we'll keep our walk close to home. Our plan takes us on a path that I frequent. It's usually the jumping-off point to much longer walks, so I'm very familiar with this brief stretch of trail. And as much as I enjoy the morsel of nature it offers, I may have allowed myself to become too familiar with it, brushing by without noticing its gifts as I head for more interesting destinations.

On this particular morning, because I want to make our short walk special for Bub, I pay attention, making myself especially attuned to the beautiful, mystical discoveries awaiting us so I can point them out to Bub.

It's not yet 10:00 AM, but we feel the potent Texas summer heat dulled only modestly within the shadowy embrace of the pines and hardwoods above us. The sun streams through openings in the trees, illuminating pine needles the color of cinnamon toast. Cicadas hum with a tinny buzz I can feel in my chest. As we walk, dried leaves, paper sack brown, give a satisfying crunch underfoot. I point out a cluster of shelf mushrooms and a spider's web, its shimmering doily strung between two thin branches of a yaupon.

Ahead of us is a large, decaying tree trunk I've passed many times. But this morning, we spend several minutes inspecting it closely. We discover areas inside the trunk that have been eaten away by time and the elements, leaving ragged, black holes that open into the earth below. It's Bub who notices the striped lizard perched on the trunk's rim, cloaked in the forest shade. As I fumble for my phone to take a picture, the lizard disappears into one of the tree's rotting holes, igniting our imaginations. The rest of the day, we talk about "the lizard that got away," fantasizing about the dark, mysterious world beneath the trunk.

Bub and I have no genes in common, no hereditary linkage; we are not kin, but we do share something significant. We both possess what I like to call "a high wonder quotient." Bub is intrigued by the world around him. I am, too.

Retirement

Linda F. Smith

The icy blue lights blinked as the plane approached Boston Logan International Airport. Welcoming. Promising culture, recreation, and cuisine. The Boston Symphony as well as the Pops. Boston Museum of Fine Arts and the Isabella Stewart Gardner. The quadruple threat of Red Sox, Celtics, Patriots, and Bruins, not to mention easy access to beaches and hiking in rolling "mountains" a few hours outside the city. Restaurants serving steaming clam chowder, crispy Sicilian pizza, the original flaky-buttery Parker House rolls. Anyone would love living here.

Each summer, I visited my daughter's family in Newton, MA. Typically, I could only spend a week in August and then had to rush back to my law practice. Now my retirement permitted a more relaxed schedule, and I intended to use the additional time to fully investigate my options.

We touched down, and I texted Lindsey—they were already at the terminal, eager to pick me up. The official welcoming committee.

Some children return to their birthplaces to set down roots, others strike out on their own. I had never been upset that Lindsey, my only child, and her husband Samuel had chosen to make their home far away from me. Boston was an ideal place for their dual career challenges—Lindsay as a clinical psychologist and Samuel a pediatric cardiologist. Yet I had frequently wondered how it might have felt if they'd chosen to settle in Utah, near me.

Lindsey found me while I was still eagle-eyeing the bags. "Oh Mom, I'm so glad you're here." I hugged her back, though we'd never been a family of huggers. We wheeled the bags outside where Samuel waited in their midnight Volvo XC40. I peered into the vehicle and saw nothing but open space. No grandkids. I had the good sense not to challenge their absence.

"Nathan and Anna stayed behind so there'd be room for all your suitcases," Samuel volunteered. I accepted the plan they had arranged but silently lamented the delay in greeting the children. Swiftly, we were wending down the interstate while Lindsey interviewed me about my trip.

Yes, it had been uneventful. Thank goodness. One did not want eventful flights these days. Now that I had no deadlines to meet, I could stay as long as I liked—as we all liked—with a flexible return ticket. During summer break, we could take to the beaches in the stifling humidity. But when they were busy with work, I could entertain myself quite expertly. Chattering on about nothing sensitive, not mentioning that this trip was unlike all the others because I didn't have a job to return to.

Retirement is supposed to feel wonderful, liberating, adventuresome. Couples plan and plot their retirements so that they can take the grand tour, whether a KOA-based journey across the US of A with a fifth wheel or a barge trip through the Rhine valley or a cruise in the Greek isles. But I had experienced none of that. First, I wasn't part of a committed couple anymore. Dave died three years ago, suddenly, of a stroke. He had been in perfect health, and then, bam. He'd left me. I seethed with unseemly anger at Dave for his inconsiderate and untimely exit. But he wasn't there to berate and blame. Gradually, I mourned Dave and learned to wring quiet pleasures from my solo daily activities—a stiff cup of coffee, yoga on the porch, a sunset walk. But since we'd never been close to planning a retirement together, I felt lost when retirement snuck up on me.

After Dave had abandoned me, my work held me together. I had a mission each day. While I no longer had a husband to fuss over, I filled that part of my heart with my responsibilities for the new attorneys. As the senior attorney in the misdemeanor division of the legal defender's office, I made sure they learned proper procedures and came to appreciate our clients' humanity.

These defendants weren't significantly sympathetic on their own terms. A tattooed man caught up in the spiral of drug abuse. A twenty-something emaciated hooker. Our drug-dependent client had started using after his family rejected him because of his sexuality. The hooker had been a runaway from familial abuse, then a victim of her pimp. They were far from repulsive after you came to know them. Counseling them required patience. I guided my mentees to communicate care and respect to our clients who had rarely received either. The intensity of my relationships with the young lawyers gradually filled the place in my heart that Dave had left vacant.

But new management arrived. New management conceived new structures. Each misdemeanor attorney would be mentored by two or three of the senior attorneys in the felony section. The office no longer needed me to supervise the misdemeanor unit. Every attorney would carry a full caseload themselves—a move to save money if not to improve service to clients and instruction of newbie lawyers.

Of course, I still had a job. I could handle misdemeanor cases myself and continue to give my care and concern to the tattooed addict and abused prostitute. If I had the heart to do that on my own. Perhaps I could return to the felony unit. Though I'd handled rape, robbery, and murder cases before, that was many years ago and, management suggested, I might not be up to the hurly-burly of the practice today. Or maybe I'd consider working in the appellate division. I was smart, and writing briefs could be a quiet and satisfying experience. Almost like retirement.

My job had been eliminated and the office wanted—needed—me to retire.

And so, I did. Some of my junior attorneys looked bereft about my departure. Other colleagues seemed awkwardly sad that I was going. Management put on a good show of awarding me a plaque but were secretly high fiving one another about getting rid of the old gal.

I had shared none of this with Lindsey. Just that management had changed, and it made sense for me to retire now. Whoop, whoop! Won't that be great.

All my life changes had been going to something ever more engaging. Getting out of junior high to go to high school with greater course selection and challenges. Graduating from high school to enter college, living away from home, and evolving intellectually as well as emotionally and socially. Going from college to law school refined skill sets and opportunities. Moving from school to career opened worlds of possibilities to contribute and accomplish. But retirement was not that. It was retrenchment and retreat.

Samuel pulled up to their home as I kept these thoughts to myself. The craftsman-style house stood solidly under tall pines, its hatched windows winking golden light to welcome us. Samuel maneuvered down the driveway, stopped before the carriage-house-turned-garage, and shut off the motor. Though it was dark, my grandkids were still awake in deference to this being summer and bedtimes being flexible. Both Nathan and Anna scampered down from the porch to help porter my bags. Perhaps Lindsey had texted them to be ready. Nathan, aged twelve, gave me a perfunctory hug, but Anna hung on my neck whispering all that her nine-year-old mind had planned for our visit.

We lugged my stuff into the fancy guest room and gathered in the kitchen for a late-night chat. I accepted Samuel's offer of a small chef salad (mixed crisp greens, ham, and Swiss, lemony vinai-grette) and the kids had a bowl (or perhaps an extra bowl) of Cherry Garcia ice cream. Lindsey and Samuel limited themselves to herbal tea, the calming aroma designed to help them sleep so they could be fresh for work the following morning.

During my typically brief vacations, I had luxuriated in a week of sleeping in. Now I almost resented that Lindsey had something to accomplish each new day.

Anna extracted promises to visit favorite spots and play card and board games she would teach me. Nathan chimed in that he would participate but that he had multiple soccer practices and responsibilities with his friends, including a new rock band that practiced in the basement. I expressed interest in hearing what they were able to play but relief that the guest room was on the second floor. Everyone sounded positive, even excited about the visit.

The next day, the parents went off to their jobs and left me with a car and two kids. We conferenced in the cozy kitchen over-looking the garden and debated where to go. We settled on the New England Aquarium, located on Boston's central wharf, and decided to take the MBTA rather than drive. A welcome relief, since the older I've gotten, the more I've hated traffic. Nathan impressed me as a confident and independent user of public tran-sit. He directed us to the ideal place to wait for the Green Line trol-ley, and then to the optimal stop for a transfer to the more modern Blue Line.

Once we arrived, Anna asserted herself in planning our expedi-tion. Her class had visited the aquarium last year, and she knew to check the schedule for "animal encounters." We observed scuba divers, floating silently, and distributing food to fish in the Giant Ocean Tank. We watched the sea lion show, sitting far enough away to avoid being splashed by the briny water as they flipped over and flapped their tails on the surface. On prior visits, I'd needed to rush after my grandkids as they ran from exhibit to exhibit, but that had changed.

Nathan had remembered to wear his glasses and took the lead reading information at each exhibit. Anna still scurried from tank to tank but then stopped and studied the interesting creatures—the slowly pulsing translucent jellies, the eerily waving tube fish—pointing out what she found fascinating about each one. She swung her long dark curls from side to side, then expertly caught them in her left hand and twisted a purple scrunchie with her right to make a ponytail. When it was time for lunch, she announced that we should go to the restrooms to wash our hands and trotted off alone to do so.

Lindsey, always organized, had packed lunches for us, and after a morning of learning about fish, we ate peanut butter and jelly sandwiches outside and watched harbor seals frolic. Following our meal, Nathan insisted that we stop at the Anderson Cabot Center for Ocean Life, learn about climate change's effect on the oceans, and watch a movie about solutions. Apparently, he'd subscribed to their newsletter and was considering a career in marine biology.

By midafternoon, we'd exhausted ourselves. I asked where they wanted to go next. "Home." Nathan needed to work on some soccer moves before his evening practice, and Anna had promised to play online games with her best friend. Accordingly, back to Newton we went, both kids zoning out with their headphones while I watched the scenery scroll by. They had clearly enjoyed themselves, but our activities had been elevated from prior outings when Nana was required to keep kiddos entertained. I felt a little pang at being less needed than in the past—a companion more than a caretaker.

The next day, Lindsey had arranged play dates for both kids—friends were becoming more important than family. But I told myself that the day off would give me the opportunity to explore the housing market. I set up my laptop on the guest room desk overlooking the back garden. I googled "real estate Boston suburbs" and scanned the prices. Chestnut Hill home for two million, one in Newton for a million and a half. Did I really want to invest all the proceeds from my house and a big chunk of my retirement account in such housing? I switched to looking for condos. At my age, it would be better to downsize and get rid of any yard care responsibilities anyway. Condos were much more reasonable, but tiny—483 square feet in Boston for $345,000. Could I live like that? I refined my search to condos in Newton. If I wanted to move to be near my family, certainly it made sense to be in the same town. After locating a few apartments-converted-to-condos that were affordable but with no character, I decided to contact a real estate agent. We made plans to meet on Friday when the kids had another set of play dates.

Next, I logged on to Our Time, my dating account for singles over fifty. I had used this sparingly in Utah but decided I should try it in Boston. Maybe I should sign up for eHarmony as well since it was the most highly rated service. I spent the rest of the day doing relationship research.

Lindsey and Samuel liked to make dinner for the family each evening. The only exception being a picnic or take-out when Nathan's soccer game required us all to be away from home. I'd volunteered to help. I could make a decent Cesar salad as well as Julia Child's French Onion Soup. But they didn't want to tie me down or impose, and they had their recipes and routines—I'd earned a vacation from cooking. I told myself I should understand their declination of my help as a gift rather than an insult.

Over dinner, Lindsey gently probed. "Any big travel plans for your retirement?"

"Not yet." Retirement was still new.

"How about Road Scholars? Colleagues of mine have gone with them. You might meet someone."

I agreed that I needed to explore some of those trips. If not with Road Scholars, then maybe with alma mater alumni travel programs. "But if I met someone, I'd like it to be someone who lived near me."

"Makes sense. Aren't there trips run by the U of Utah? They'd have mostly folks from Utah."

"That's a thought." I took another bite of salad. "I did sign up for a dating service."

"Good for you."

Some adult children resent their widowed parent looking for another partner. But not Lindsey. After Dave died, Lindsey asked me if I would consider remarrying, or at least dating again before even my friends had broached the topic. Perhaps it was her training in psychology and knowledge that relationships are the most important thing to stay happy and healthy. Perhaps it was her recognition that I was a private person who benefited from a committed relationship. Perhaps it was her knowledge that thousands of miles away, she couldn't give me the family that I might need.

I'd explained to her that work provided me with plenty of family-like relationships, especially with my mentees. She'd accepted that, no doubt feeling relief that others filled the role she might have assumed. Now that I had retired, we didn't turn to discuss how my loss of those work friendships affected me. Thank goodness Lindsey did not intrude into that sensitive topic.

"I might even have a date here."

"Really?" Lindsay's eyes opened wider than usual, and her eyebrows arched up to disappear into her auburn bangs.

"I thought a few dates might get me out of your hair, let me see a show or concert without you needing to arrange it. Particularly since I might stay longer than usual."

"Makes sense." Lindsay studied her salad as if trying to determine the perfect bite.

"I also might investigate the Boston hiking meetup group. In case there's a day the kids are busy, just to keep myself occupied."

"Sounds good. I'm happy for you to do your own thing whenever." Lindsay smiled, accepting that I should be more independent given I was staying longer than a week, maybe even a month, this visit.

Lindsey hadn't considered I might want to move to Boston. She didn't count on me to fill in as childcare provider but welcomed my optional presence as "fun Nana." Perhaps it would have been different had the kids been younger, enrolled in preschool or afterschool programs. But now, they were so self-sufficient and involved with peers and play dates, they didn't need me.

When Lindsay had been pregnant with Nathan, Dave and I briefly considered moving to Boston. Dave's work in IT could have been done remotely, and he brought up the idea. But at fifty-four and very invested in my career, I didn't want to stop working to become Lindsay's nanny. And it would have been too difficult to carve out a new legal practice in Massachusetts. We never broached the topic with Lindsey. Maybe that had been a mistake. Maybe I should have seen the value of being near family back then.

Over the weekend, Samuel and Lindsey arranged a trip to the beach for everyone. Not to the rough waters of the Cape for body surfing in the waves. Instead, sheltered sandy shores nearer to town offered opportunities to cool off in the water and build sandcastles at leisure. Lindsey dove into a novel she'd been waiting to read, while Samuel flew kites with the kids. I held the butterfly-shaped kite for Anna while Nathan and his dad launched a dragon kite with red and gold streamers. Then, with two kites soaring high above us on the ocean breezes, Samuel attached them to Lindsey's chair and started a relaxed version of beach volleyball. I'd been a good athlete in my day so after a while I stroked out into the water, and we transferred the volleyball game to the ocean. The blazing sun, humid heat, and sea water resulted in an exhausted family, happy to order pizza for dinner so no one had to cook.

If I lived here, there would be more easy days like this. Times I could kick back and have fun with my grandchildren and their parents, all of us focused on the mindful present. It would be good for me, this discipline of savoring the moment and not worrying about work that needed doing. But as the children grew and accumulated more responsibilities themselves, such days would be fewer and fewer. My mind returned to our failure to relocate when Nathan was a baby, and we could have become an integral part of their family.

The next week involved trips to the zoo and the city harbor as well as time to see condos and small houses with a real estate agent.

On the dating scene, I received an invitation from a gentleman for lunch at Harvard Square. "Since you have Nathan's soccer game Saturday morning, I thought I might sneak away and meet someone for brunch," I told Lindsay.

"Really? Who?" Lindsay's eyebrows raised as they had when I first mentioned dating here.

"Some retired professor from MIT— a Mitchell Van Deusen. I don't know him well. We've texted and talked a bit. He's invited me for a meal at Harvest."

"Ooh. Sounds fancy."

"Maybe. I gather it's his favorite restaurant."

"I'm sure Nathan will forgive your absence in the peanut gallery." Lindsey laughed, "Let us know if this date is a Van-Doosey or not."

He was not. The restaurant's elegance—ivory linens, sparkling silver, and locally sourced food—did not make up for Professor Van Deusen's mediocrity. He seemed much older than advertised and had trouble hearing even in an unusually quiet restaurant. He had recently lost his wife and talked about her a great deal. He did have a healthy appetite for music and art, but it seemed doubtful we could attend concerts or visit museums without him filling our time with reminiscences about his late wife.

Lindsey sighed at my description of the date while we were enjoying a post-dinner coffee. "How about back in Utah, Mom? Any action there?"

I smirked at her framing. When Dave had been alive, he regularly took the lead in arranging activities with mutual friends. After his death, relationships at work served my social needs. Now that I'd retired, establishing an equivalent richness of outside friendships would not be easy. "There's one guy who I've gone out with a few times. He's a retired professor, theater department, always eager to give you a critique of whatever is playing."

"Sounds okay." Lindsey's brow wrinkled as if unsure of her support.

"He's smart," I admitted. "But I'm not sure if he's interested in me or just having an audience for his commentary."

Lindsey snorted then tried to cover her laugh. "You need people who are there for you emotionally."

"Yeah. He's better than Van-Doosey in the empathy department, but just a bit."

Lindsey sighed as she stirred, spoon clinking on the china cup. "Is that why you're thinking of moving here? To have more emotional support?"

Surely my face showed my surprise that she'd ferreted out my scheme.

"I've seen real estate agents picking you up and dropping you off. When were you going to mention anything to us?"

I put a teaspoon of sugar in my coffee, though I really don't like it sweetened, and stirred it around. "I was just exploring the idea. Not really seeking emotional support so much as I thought I could be useful, help with the kids, take some of the load off you and Samuel."

Lindsey got up, fetched the coffee pot, and refreshed my cup, helpfully diluting the sugar. "You're always a help when you visit. And it would be great to have you closer. But becoming our nanny doesn't strike me as the best plan for your retirement, Mom."

I thought back to the time Dave had proposed moving to Massachusetts and I rejected the idea. Now the children were quite independent, and the family's well-established routines didn't need a nannying granny.

"I'm not sure of the right way to do retirement. Your dad and I hadn't thought about it at all and then it just snuck up on me. Now that I've stopped working, it doesn't feel as if there is anything important for me to do in Utah."

"You didn't want this retirement. I can tell." Lindsay went on without waiting to hear my response, permitting me privacy. "If you moved, could you do legal defender work here?"

"Not a possibility, no way. I'm not licensed in Massachusetts, and I don't know the law or the procedure. Even more importantly, I don't know the programs that could help my clients. It would be a steep learning curve to get to where I have been. Not to mention no one would hire a 66-year-old woman. The curtain has come down on that stage of my life." I took a sip of the still-too-sweet coffee.

Lindsey frowned. "You couldn't be useful here as a lawyer, just a granny?"

Retirement had taken away my chance to be useful as well as my emotional connections. As Freud said, "*lieben und arbeiten*— love and work, work and love, that's all there is," and I had found both in my office. Could I replace them both through Lindsey and her family? Perhaps that was unrealistic.

"Could you find other ways to be useful besides practicing law?" Lindsey returned to the topic. "How about other volunteer work? In Utah or here? You're smart and organized. You could be helpful—be a leader even—in lots of other things."

"I guess I haven't contemplated the rich menu of volunteer opportunities," I smiled.

"If you were here, there's a CASA program—court appointed special advocates. They speak up for kids in foster care."

"We have CASA volunteers in Utah, too. That's an idea." I smiled to think of my daughter doing therapy with me around the creation of my new identity as a fulfilled, retired widow.

Our conversation ended without any resolution. In fact, I felt more confused than ever. Lindsey hadn't seemed excited by the prospect of my moving to Massachusetts. But she hadn't rejected the idea either. Instead, she had tried to help me think through what plan would be best for me—not the help I'd sought but perhaps the care I needed. I kicked off my shoes and lay back on the guest room bed. Plenty of time for me to chart my next course and no immediate need to make permanent commitments.

Time passed and I heard Nathan's band perform, learned numerous card and board games with Anna, and accompanied the kids on back-to-school shopping sprees. I continued to look at condos in Newton, but not with the same excitement. I took some hikes with a club for seniors and discovered a Silver Sneakers exercise studio nearby. I went on a date with another unremarkable but highly educated gentleman. I googled "volunteer opportunities" and confronted an overwhelming number of tasks nonprofit and governmental entities were looking for private citizens to undertake. I had been away from home for longer than ever before.

On the first day of the kids' school, I received an email from the chair of the Utah bar's criminal defense section. She wrote about a project to provide more support to defendants released from jail or prison. They'd received a grant to facilitate greater social, educational, employment and legal counseling for these folks. Would I be interested in participating? Since I had retired and had time as well as deep insight? I chuckled at the "deep insight" hook, figuring they must be desperate, but realizing I might have both time and inclination.

Before I could reply I saw a text, this time from Xan, the theater professor. "Can U go 2 play 9/10?"

I hadn't planned on returning to Salt Lake so soon. But there really was no reason I couldn't arrange it. The kids would be busy with classes, sports, and music lessons. Our summer fun was at an end.

"Yes. I'd love to go with you. What will we be seeing?" I texted, avoiding those abbreviations I hated.

That evening as we shared our meal, I told my family that I

planned to go back to Utah within the week. Lindsey and Samuel both nodded their acquiescence.

"So, I guess you haven't found the perfect condo to buy?" asked Lindsey, reaching for the bowl of fruit.

I admitted that nothing had seemed right and perhaps I hadn't completely made up my mind to relocate. I began to slice a pear and Lindsey offered me a chunk of cheddar cheese to accompany it.

"We've thought about making our garage into a separate housing unit," Lindsey said. Their garage had been a carriage house a hundred years ago, with ample space and two full stories. They had insulated the building and installed new windows some time ago to support a workshop that Samuel never had time to use.

"Accessory dwelling units are all the rage now." Samuel peeled a banana and looked my way. "Newton changed our zoning to make them legal. I think we should go for it."

"Would it have a bathroom and everything?" interjected Anna.

"No, silly, Nana would have to use a port-a-potty." Nathan poked Anna in the ribs.

"Let's do it! Nana can be here and in Utah so we can visit and ski." Anna pumped her fist.

"We'd want all the facilities on the ground floor," Lindsey showed me a sketch she'd made. "Avoid unnecessary stairs. But there could be a loft—a sitting room or second bedroom."

My head spun. Lindsey was trying to take care of me, to offer me options, to help me avoid giving anything up. I had no experience with other people tending to me in this way.

"Someday you might need to be nearer to us." Lindsey said. "I know you're a young sixty-six and don't need anyone. Now. But you could have a health issue. An injury. Need help—groceries, errands, trips to the doctor. We could pitch in if you were close by."

I hadn't considered the possibility of my needing them. I surely wasn't old. I hadn't imagined Lindsey would contemplate these scenarios. Hadn't she always appreciated me as her independent, self-sufficient mom? I didn't feel entirely sanguine that my prospective move was now premised on my needing their assistance rather than my providing help to them.

I smiled and took a bite of the juicy pear and cheddar. "I think that would be lovely, Linds."

After the dishes were cleared and I had returned to the fancy guest room, I logged onto my computer. I made the necessary airline reservations.

Then I sent an affirmative response to the Utah criminal law section chair.

We Happy Few, We Band of Sisters

Marie Tollstrup

Habits swish, rustle, whoosh
as heels click-tap, click-tap in rhythm.
Organ tones surge in billows,
and choir harmonies transport spirits—
a marching *esprit de corps*.

Grand chapel walls
fly to heaven's door
carrying nuns' pleas,
vibrating vast space.
Slender gothic columns
salute vowed Sisters as we enter
God's temple, binding
our communal bond to Divinity.

Dust motes whirl
in slipstreams of light
filtered through stained glass,
a fleeting canvas for believers.
Incense swirls levitate souls
as the censer's clink
blesses with tangy gusts.
Our heart-whispers ascend.

Bell's tinkle announces
the sacred Presence,
transformed from bread and wine,
eaten in communal bond.
Chapel ambience invites visions—
tinged in gold,
resplendent in marble,
and transfixes our uplifted eyes.

As a marching *esprit de corps*—
choir harmonies transport spirits
and organ tones surge in billows.
Heels click-tap, click-tap in rhythm
as habits swish, rustle, whoosh.

Rural Utah

Lorraine Jeffery

Their children left for the excitement
and ease of the bigger cities,
seeing through the optimistic names
given to this dry land by their
Scandinavian grandparents—
Garden City, Fairfield, Mt. Pleasant.

Grappling with a new country and
religion, the homesteaders
killed rattlesnakes and coyotes,
raised hay, cattle, sugar beets,
and sheep. Built schools and sawmills,
struggled through dry summers,
frigid winters, and tried
to live in a communal order.

Life-giving water was the
alpha and omega
of all immigrant settlements—
        lakes—Bear, Panguitch,

rivers—Sanpitch, Severe, Virgin,
creeks—Cottonwood, Hobble, and Pine.

They built forts to ward off Utes
and Paiutes while spreading
their culture and heritage.

Settlers rethought town names and
changed them:
>   Skin Town to Centerfield
>   Union Bench to Mapleton
>   Hog Wallow to Gunnison

Now, their descendants are rethinking
the value of small hometowns
where histories and people
are not forgotten.

IF GRIEF COULD BE WASHED AWAY

PAT PARTRIDGE

I wish grief were like mud. Something I could wash away with some miracle soap for the soul and watch it disappear down the drain and into the sewer to blend and merge with the pain of others who grieve. To be sanitized, sterilized, purified.

But my grief clings to me, clings to my heart and what passes for my soul. Its hold on me is unbidden but as real as my gray hair, my wrinkled skin, my tired, reddened eyes.

My grief is a messy distraction, the Stoics would say, keeping me from moving forward, from pursuing value and virtue, the proper role of a man. Grief offers nothing but sorrow and pain, they'd tell me. It's selfish. Indulgent. Cry and get over it. Move on, they'd say.

It's what my brother said to me before he was gone.

"Nothing good is going to come from crying over me." His face was stern. Then he smiled. "But you've cried over sillier stuff. Like stories of lost dogs. Especially when some lost mutt was found. You cried at weddings. For God's sake, if you want to cry about me, go right ahead."

"I'll cry when I want to." I punched his shoulder lightly,

pretending to be defiant, knowing he would see through it. That my bravado was a thin varnish over my sadness.

He was home, my home. Where he belonged. No longer in a hospital. No longer connected to IVs and monitors that casually reported his heart rate was weak, his blood oxygen low.

He was home to die.

I sat with him as he sprawled on the bed. Out the window a flock of glowing orange clouds filled the sky as the sun slipped below the horizon.

"Remember the good times," he said.

He grabbed my hand and let out a belly laugh stronger than I thought he could manage. A laugh I'd heard countless times. Irresistibly, I laughed too.

"Remember the time we borrowed Dad's wooden fishing boat without his permission?" he said. "We snuck two girls and three six-packs on it for some nighttime fun. Then the motor died. I made you get into the water in your underwear and push the boat back to shore."

"Yes, I remember."

"You shivered and whined like a six-year-old. Those girls were pissed and happy to dump us. And we had to pay Dad for the repairs." He coughed as he laughed. "That was a good time."

"It was."

"Remember the time we emptied the gunpowder from two boxes of shotgun shells into a coffee can? And we packed the can inside a small metal box and poured in quick-drying concrete to add compression. And then one boring Friday night we buried our little bomb in a sand trap on the seventh green at the country club."

"Yes. The explosion blew out half the sand and rattled nearby windows. And we never got caught. And we never told anyone, although we really, really wanted to."

He nodded, smiled. "That was a good time."

"Yes. Unforgettable."

"Remember your wedding? God, what fun! You tried to say your vows, and I kept whispering 'are you sure' standing next to you. And you kept grinning and messing up the words. Suzy was ready to dump you right at the altar and hang me by my balls. Did she ever forgive me for that?"

"Eventually."

"That was a good time."

"Yes."

"Remember when your first son was born after you two had tried so long to have a kid? We threw a surprise coming-home party, and the baby slept through the racket. Suzy was exhausted and wanted us all to leave, but she didn't say anything until after we finally left around midnight. Then you got an earful. Did she ever forgive you and me for that?"

"You, yes. Me, no."

"That was a good time."

"Yes."

"Remember when I joined your family for that houseboat trip, and I taught your kids how to water ski? And then I drove the ski boat while you skied. I took you in a circle faster and faster until you finally went flying out of your skis and hit the water so hard it ripped off your swimsuit. Your kids thought it was hilarious!"

"Yes. They never let me forget."

"That was a good time."

We talked long past the warm glow of the sunset, deep into the night. Because we'd had a lot of good times, and he wanted to remember them all. Because he wouldn't be able to remember any of them soon enough. And then, he knew, he would only be a memory.

Is that true? Is that all my brother is now, a memory? Or really a tapestry of memories that will fade and unravel as the threads in my aging brain weaken, loosen, and break?

Are happy thoughts and warm feelings the only ones I'm allowed? If so, why can't I just cut through this Gordian Knot of sadness, anger, and loss that binds me to him still? Why can't I wash this messy grief away? Or bury it deep in the ground?

Why aren't happy memories enough?

I know the answer, of course, but I wish it provided more solace. It's a simple one. I loved him.

If love were only about good times, we might never truly love. He knew this too. His life, my life, everyone's, can never escape pain, never avoid sadness, never flitter like a butterfly among pleasant memories only.

I left him that night when he tired and the memories became harder to recall. I got up to go to bed, but first I said something to him I'd never said before.

"I love you." I squeezed his hand.

"Back at you." He gripped my hand hard and winked. "Tonight. We had a good time."

"Yes," I said.

But I didn't cry. Not then. At least not on the outside where he could see.

The Stoics were wrong. I grieve as a brother, for a brother. I grieve for no hand to grasp and none to grasp mine. Time will soften my loss, I'm told, but for now my grief still muddies my soul.

My grief is love with nowhere to go.

What Do You Write?

T. Rodriguez

Quills 2023, Friday 8:00 a.m.

The woman to my right was juggling a rolling black suitcase, a flower print shoulder bag, and a cup of tea from the complimentary coffee station in the vendor's hall.

"Can I help you carry something?" I offered, finishing the preparations on my own tea.

She handed me the bag. "Thanks. I'm Theresa."

As we walked up the carpet covered ramp leading into the hotel lobby, I introduced myself and went through autopilot answers regarding my unusual name.

"What do you write?" she asked.

My grip on my tea tightened. Why would she ask me such a personal question after just meeting me? My lid popped off, and tea spilled onto the carpet. Using a napkin to clean the mess was a welcome distraction. Theresa paused. I couldn't answer that question for myself, let alone someone I had known for less than two minutes. When I finished cleaning, we resumed our walk.

"So, what do you write?" she repeated.

I guess it was wishful thinking to hope she had forgotten her question. Since we were at the Quills Writing Conference, I suppose it was a reasonable thing to ask.

"Umm, well, I am kind of working on writing how my parents met. It's better than fiction, and I am kind of writing like a memoir in a cookbook." My reply was clear as mud, but Theresa nodded her head as if I hadn't given an incredibly ridiculous answer. My turn. Fair is fair. "What do you write?"

"Supernatural," she said.

We made small talk all the way to the elevator. "What class are you attending first?" I asked.

"I'm presenting a class during the second session on tropes and clichés," Theresa explained. "I need to make sure I know where to set up."

I am such an idiot. She was one of the presenters I had researched. Not only was it presumptuous of me to talk to a published author and presenter, but it was so like me to not recognize her. I'm sure she wouldn't be talking to a nobody like me if she hadn't needed help. I kept my face neutral and hoped I didn't look as stupid as I felt. "Your class is one I plan on coming to."

"Awesome. Maybe I'll see you at lunch; we can talk then," Theresa said.

Why would she want to eat lunch with me when she could talk to other people of her own talent level? She was probably being nice —like when someone says, "Let's get together sometime," but *sometime* is an ambiguous *never*. No matter. Since I hadn't purchased a meal package, I wouldn't be there for the inevitable disappointment.

I headed to my first class with Rachael Bush and Terra Luft. Rachael taught the creative writing class that led me to volunteering at this Quills Conference and joining her Blue Quill Chapter. This session would help new attendees make the most of the conference. The information would be valuable, even if I was spending half my time volunteering.

Their class was in the ballroom filled with white linen-covered, circular tables. Scattered around the room, small groups of friends sat at half empty tables. Asking strangers if I could join them might lead to a conversation, but it could also be uncomfortable if the friends were engaged in a private tete-a-tete, making me—the outsider—feel the need to look at everything around them, but never at them, so they wouldn't think I was intruding on their personal conversation.

I chose an empty table near the tech crew set up. I wanted to say hi to Rachael, but she was busy, and it was unlikely she would want to interact with me here.

"Do you want to start?" Rachael asked Terra when the mics turned on.

"Not really." Terra sipped her coffee.

Rachael scanned the audience. "Welcome to Quills 2023. How many of you are here for the first time?" Almost every hand went up. "This session is about making the most of your experience. First, we recommend you talk to new people. The League of Utah Writers believes in supporting fellow writers."

"Sometimes people like your spouse don't understand what it's like," Terra added. "Meeting new people going through the same things as yourself is important. Wait. This is being recorded?" She turned and looked directly into the camera.

"Yes. It is." Rachael confirmed.

"Hi, Honey." Terra waved at the camera. "I wasn't talking about you specifically." Terra looked at Rachael. "He might see this."

Rachael raised one eyebrow.

"Never mind. He's never going to watch this." She shrugged one shoulder and turned back to the audience.

Rachael had mentioned she had a good friend and critique partner that wrote horror books. Terra must be the horror writer to Rachael's romance. She didn't look like a horror writer, but what does a horror writer look like? I refocused my attention. Rachael was explaining The Quiet Room.

"They don't permit me in there." Terra said.

"It's true. It's not for people like you. Drink your coffee," Rachel fluttered her fingers in the direction of Terra's cup.

"It's empty. I need more," Terra deadpanned.

Their interaction reminded me of my best friend. It had taken me forty years to find her, someone other than family to appreciate all my quirkiness. People generally only enjoyed me at a superficial level. I felt drawn to these women and recognized an emerging hope to know them better, but I reminded myself that it was unlikely they would reciprocate those feelings.

Quills 2023, Friday Mid-morning

I entered the room where Theresa was presenting, sitting in the last row of rectangular conference tables at the back of the classroom. I set my backpack on the chair next to me and took out my notebook. A young gentleman approached and asked if he could sit in the chair next to my stuff. When I nodded, he smiled and took a seat.

Rachael had said introducing yourself to people would make your conference experience more memorable, but I hesitated. I thought of all the times I had tried opening a conversation with a stranger, only to earn a weird look. The worst was when someone pretended you hadn't spoken at all. I still hadn't figured out how to handle that scenario. But here goes nothing.

"Are you enjoying the conference?" I made eye contact for a fleeting second before turning my gaze to stare at a non-committal zone in front of him, in case he ignored me.

"Yeah. Did you come yesterday?" He turned his body to face me, giving me a direct view of his boyish grin beneath a full beard, almost masking his youth. He was probably the same age as my sons.

"No. How about you?" I asked.

"I went to an amazing workshop session yesterday. So, what do you write?" he asked.

Again. Are you kidding me? We didn't even know each other's names. Why was he getting personal? If Theresa hadn't asked me earlier, I would have dismissed his question as the rudeness of youth. Didn't these people know that saying it aloud would be tantamount to admitting it? If I didn't tell anyone, and I was terrible at it, who cared? I wanted to quietly explore writing without judgment. If I said it aloud, I opened myself up to potential failure. Not to mention it was presumptuous to tell people I wrote and assume anyone would want to read it. And what *did* I really like to write, anyway? Not only had I not written enough to know the answer, but my brain ping-ponged too many places to choose one preferred genre.

When I had told my children I was volunteering at a writing conference, I emphasized the volunteer part. No one but my husband knew I was attending chapter meetings. When my kids learned I was taking a writing class, my most talkative child looked at me from half squinted eyes and said, "Oh. Okay," and left the room.

The bearded young man waited for my response. If my neurodivergent brain didn't process my thoughts quickly, the pause might have become awkward, but the lag was only ever long enough to be awkward in my own head. There was no polite way to get out of this question. "I am writing how my parents met and a memoir cookbook combining recipes with my memories of family members." I'm not sure it made any more sense than the first time I said it, but at least I wasn't stumbling over my words.

"That's interesting."

Was it? He couldn't possibly think so.

The best way to stop talking about me was to ask him the same awful question. The twinkle in his eye told me he had been waiting for me to ask about his writing. The collection of modern-day fables he described was intriguing. I found myself disappointed when the start of Theresa's presentation interrupted our conversation because I wouldn't be able to hear more about his ideas after the class. I had to report directly to my first volunteering assignment.

Quills 2023, Friday Afternoon

While I waited for Rachael to set up my laptop to help with virtual pitches, Terra joined us, and we were introduced.

"I liked your presentation this morning. I didn't think I would laugh so much at an intro session." I told Terra.

"Thanks. We aim to please." She flipped her full head of wavy hair over her shoulder with a dramatic flourish.

"When the League knows me better, they will intentionally keep me away from The Quiet Room, too." The edges of my mouth quirked up.

"Oh, are you one of *my* people?" Her eyes crinkled at the corners above the mask she was wearing.

I continued, "Why don't they give people like us a room? Why do only quiet people need a safe space?"

Terra laughed. "Yeah. We should make a safe space for people who get kicked out of quiet spaces."

"I'll be in there with you." The boisterous part of my soul had no problem matching Terra's energy.

"What do you write?" she asked.

By now I realized how naïve I had been to be shocked by this question. It was the customary and expected greeting, heard in every corner of the conference. It didn't make the question less scary for me.

I thought back to the day I told my husband I wanted to take a writing class. As he walked into our sitting area from the garage, I asked, "Do you have a minute?"

He sat on the couch, angling his legs towards me, our knees touching so he could look me in the eye. "Yeah. What's up?"

"I think I want to write a book."

"That's great. You would be really good at it."

No hesitation. He didn't even blink. Why had I been worried? This was David—the man who thought I was capable of anything.

He stood up. "Is that all you wanted to tell me?"

I tugged at his hand until he sat back down. "You *do* know it would be a ton of work, right?"

"You know I will support you with anything you want to do. If you wrote a book, I would *even read it.*"

I laughed. The only thing he read was his scriptures—and only because you're supposed to. He used to read the newspaper, but now he could watch the news on video apps.

I channeled my husband's faith in me, mustering the courage to answer Terra's question. The answer itself hadn't changed, but I was getting used to hearing myself say it aloud.

Quills 2023, Friday Evening

Twilight cast dampened shadows through the full back wall of windows into the foyer outside the ballroom. Today, I had interacted with many of the diverse cast I saw milling about: younger and older, professional and casual, queer and straight, conservative and not. There was only one hour left and a choice between the After Dark Horror or Romance Panel Discussion. Both sessions came with a content warning. But what did that mean? Content warnings could reflect a wide range of topics. Throughout the day, I had asked seasoned Quill attendees what they knew about the

After Dark Sessions. I smirked as I realized none of them had commented to me about the Horror Session. Whatever a horror writer looked like, I apparently was not it.

One reason I didn't like being asked what I wrote is because I didn't have good experiences with people seeing the real me. My friends existed at the acquaintance level; few spent time with me outside of work or church.

Several people warned me against attending the Romance Session. I didn't know who was more surprised when it was evident I wasn't giving credence to warnings without basis: me or them. Hadn't they listened when I gave my answer to that all too dreadful question, "What do you write?" I was writing a meet-cute about my parents. Maybe I had been in my incoherent-answer stage. Each time I didn't accept face value answers, I found myself being scanned from head to toe, the observers adjusting their assessment of me with puckered faces. Unfortunately, I was all too familiar with that evaluation.

Eventually, I learned enough about the session to know it might have helpful advice. Besides, Rachael was a panelist, and I wanted to hear her talk as an author. I took a seat near the door in case the topic turned into something I was uncomfortable with. An older woman in her seventies sat down next to me. She looked at my name badge. Since I only wore it as a polite formality, I waited to see how she would handle my unique, non-phonetic name.

"Do you play the violin?" she asked.

I chuckled and mentally gave this woman props. "No, but you obviously know something about my name if you're asking me that." Not only did she skip the question about what I wrote, but I rarely got that knowledgeable of a response to my name. It struck me, in that moment, how ironic it was that my very name represented the dichotomous person I was. How many devoutly religious mothers name their daughters after operas that feature coveted French courtesans?

The woman replied, "I gave your name to a character in the story I am writing. Would you be willing to read it and tell me what you think?"

Even if she was only asking me because of my name, I was surprised but honored that she would share her story with me. How could I pass up an offer to work with her as a writer? I gave her my email without hesitation.

———

Quills 2023, Saturday Afternoon

My laptop rested on a small coffee table between me and another matching chair that made up a sitting arrangement in a private corner of the foyer. I ended the last virtual pitch for the day. Over the edge of the screen, Virginia was sitting in an identical arrangement two feet over. She had been the site tech for the After Dark Romance Panel last night but contributed as much as any panelist to the discussion. At the last chapter meeting I attended, we interacted for about two minutes. I doubted she would remember me. She hunched over a laptop, her full head of unruly waves pulled back loosely away from her face.

Rachael came to a stop in front of me. In her hands was a plastic container with one remaining cupcake inside. Its creamy white frosting was topped with a purple drizzle and a fresh blackberry. "Have you had this brand of vegan cupcakes before? They're the best." She extended the container out to me. Every time Rachael greeted me, my earlier worries about her not having time to say hello disappeared. Not only did she act happy to see me, she was constantly sharing her food with me. Rachael looked over at Virginia. "Have you two met?" With that, my inevitable acceptance of the cupcake was assumed.

"You were at the romance panel last night," she asked. "What are you working on?"

I told her about my parents' meet-cute.

"I remember that now," she said.

I nodded. "You both did a great job last night. I'm glad I went, even though people tried to warn me off." The three-author panel had focused less on sex and more on how to build meaningful intimacy between characters. Rachael was the only panelist who didn't write closed door romances.

"Who warned you?" Rachael asked.

Oops. Not a good choice of words. Rachael gave me the same head-to-toe glance others had yesterday. This time, it was for different reasons. They had judged my faith and found me as less-than. Would Rachael decide I was the opposite: too religious? In less than 24 hours, I had found myself in a summarized version of my life. Everything I had experienced at Quills so far made me hopeful I might be accepted into their community, but this was the kind of conversation that reminded me I belonged nowhere.

I was a multi-racial, faith-abiding, educated mother, married to my opposite in almost every way. We maintained close relationships with our trans child, agnostic child, and my lesbian aunts. Growing up in the San Francisco Bay Area meant diversity was a way of life. Asking someone their nationality, gender affiliation, or religious beliefs was something everyone did because they wanted to understand and respect each other for what each person uniquely represented. But it wasn't like that in Utah. I had two separate close friends leave our faith, and with it they abandoned me. On my part, I thought our friendship was about more than religious beliefs. It was about who we were together: always full of fun, laughter, and support. The pain of those losses never went away, but I accepted I never completely fit into anyone's world; too open-minded for some and not enough for others.

Rachael was still waiting for my answer. Despite being rejected repeatedly for being myself, I had never changed for others. I wasn't going to start now. I scratched my head. "Um. I kinda dress modestly. I think people could tell I'm religious and were trying to be helpful to me." Saying it aloud was awkward given Rachael dressed more conservatively than me but wrote spicy romance novels. "I thought the panel was well done, and while there were suggestive things warranting the warning, it wasn't explicit like people had hinted." Did I even take a breath? I waited for Rachael's assessment.

She casually turned to Virginia, "How did we write the class description?" They pulled out their phones and Rachael read it aloud. She looked up at me. "We were trying to dispel misconceptions and write it accurately. Did we not do that?" They both stared at me, sincerity in their eyes.

Well, then. I had expected them to politely demure or dismiss my thoughts. Apparently, they were still interested in my ideas. Together, we dissected the wording, brainstorming ways to write an accurate depiction of the class for next time. When we finished, Rachael asked, "Are you coming to the banquet?" with the same enthusiasm she had used to include me in her happy bubble all day.

My heart stuttered. Was she really hoping I was coming, or did she talk to everyone like this? I think both. Terra joined us, reminding Rachael to change for the banquet. We hovered in the lobby for a few minutes, talking.

Most of the time I can manage my ADHD, but when I feel elated, an overwhelming energy surges under the surface of my skin, needing an escape outlet. The excitement of making new friends was giving me that buzz. I laughed at a sarcastic comment Terra said, and before I knew what was happening, my arm went around Terra's shoulder, squeezing it in a side hug.

Terra froze. What was I doing? I didn't know Terra well enough to cross into her physical space. Why did my body decide to be impulsive, in this way, at this moment? I dropped my hand and pretended it never happened. Terra made an excuse to leave.

Sometimes it made complete sense why people didn't want to be around me. If Virginia hadn't stayed and talked with me, I would have found a quiet corner to bang my head on the wall and call myself, "stupid, stupid, stupid," with each thud.

"Let me give you my number. Call me whenever you have questions," Virginia said. Whether it was my present state of mind or my awe that a successful author would offer to help me beyond a polite interaction in the lobby, her generosity was unexpected. Maybe I had messed up with Terra, but I had not been this unabashedly accepted since I lived in the Bay Area. I had worried about people asking me what I wrote, but everyone sincerely seemed to want to learn what creatively inspired me and what mattered to my heart—even if it wasn't the same as themselves.

As I drove home, my mind raced to search for the right words to express to my husband how amazing my weekend at Quills had been. I didn't know how I could possibly wait a month to attend the next chapter meeting.

September 2023

I smacked my hand at random objects on my nightstand, blindly trying to find the off button to my phone alarm waking me up at four a.m. Was it an unreasonable hour to wake up? Yes. Was it the only time I could dedicate to writing daily? That too. I went through the motions to get out of bed until I was awake enough to remember how discouraged I felt after last night's Blue Quill Chapter Meeting. I had volunteered for critiques, and it hadn't gone well. At least not in my mind. Maybe I would go back to bed instead. I had grown up watching my dad say and do impulsive things. Some people found him embarrassing; I thought he was endearing. Inheriting the same impulsiveness? Not endearing.

I should have never volunteered when I knew my piece wasn't quite right. When I didn't know how to back out of sharing, I should have chosen to go first before the high-quality presentations by everyone else. Ugghhh.

All right. Time for a pep talk.

I was writing for myself, and no one but my family would ever read my stuff, so it didn't matter. I had found an activity I enjoyed. Even if I was terrible, it brought me peace and joy.

I opened my laptop. My mouse hovered over the file of the cookbook memoir I had read from last night. I thought about the feedback for revisions I had received. Instead of opening my story, I opted for procrastination in the form of perusing my junk mail.

At the top of my inbox was a message from Inna, one of the Blue Quill Chapter members and winner of eight awards at the Quills Conference. At the start of last night's meeting, I asked if we would get to read the actual stories of the Quill's winners. Inna said if I emailed her a request, she would share her work with me. I had emailed her before my fated reading had started. Her reply email included four of her favorite pieces. I opened the first story and kept reading until I finished them all. Her writing was creative and intelligent. When I was done, I emailed her a thank you, telling her I hoped one day I could write as well as she did.

The next morning, I woke up at four a.m. again. I planned to check the latest sales at Old Navy, but there was another email from Inna. I hadn't been fishing for a pep talk, but she had written me one anyway.

Hello New Friend,

Someone famous once said, 'Writing is a lonely job done in groups.' It has become my motto. We do write alone, but we all need other writers' opinions, critiques, and support. The people in the League of Utah Writers understand that and try to help others on their individual writing path. You are in good hands. Don't be afraid to ask questions or to learn how to write. This is a learnable trade. I'm not the greatest writer (yet!), but I have studied what it takes to be one. You can always ask me a question. How is that for beginning a career as an author?

Pretty great, Inna, pretty great.

I opened a new file and started writing an idea I had gotten in my sleep. It might be a good submission for the fall writing contest.

———

November 2023

I sat on the bottom bunk of the room I was sharing with Michelle during the Blue Quill writing retreat I had helped Inna coordinate. I was trying to get as much written as I could before Inna returned from an errand. She wanted to critique my first finished piece. I hadn't put myself out there since my first failed attempt. Before Inna left, I had told her I was only ready to share my piece with her alone. She had become my personal mother hen, and I felt safe in her hands.

When Inna returned, she perched herself on the edge of the bed, worktable on her lap, pen in hand.

"Are you ready to read your piece to me?"

Before I could answer, Michelle walked in and plopped on the floor, sitting cross-legged in front of the bed. "What are we doing?"

"We are doing critiques," Inna said.

"Can I join?" Michelle asked.

I waited for Inna to tell her the polite equivalent of no in the writing world. She didn't say anything. As always, the pause was agonizing in my own head, not noticeable to others. Inna and Michelle were nice enough that if I actually let on I was uncomfortable, they would let me bow out.

"Sure," I said.

Drat. This is how I had gotten into the mess of reading my story at the Great Failed First Critique. But I reminded myself this was different. I was as ready as I could get.

I read aloud, keeping my eyes glued to the words on my screen, not wanting to look up at their reactions. When there was one paragraph to go, I took a deep breath and prepared myself to hear the worst about my two-and-a-half-month labor of love. I dared to look up.

"I loved it," Inna said. "Your pacing was good. It kept me interested the whole way, and I didn't expect the ending."

"Yeah. I liked it too," Michelle said.

I did it. I did it. I did it. I wrote something worth reading.

Inna and Michelle proceeded to give me more specific feedback. Instead of dreading what I might hear, I was excited to brainstorm ways I could improve.

January 2024

Our Blue Quill members lingered in the parking lot of Social Axe Throwing, torn between talking and wanting to escape the cold seeping into our bones. It was a miracle we could attend this event, given it had snowed all day. I hadn't seen some people in our group since either Quills or the retreat.

Rachael had joyfully stuffed me with vegan pizza and zeppoles. Sharing food with her was more of an experience than simply eating. I looked over at Michelle, who had coordinated tonight's fun. She was leaving for Thailand soon, and I would miss her, but I was excited to be a part of the advanced reader team for her first novel. Terra opened the passenger door to her black pick-up, turning for a final goodbye before getting in. She opened her hands towards me in a subtle invitation, "Are you a hugger?" After Quills, I hadn't thought *she* was a hugger or that she would want to hug *me*. Relieved I hadn't permanently ruined things, I met her the rest of the way and squeezed.

"Yeah! We have a hugger." She squeezed me back with a slight rocking motion, a genuine smile lighting up her face. It was a perfect ending to a perfect night.

————

In My Future

At my next Quills conference, when someone asks me that wonderful question, "What do you write?" my joy will shine through when I say, "I write short stories that come from my heart. What do you write?"

Get Your Goat

Alexis Hansen

Magic weaved between Desher's fingers. After weeks of study and practice, the spell was finally coming together like an intricate tapestry. The glistening threads were fragile and delicate, ready to snap at a moment's notice. According to every how-to book he'd read, intense concentration was a requirement for mending magic, as were steady hands.

Sweat beaded on his brow. He kept his movements slow and precise as he visualized the twisted, fractured metal in front of him as whole and unbroken. Any wrong maneuver could cause the spell to unravel. Almost finished...

A thud sounded on the roof above him.

His finger twitched. The web of magic held together, but only barely. Focus. He needed to maintain the visualization.

There was another thud, followed by rhythmic clattering.

The spell fell apart, glowing strands dissipating before his eyes. Desher's head collapsed into his hands, and he had to take a steadying breath before pushing aside the broken latch he'd been trying to mend. He marched to the entryway of the cottage, barely taking the time to grab a broomstick and a lantern before wrenching the door open.

A large shadow silhouetted against the nearly full moon let out a disgruntled bleat at his appearance. The darned goats were on the roof again.

"Newt," Desher called from his front porch. "Get down."

Newt, of course, ignored his demand.

Sal trotted up to the buck's side and gave the shingles an experimental nibble. There was nothing edible up there, but that certainly didn't stop them from trying.

"I'm warning you." Desher brandished the broomstick.

Sal flinched away; the doe had never quite gotten over her skittish phase. Newt merely pawed his hoof against the tiles before folding his knees and plopping his wide belly on the roof below him. He stretched out his legs contentedly and started chewing his cud, ignoring Desher and his broom altogether.

A cacophony of hooves thundered over the cottage as the kids chased each other across every inch of available space, followed by the clacking of Sal's and Ax's horns clashing together. The whole lot of them were prancing on top of his house like it was the Centennial Celebration and not *three in the lousy morning*.

No one had told him that goats were apparently nocturnal. And escape artists. And stubborn as—well, a goat.

In hindsight, he should have figured that one out.

Desher trudged to the side of the cottage, where, as suspected, the firewood shed's outer wall had collapsed. Again. Logs spilled out, forming a precarious but functional ramp to the shed's now-sagging roof, which in turn led to the cottage roof.

They had broken the latch the other day, but he thought the temporary fasteners would hold at least until tomorrow. How had they managed to knock it down?

As if on cue, another crash of colliding horns answered that question.

This wasn't how he wanted to spend his night. Hyran would

be leaving town tomorrow (or was it now today?) to return to his fancy pants wizard school, which meant Desher only had a matter of hours to figure out this spell so he could wipe that stupid smug grin from above that stupid cleft chin.

"You'll never hold a candle to a *real* wizard with self-taught magic, Desher," he mimicked Hyran's falsetto, setting the lantern aside. "Why don't you just run off and frolic with your bone-headed goats, Desher?"

Keeping a firm grip on the broom, he scrambled to follow the goats up the loose log pile. Slipping more than once—he had *hands,* how were the four-legged demons still better at climbing than he was?—he eventually crested the eaves, huffing and puffing.

Ax, ever the hugger, immediately disengaged from her legendary duel with Sal to bound toward him and throw her entire body weight into rubbing up against Desher's side, tail wagging. It was a small miracle he didn't go tumbling off.

Seconds later, his trousers were almost yanked down as Frog nibbled at the seams, staring up at him with unapologetic pale blue eyes. Toad planted her small, white-socked front hooves on his legs, bleating up at him, no doubt after his hair. She still hadn't figured out it wasn't food.

Shooing the kids to the side, Desher set about waving the broomstick around and raising his voice to scare them all off the roof.

"Yes, go on Salamander—come on, off you get, you two—I adore you too, Axolotl, now get down—"

Unsurprisingly, Sal, the most easily spooked, was the first one down. Frog and Toad, the twins, followed their mother, kicking their legs out in the most adorable manner whilst still in mid-air before running off into the field. Ax was undeterred by both the broom and the noise, flicking her speckled ears at Desher before she begrudgingly clambered down with some gentle and *persistent* prodding. Newt didn't move a muscle.

Desher stood over the buck and nudged him with the broom.

Then nudged harder. "Newt." The handle was going to snap at this rate, and Desher had a grudge to get back to. "*Get up.*"

Newt grunted, turning his head to scratch at his flank with one of his long, twisted horns before resuming his rumination. With a groan, Desher chucked the broom somewhere in the vicinity of the front door to retrieve later and crouched, proceeding to shove the two-hundred-pound goat along the uneven surface of the roof.

They made it five feet before Newt grew tired of the treatment and stood. He must have taken pity on Desher because he jumped down without complaint, leaving the man to fumble his own way to the ground.

The yard was a mess of scattered logs and splintered planks. If he wanted to get any sleep tonight, *without* waking up to hooves pounding above his head, the shed would need to be fixed now. With such a task in front of him, any hopes of upstaging Hyran before his departure dissipated faster than the threads of his failed spell.

Unless...

He unearthed the collapsed wall and propped it against the remains of the shed, drawing in a deep breath and stretching his hands out in front of him. This was what he wanted to learn mending magic for, after all—outside of rubbing it in Hyran's face. Ignoring the fact that he had yet to successfully complete the spell and that this task was much larger than anything he'd attempted so far, he pulled the magic to him again. Why not learn on the job?

Golden strands threaded between Desher's fingers, weaving together as he visualized the wall strong and secure, the spell growing more intricate, the threads beginning to tangle and fray, but he just needed to maintain his focus and keep trying—

The shed groaned as Newt put his weight on the untethered, rickety wall, attempting to use it to get back up to the roof. The spell disappeared in a puff of glittering sparks.

"Oh, *no you don't—*"

Once Newt was satisfactorily chewing on a patch of grass a reasonable distance away, Desher knelt, closing his eyes. After this many tries, he didn't expect the visualization to be the hard part, but the picture in his mind wouldn't hold still. Sleep would no doubt fix the problem, as would not having to keep an ear out for his goats wreaking havoc again, but weren't there also some people who didn't have an inner eye to begin with? And surely even a skilled wizard couldn't guarantee a distraction-free space. Or was that why they holed themselves up in towers all the time? Did no one cast spells out in the real world?

No, his books had to have something wrong.

Desher pitched forward with a grunt as small hooves slammed into his shoulders. At least the twins were having fun, racing around in circles and literally bouncing off the walls—and his back.

It must be nice being a goat. They didn't need to study or fix fallen walls and broken latches or have a reason to visualize outcomes.

They could still hold grudges, though, more so than anyone he'd ever met.

Actually... perhaps that was exactly what Desher needed. Not the grudges bit—he already had one—but maybe it was time to forget everything he'd learned and start from scratch.

Initiating the spell once more, this time he didn't think about the end result he wanted. Instead, he stayed in the present moment and molded each new filament as it coalesced into his palms. There was still a purpose to this magic, but when he let go of the iron grip he'd had earlier, the magic was free to dance.

The goats still played, but instead of holding onto the irritation at each distraction, he let it drift like a ballooning spiderling and watched the magic work.

He touched his hands to the planks, and a surge of light illuminated the yard. Shimmering filaments stretched across the wall, seeping into the wood grain, and lashing to the rest of the structure, binding it into place. Then the threads faded away one by one, leaving a sturdy, flawless shed behind.

Well, maybe not flawless—the repaired wall was a bit crooked —but it wasn't bad for his first successful spell.

He'd done it. He used mending magic.

So much for intense concentration and visualization being a requirement.

Exhaustion from the long night taking hold, Desher collapsed onto the grass, staring up at the dimming stars. Dawn wasn't far off. His muscles ached, fingers still tingling with the feeling of magic, and chest warm from the feeling of accomplishment.

He ought to celebrate by treating himself to a cozy day spent indoors. If the goats would allow it, of course.

The image of Hyran's smug grin drifted through Desher's mind, but it was quickly replaced by the much more appealing picture of his own bed, a gentle fire, and a hot cup of tea. He was too tired to go anywhere. He might even fall asleep right here and now. Hyran could keep his cleft chin to himself.

Toad's face appeared above Desher's. She gave a happy bounce and proceeded to chew vigorously on his hair.

A warm body lay down at his side, and he lifted a hand to scratch between Ax's horns. She leaned into the touch. Sal and Frog weren't far, settling down for the night—in the middle of the field instead of the warm, perfectly adequate shelter that took him weeks to build, of course.

He smiled. They might be hellions and a massive pain in his backside, but they were *his* hellions.

Newt's horns came into his field of view, silhouetted by the nearly full moon. He let out a disgruntled bleat.

Desher snapped upright. The darned goat was on the roof again.

ALL IN A POT

MICHAEL SHOEMAKER

One November late afternoon
    slanted shadows
        fell on white sidewalks
           on a dead-end street.

My missionary companion and I
in Córdoba, Argentina,
pressed our bicycle hand brakes
seeing something we had never
seen before.

A man was stirring
something in a huge pot over a wood stove.

I asked him, "What is this?"
Without looking up, he replied, "A pot."

I asked, "What's it for?"
Not looking up and with a dragging
tiredness he said, "*Comida, Comida.*"
"For food, for food."

Not wanting to bother him
and appreciating his economy of words
we withdrew our bikes to the curb
to watch a scene unfold.

A young girl skipped by
handing the man
a softball-sized white onion.
Chop, chop, chop, and into the stew.

Young and old came
with lima beans, diced tomatoes, radishes,
beets, carrots, peas, squash, potatoes,
and a butcher found some ends of beef.

All who gave one thing
returned and partook
of what seemed to be new.

Laughing, clinking of glasses, guitars and singing
waft with the wind through open verandas
while all who used to be only one were now filled together.

FORTY-TWO GOING ON TWENTY

M. ROHR

My brother has been smarter, faster, and better than me at everything since the moment I was born. Or so I thought. That same brother, gifted by the fates with a four-year advantage, is going back to an emotionally abusive relationship after living in my basement for the last few months. I wave from my porch as he drives away, stunned by the realization that my forty-two-year-old, better-at-everything brother is in the same developmental place I was when I was twenty.

He's me, twenty years ago.

My brother enlisted the day after high school graduation and never looked back. He called from Italy, his first duty station, drunk on Limoncello while I could only afford to buy oatmeal, rice, and beans. He got a signing bonus in the tens of thousands of dollars while I rode a bike with a flat tire to work every day. The military paid for him to get his college degree. I would have to waitress for mine.

My brother and his military roommates shared a house in the Tuscan hills, enjoying independence, financial freedom, and the luxury of getting paid to live in a foreign country. I lived with my mother, who made comments nearly every day about how hard it was to deal with me because I left my shoes by the couch or my cup on the counter, or because I didn't fold kitchen towels right.

My senior year of high school, my brother lived in Italy and traveled Europe at his leisure. I would've sold my soul for the freedom to leave our mother's nest like he did. I couldn't. Or that's what friends and family told me. My mom told people she was in a bad place financially and emotionally. Those people then told me how hard my mother had worked as a single mom to give my brother and me a good life and suggested that if I really loved her, I would stick around to support her.

Being the good child, I applied to the local college and agreed to live at home so I could continue helping her pay the mortgage.

Everyone congratulated me on making the right decision.

I stuck with my plan until the day of high school graduation, when my mother unleashed a torrent of anger and blame on me. A few days later, I packed, and I left. I was prepared to live in my car. Instead, an acquaintance said her grandparents had basement room they sometimes rented. I met them, they agreed I could stay with them rent-free, and I moved in.

One might think I responded to this new family's acceptance and generosity with open-hearted reciprocation.

I did not.

They were grandparents in their early eighties. They, their children, and their grandchildren had lively Sunday dinners with extended family. They talked loudly at the kitchen table when they disagreed. The siblings vocalized disapproval of each other's life choices then smiled warmly as they held hands to pray.

I'd never been allowed to criticize. Or talk loudly.

I ate meals in the basement bedroom they'd given me because I assumed I was in their way if I went upstairs. I cleaned every plate, sink, and speck of dust I created in order to minimize the trouble of my presence.

I'd been there six months when the grandmother, who would become a second mother to me, turned to me and said, "Dear, it's time for you to take up space."

"Okay," I said because I wanted to make sure I did anything and everything they expected.

"No, dear. I mean, this is your home. Live in it. Really live."

She smiled like she knew I had no idea what she meant. Then she went back to her book while I tried to figure out what she could possibly be asking me to do.

On evenings I didn't spend working or studying, the grandfather of my new family spent endless hours sitting in the front room with me, talking to me about life. I was amazed that he always spoke so kindly and seemed to have so much patience. I couldn't begin to imagine why he and his wife spent so much time with me. My mother had rarely, if ever, listened with such interest. If she did, it inevitably led to her explaining the things I had done wrong.

As months passed, I began sitting at the kitchen table to study. I accepted their offer to eat freely from the fridge and pantry. I joined them in the family room while they read or chatted. I joined Sunday dinners. One particularly daring night, I left a dirty cup next to the sink instead of in the dishwasher.

Shockingly, they treated me the same, whether I left clutter on the table or laundry in the dryer or a light on in the hall.

I started socializing with people I met in college, something I hadn't done while living with my mom. I went on some dates.

When, two years after moving in, I started spending too much time with boys that weren't good for me, my second family said something gentle about how I could do better. They didn't yell or suggest I was a disappointment. Somehow, in a way my young, poorly adapted brain couldn't comprehend, they made it sound like encouragement.

With their loving support, I graduated college, went on to get a masters, and gained enough confidence to move out of their safe haven so I could try adulthood with a little more independence. Ten years after they first took me in, I met someone kind who made me laugh. He was patient with what he described as the bubble I kept around myself, my thoughts, and my feelings.

He was close with his parents, his siblings, his cousins, and his grandparents. They hung out together at Grandma's house on Sundays. The cousins were the first to point out each other's mistakes and shortcomings, but they never missed major holidays or life events.

His parents were eager to know me and were abundant with their generosity. I knew immediately that they had nothing but love for their children and for anyone their kids brought home.

They reminded me a lot of my second family: vocal in their opinions but trusting in their unconditional love for each other.

Their home felt like that of my second family. When I arrived, I tossed my shoes in the pile of others. My jacket went over a railing by someone else's. I sat down on the worn couch, put my feet up on the ottoman like everyone else did, and smiled as they argued about which sporting event they should watch. It was so similar to my second family's home that it brought tears to my eyes.

I felt *safe*.

I'd been married for ten years and had two children when my brother came back into my life. His wife of eighteen years wanted a divorce. In that emotional crisis, he reached out to his family.

And so, at long last, the prodigal son made his return.

For the first time in two decades, my brother came home for a visit. At that point, it had been so long since he and I had spoken that I didn't have his phone number. I watched with envy as my mother doted on him and praised him. She told family, friends, neighbors, and coworkers what a wonderful person he'd grown up to be—then told me how impressed those people were when she told them. She extolled not just his respect and politeness, but described in great detail how careful he was to remove his shoes when he entered her house, how he helped not just cook but also clean up, how he helped carry groceries, and, of course, how he didn't need to be asked to do any of those things.

Where my brother could do no wrong, I could do no right. When I went to my mom's to spend time with them, she pointed out that I dripped water on the kitchen floor, that I only spent time with my in-laws because they had money to buy me things, and that not only were my kids too noisy, but I was doing a terrible job raising them. I obviously didn't love her enough to not drip water, to supervise my children, or to raise them the way she thought they should be raised. Meanwhile, my brother was praised for loving her enough that he took the time to fold the dish towels correctly and hand wash all my mother's antique dinnerware.

After a few token visits to my mom's house to be polite, I felt like my presence had trampled on my mother's happiness enough. So, I kept my distance and tried to be happy that my mother had her son back and that my brother had his mother in a time of need.

Like a punchline to the joke that was the last twenty years of my life, my perfect brother had come home so that I could be jealous up close instead of having to watch from afar.

I should have expected that the prodigal son would find an equally outstanding girlfriend.

When he brought her home for Christmas the following year, I was perhaps not as happy for him as I could have been. His girlfriend was attractive, polite, charming, and outgoing. She had a musical laugh and a friendly face. She was gracious in every conversation we had. It was impossible not to be charmed by her.

In the way of all siblings of prodigal sons, I was immediately jealous. While I'd struggled for a decade to navigate my mother's dislike of my husband, my brother had found a superb life partner, whom my mother adored immediately.

Perhaps it was the jealousy that made the difference. Because as ridiculously happy as they seemed, I noticed things.

They were little things at first. They'd been together for a year and a half, but she seemed to struggle if my brother's attention wasn't wholly focused on her. She seemed to be overly involved in my brother's interactions with other people. She seemed disproportionately offended when someone in our family didn't immediately like her.

She did not have a job, though my brother stressed about finding employment after his upcoming military retirement. They didn't have kids, and she seemed active in social activities, so I asked how she spent her time. She listed several entertaining hobbies, then said it wouldn't be fair of her to commit to even part-time work because she and my brother might move sometime later in the year.

After they went home, I made a concerted effort to keep in touch. That went well, initially. So well, in fact, that six months later they came to stay with my husband and me for a week.

It was then, with the microscopic view provided by living in close quarters, that I became seriously concerned.

While we were out to dinner one evening, the girlfriend wanted my brother to go with her to the buffet-style dessert table. My brother was engaged in a conversation and told her to go ahead without him. She repeated her request. He declined. She insisted.

He finally got up and went with her. I stared at their empty seats after they'd gone, concerned that she was both unable to get dessert by herself and unable to let it rest.

Another day, my brother and I sat in the kitchen eating left-over pizza for lunch. The girlfriend came into the room and expressed frustration that my brother hadn't offered to prepare some for her. My brother offered her the dish of leftovers and went to get a plate for her.

"I don't like it cold," she told him. To me, she said, "He knows better than this. In our home, if one of us is getting something out, we offer some to the other person."

I thought it was charming that my brother had hopped up to get her a plate.

After the cold pizza incident, the girlfriend explained to me how my brother needed to work on his communication skills.

"Your brother can't make good decisions," she told me. "I have to give him two choices to pick from."

My brother was well within hearing range as his partner compared him to my four and five-year-old children.

Later in the week, we had plans to go sightseeing, but she stayed downstairs in our guest bedroom until nearly six hours after we were supposed to leave. I caught my brother rummaging in the fridge and asked if they needed anything.

. "Nah, I'm just grabbing her some lunch," he said, with no indication of what was causing her to stay in the basement for the day when we'd clearly made plans.

For the rest of the day, his forays into the kitchen happened only while I was occupied with my children on the top floor of our home. With a sinking heart, I concluded he timed his comings and goings so that he wouldn't be in a situation where I might ask an awkward question.

The next day, the girlfriend told me that my brother needed to work on his fear of commitment so he could propose to her. Her tone was critical and accusatory. My brother sat beside her when she said it.

That evening, as I started cooking dinner, the girlfriend announced she was in the mood for takeout. My brother called in her order and went to pick it up while she played a game on her phone. She ate while my brother sat next to her—not eating—and I prepared the dinner I'd planned for all of us to share. When she was done, she announced she was going to bed. And then she went downstairs—taking my brother with her—nearly an hour before my husband even got home from work.

As my family and I sat down to eat that evening, I texted my brother. "If you're hungry, you're welcome to join us."

He texted back a few minutes later. "I'm fine, thanks."

Perhaps he had granola bars in his suitcase. It seems more likely that he went to bed hungry.

Finally, the night before they traveled home, my husband said to me, "She's your *mother*."

Yes, she was. The conditions she placed on her love and affection, the control she demanded, the fear of my brother being out of her sight, and the way my brother spent more of his visit taking care of her than getting to know my husband and children (or even me), were all behaviors I was intimately acquainted with.

It was precisely the way my mom treated me: excessive demands, conditional love, and emotional manipulation.

"You need to tell him," my husband said.

My brother—my older, better than me at everything, world-traveling, paragon of success brother—needed to be told he was repeating a cycle of abuse.

In the hours before my brother and his girlfriend started their cross-country drive home, I pulled him into a bedroom in the upper level of my house, closed the door, and whispered that I was sorry to trap him like this, but I was seeing behaviors in his relationship that made me worry a cycle of abuse was being repeated.

To my surprise, my brother collapsed into a chair, looking completely and utterly defeated. "It's awful," he said. "It didn't start like this."

"She treats you exactly like Mom treated us growing up."

He agreed. "I don't want to live like this, but every time I try to talk to her about changing things, she tells me it's all my fault."

I insisted that he was worthy of unconditional love, that he was a good person, and that he could find someone who didn't control or manipulate.

The conversation couldn't have been more than five minutes. Still, when we returned to the main living area, the girlfriend immediately demanded to know what we had been doing.

I reassured her exactly as I would've soothed an accusation from my mother.

A week after my brother and his girlfriend went home, he texted to say he was breaking up with her.

By that point, he was retired after two decades of military service. He'd been submitting resumes for the past six months, but he still hadn't been offered a job. He couldn't afford rent on his retirement alone. I invited him to live with us while he sorted out what to do next.

As he settled into his new life as a single and unemployed veteran living in his little sister's basement, I felt like Orphan Annie finding a family. I assumed I was getting the brother who had been better at climbing trees, catching frogs, and building forts. The brother who had been my Jedi master, the Smokey to my Bandit, the Mario to my Luigi. My brother who was my only connection to magical childhood memories, and I was thrilled to reconnect with him.

With this newfound proximity, the shared connection from that week he'd visited with the now ex-girlfriend, and the emotional intimacy of the whispered conversation about getting out of a cycle of abuse, I expected him to open up about his recent break-up. In my home, we talked openly about thoughts and feelings, and I felt like we had shared something difficult that warranted a deeper relationship.

"Yeah," he said with a shrug when I asked how he was feeling about the breakup. "It happened."

"You want to talk about it?"

"Not much to say."

"I can listen if you need someone."

He never brought it up.

Since the ex-girlfriend seemed to be off-limits as a conversation starter, I asked him about his marriage that had ended just before he'd met his now ex-girlfriend.

I was shocked at his answer. Referring to the woman he'd been married to for eighteen years, he said, "She was never... nice."

I asked why he'd stayed married to someone who wasn't nice.

From what little he said, I concluded their marriage had consisted almost entirely of my brother fixing her problems, absorbing the guilt for what went wrong in her life, and making her as comfortable as possible.

That described my relationship with our mom, as well. But my marriage had never functioned like that. Never. And he'd spent eighteen years with her.

I joked one day about how he carefully removed his shoes in my house. I have small children, and the carpet is understandably doomed.

"I've been trained well," he said with a straight face, as though this was a fact and not a joke.

It was more than just his caution about the carpet, though. As weeks and then a month passed, he never left a book on the table or put food in the pantry. He never left a sweater tossed over the railing—or even hung up in the coat closet. He only used the TV when we weren't home. The remote was always in the precise location it had been when we left the house. He joined us for dinners but never prepared food in the kitchen. I suspected he ate granola bars in his room during the day.

On an evening I had planned takeout for dinner, I asked if he preferred pizza or salads.

"Either's fine," he said.

A couple of weeks later, we tried to include him in our family vacation. We didn't need an RSVP; we just told him frequently how much we'd enjoy it if he came. He answered with the equivalent of, "It sounds like fun," until the day we left, when he finally said he probably wouldn't make it.

The pattern became painfully obvious: my brother couldn't express a preference on anything personal. He could talk for an hour about national politics but gave only vague deflections when asked how he was really doing or what he wanted.

And then, over coffee one morning, the words my second mother said to me nearly two decades prior fell out of my mouth: "It's okay to take up space. This is your home, too."

"Yeah," he said. "Okay."

My second mother's smile came to mind. I hadn't understood it twenty years ago. But as I gave my brother a smile that I meant to be reassuring, I knew he had no idea what I was asking him to do. And I understood why my second mother's smile had seemed so unfathomable.

With the help of a therapist, I've recently discovered that my mother likely lives with undiagnosed Borderline Personality Disorder (BPD). In sum, she loves us; it just sounds like shame and anger when she expresses it.

I hoped my brother would see a therapist, as well. I even offered to pay.

"I'm all right," he said.

When I first moved in with my second family, I thought I was fine, too. Now I can look back on a decade of their unconditional love and see how very *not* fine I was. It took years for my second family to teach me it was okay to share my thoughts and, eventually, feelings. Since then, I've had a decade of my in-laws' loud, generous love as a safety net where I can be myself without fear of criticism.

It seems I was wrong about my brother's perfect life.

All that world traveling he did? Yes, it was awesome. But what he described is a series of acquaintances with whom he occasionally traveled and had fun. He has no close friends, no family, no safety net. I envy him his adventures, but if I had to trade my second family and in-laws in order to have those experiences myself, I wouldn't even consider it.

The ex-wife he spent eighteen years with didn't have to be nice. After being raised by our BPD mother, my brother was well-trained at prioritizing manipulative demands and convincing himself that he didn't deserve to have needs or wants. He transitioned easily from a BPD mom to an unkind and controlling wife.

The opinions about his thoughts, feelings, and preferences that he can't express are classic symptoms of codependency and the emotional trauma of children raised by a BPD mother.

Like a map I've been looking at upside down, my perspective shifts, and the difference between my brother's life and mine finally makes sense.

After living with my family for several months, my brother has decided to move back in with the ex-girlfriend. His last week with us, I watch him pack his things and load his car with a ridiculously happy grin on his face.

"Do you want to talk about it?" I ask multiple times, hoping we can discuss relationship skills.

"Nah, we're good," he says.

My gentle, trying-to-be-sensitive attempts to ask how they've worked everything out are met with vague comments like, "She took a class about boundaries," or "I'm reading that book."

The book he's reading is *Walking on Eggshells*, an excellent text for loved ones of a person with Borderline Personality Disorder. I bought it for him hoping it would help him understand himself, our mom, and the girlfriend.

I applaud him for reading it. Still, I desperately want to tell him that his life experience has not prepared him to live comfortably with a BPD girlfriend. It took me decades to find some semblance of emotional safety. I had a lot of people to help, and I still don't know how to interact with our mom in a healthy way.

But my brother is not accustomed to his little sister questioning his life choices. I recommend that he find a therapist to help them continue improving their relationship. He's confident they'll be fine.

I stop with the suggestions he obviously doesn't want. It's more important to preserve the relationship with him than to point out the cycle he's returning to—the cycle he was born into, then married into, and now wants to commit the next portion of his life to. The cycle my second family nudged me out of. The cycle that is so foreign to my husband and in-laws that they honestly can't comprehend it when I try to explain.

So, I make sure my brother sees me smiling, not crying, as he finishes packing his car.

The older brother who has always been smarter, faster, and better than me is now twenty years behind developmentally: damaged, codependent, and incapable of expressing himself because his self depends entirely on the toxic expectations of someone else.

After his car turns the corner and he's out of sight, I go inside, kick off my shoes in the middle of the entry, toss my coat over an easy chair, and call my mother-in-law.

"Thank you," I say when she answers.

"For what?"

"For loving me."

THE RIGHT WORDS

M. LEE HOLMES

"I'm just struggling to get the right words," Kelsey says, leaning against the Queen Anne hutch. It's piled high with old newspapers and unopened mail. Kelsey glimpses a post-marked date on a dusty envelope—2017. *Jesus. This is going to be a helluva mess to sort through.*

Jonathan has turned his back to Kelsey, his eyes scanning the green field just beyond the kitchen window. As far as Kelsey can tell, he isn't really looking at anything.

"I just need something from you, anything," Kelsey begs.

His father sighs, the sound of it so deflated, so defeated, it nearly knocks Kelsey over. And as Kelsey stares at his father's back, he notices for the first time the slumped shoulders, the ridged frame, the shuddering of back muscles as he breathes in and out, as if this labor is too much. As if the labor of hearing his son speak is too much.

"Look," Kelsey says, trying to reason with the old man, "I know I've been gone a long time. I know I left for a career you disapprove of. I know you hate the way I dress, the way I present myself to your railroad buddies, the way I chew my food. The way I'm tapping my pen against this paper. I know you hate my NYU stuffiness, the fact that I left Bridgetown, left the railroad, left Avery and Colton to pick up your pieces. I know all of that. But I can't write about that stuff. You've got to give me something." Kelsey waits, still tapping his pen. His father doesn't turn, doesn't even sigh anymore. He just stares out that damn window. No acknowledgement whatsoever. Whiskey bottles line the countertop on either side of Jonathan. Some empty, some not. Some turned over. Some broken. Old food sits rotting on the stove. Pots boiled over during the incident, and no one had bothered cleaning them up. At least someone had been thoughtful enough to turn off the burners. Flies flitter around the hot kitchen, sticking to the sweat on Kelsey's forehead.

"Just give me anything!" Kelsey pleads.

Jonathan turns, not fully to Kelsey, but towards the hallway. His footsteps are totally silent as he shuffles out of the kitchen. His jaundiced hands are trembling. Kelsey watches him go with a scowl.

"Fine! Old bastard. Be that way! Now I remember why I left in the first place."

Kelsey throws down his pen, his eyes falling to the empty spot where his father had just been standing. He looks over the bottles again, the afternoon sun glinting off green and brown glass, casting glowing orbs on the walls of the otherwise dark and dreary room. The Queen Anne hides in the dark, dust from the top of it clinging to Kelsey's sport coat. He rips the coat off, wondering why he wore it for so long in this sweltering heat. Beads of sweat drip into his eyes. Then his eyes swell with tears. He wipes them away, puts his face in his hands, and lets out a silent sob.

Avery and Colton arrive that evening, having come straight over after their shifts at the railroad. Both had taken after their father, becoming signal maintainers. Kelsey thinks it ironic that his father spent his life fixing lights, and he couldn't even get the lights in his own house to work properly. He'd been trying to clean up the messes in the kitchen, flipping light switches, only to discover one or two bulbs popping on, casting dim glows that only made the shadows of the house worse.

"Wow. It's weird to actually see a countertop," Colton says, stepping into the kitchen. He grabs a partially filled whiskey bottle that Kelsey had stacked in the corner near the fridge and pours two glasses. He hands one to Avery, then tilts the bottle in Kelsey's direction.

"I don't see how you can drink that swill," Kelsey says, scowling at the liquid in the glass. He turns away from his brothers, focusing on the wet rag in his hand as he wipes down the sticky counter.

"I don't see how you can live in New York City and *not* drink it," Avery says, shaking his head with much the same disapproval as their father.

"I have an occasional glass of wine with dinner, but I moved to get away from all of that, remember?"

Neither of Kelsey's brothers say anything. He has a feeling they are exchanging glances behind his back, but he doesn't care. He throws the rag into the sink and looks up, through the same kitchen window at the same green field. The field is dark now, almost black, like the sea at nighttime. The moon crests over the hills, but it isn't bright enough to give Kelsey any sort of bearing. He thinks of his paper again, the one still sitting on the Queen Anne, the one he'd abandoned because it was impossible. He'd scribbled one sentence so far; *Jonathan Hurst, my father, worked hard all his life...* That was it. That was all he could get down. He stares at the field, thinking maybe the answer is lost out there in the darkness. Maybe it ran away, like he did all those years ago.

"Yeah, well, sometimes after a hard day of work, the warmth of the whiskey is all you crave," Colton says as he sips loudly from his glass. He pulls out a barstool and plops into it, as if he owns it. As if he has owned this whole kitchen his whole life. Kelsey scowls at the smugness of Colton's face, at the sense of ownership in his posture.

"I have hard days of work, too."

Both Colton and Avery snort. Avery cracks a smile. "Pretty hard sittin' at a desk typin' all day, is it?"

Kelsey grunts and turns away from his brothers. He could argue with them, sure, but they would never understand that mental labor could be just as difficult as the physical. Colton and Avery would never know the anguish it could bring, trying to find the right words.

Kelsey studies journalism at NYU, which means he's going to spend his life writing about the problems of others, but he'd dabbled in some nonfiction pieces about his own life, mostly for class projects. Each time he handed in a paper, his heart skipped a beat or two, knowing his professor and his entire class were going to read it and judge him, not only on the structure and prose, but also on his past, on his shameful departure from his home, leaving his father with the ailing liver behind in the hands of his younger brothers while he pursued a better life. These were the only things he could write about. He tried once to write a piece about his mother, but she was so far gone from his memory, the piece read more like a work of fiction than reality. All he had to write about was his father, the way he would stumble to work in the mornings, groggy and sleep deprived. The way he would stumble home late at night smelling of whiskey and perfume. The way he'd demand Kelsey get out of bed at twelve, sometimes one o'clock in the morning to make him a sandwich, a duty that had passed to the eldest son after his mother's disappearance. His father raised his voice often to Kesley, but he never raised a hand to him. That didn't make his drunkenness any easier to deal with. Sometimes, Kelsey found himself wishing his father *would* hit him. He'd come close on several occasions, his watery eyes twitching with anger, his whiskey-soaked breath pummeling Kelsey in the face, his trembling hand clenching then unclenching just as quickly. *The second he strikes me, I'm out that door and gone,* Kelsey had always thought.

"You know, dad wasn't that mad at you," Avery says. His words are already slurred, as if he'd had one or two drinks even before arriving at their father's house, which meant he kept a bottle of something stashed in his car. "He thought it was good you got away. He told us to do the same, but someone had to stay."

Kelsey turns, stares at his nearly blank paper from across the room. *Maybe there's something there, then? At least a little something I can mention.*

"I don't think dad would ever say that," Kelsey says to Avery, fishing for more information.

"He did. Swear on my life. He wasn't too thrilled about your career choice, but he was glad you got out of this small town and experienced the world outside. Of course, he knew that meant you thought his job at the railroad was something to be ashamed of."

Kelsey grimaces. "I don't think that."

"Sure, you do," Colton chimes in. "Just like you think staying in this uneducated, piss-pot town is something to be ashamed of." Colton drinks the last of his whiskey, then stands and sets his glass in the sink. "You just couldn't get away fast enough. You left even before you finished high school."

At the age of sixteen, Kelsey decided he couldn't wait for his father to hit him. He left. Gone to New York to live with Aunt Tammy. Left Colton and Avery behind to take care of the old man. To follow in his footsteps. To be doomed to the railroad, which was the only prospect for young men in this lousy town with a population of less than a thousand.

Colton glances around the kitchen, staring at the pristine countertops, his eyes finally settling on the nearly blank paper on the Queen Anne. He moves closer to it, reads the one line on the page, then sets it down, shaking his head. "You don't have to clean up anymore. That's mine and Avery's job. Just write the damn thing. That's all you're here for."

Avery and Colton both leave the house through the back door, following the dirt road towards town. They leave their cars and walk. Kelsey knows they are heading to the bar. Maybe they'll come back later, hammered out of their minds. Or maybe they'll each go to their houses, fumble in the dark for their beds, trying not to wake their wives and kids. Kelsey is half tempted to join them but moves across the kitchen instead to the paper. He picks it up and begins wandering aimlessly through the house, peeking into rooms, and staring at old furniture and stacks of books. The house isn't large—three bedrooms, one bathroom—and it doesn't take Kelsey long to find himself in his father's room. The old man is there again, lying on his bed, staring up at the ceiling. Kelsey ignores him, knowing he won't say anything.

Kelsey glances about the room, seeing more unopened letters stacked on the bedside table next to a small stack of books so old and used their bindings are tearing—a collection of mysteries, the popular kind that sell millions of copies. "Easy reads," his father once said when Kelsey was a boy. In true form, Kelsey had avoided those types of 'easy reads' ever since hearing the phrase escape his father's lips.

He moves around the bed towards the closet, pushing aside a pile of unwashed clothes with his foot and peering into the open folding door. The shelves are stacked neatly, to Kelsey's surprise. Plaid shirts hang in tight rows and folded jeans line the center shelves. Boots and mud-caked shoes sit in rows along the floor, each one resting next to its mate. After the disaster in the kitchen, this orderliness is not what Kesley expects to find.

Kelsey's eyes turn up towards the top right corner shelf. He spots an old shoebox, covered in a layer of dust. Curious, Kelsey stands on tiptoes and yanks it down. It's light in his hands. Definitely not filled with unworn shoes. Kelsey takes it into the front room where there is a little light coming in through the large window facing west. The setting sun is casting an orange glow over the world, and Kelsey uses this light to look in the box and examine the old pictures and letters within.

There are pictures of him and his brothers as young boys, fishing at the lake, running through the field outside their back door, attempting to bake a birthday cake for their father. Kesley smiles at this. It was taken two years after their mother left. Kelsey is six years old in this photo, Colton four and Avery three. They are standing on stools, Kelsey with a mixing bowl and whisk in hand, a determined expression on his face. Colton and Avery are looking directly at the camera, their faces smeared with white flour, Colton's hands clutching the cake batter box. Both have large grins on their faces. The memory of this day floods back into Kelsey's mind like a broken dam. It's his first memory of doing something together with his brothers. He spots, in the background behind Kelsey's mixing bowl, the whiskey bottle sitting idly on the counter. After cake, Kelsey's father had gone for the whiskey and was passed out drunk on the couch by suppertime.

Kelsey sets the photo aside and rummages through the rest, finding a picture that makes his hands suddenly tremble. He lifts it up to the light, scrunching his eyes to see it with more clarity. He really should be wearing his glasses, but he left them in his suitcase because he didn't want to give his brothers another reason to think him a snob.

The photo is of his father and mother. It must have been just after they got married. It had been taken by a hired professional, something Kelsey had never seen in their family albums. Kelsey's father stands with one leg up on a stump and his left arm wrapped around Florence's shoulders. He wears a cowboy hat, with tight jeans, and boots. Florence, his mother, stands with her arm around Jonathan's waist. A half-smile paints her face, as if she couldn't decide whether to smile or sob. Her brown eyes are wide and bright. Her short dark hair is curled. She wears a yellow dress that stops just above her ankles and holds a small bouquet of wildflowers in her free hand. Kelsey stares hard at her face, stares as if looking at the copied face of his mother will make her spill her secrets. "Why did you leave?" he asks the photo, not realizing he is speaking aloud. His eyes glance back to his father. Jonathan has a stern but proud look on his face, a genuine expression.

Kelsey rummages through more photos, finding another one of his parents. This photo had been taken at a dance, probably the fall festival dance that Bridgetown puts on every year, the Harvest Ball. Kelsey has no idea who took this photo. His father is holding tight to his mother as he spins her around the dance floor. His smile is big, on the verge of a laugh. His mother's face is blurry from the motion, so Kelsey can't see her expression, but she is wearing the same dress as in the professional photo. He reaches into the box, hungry for more pictures, and finds one that had been taken many years later. Again, Kelsey has no idea who is behind the camera, but there stands Kelsey's father, holding a young version of Kelsey on his shoulders. Kelsey must have been two in this picture. He's grasping Jonathan's hair tightly, as if terrified of being let go, and Kelsey's father is laughing with a tumultuous joy, one that Kelsey can sense even through the barrier of photo and reality, past and present. Florence is holding a baby in her arms, baby Colton. She isn't smiling. Her hair is a bit disheveled, as if she'd just gotten out of bed, and she wears overalls with a red shirt, clothes that are too big on her. She clutches Colton tightly, glaring at the camera, as if she'd not been expecting to have her picture taken.

Kelsey's hands are shaking as he sets the photo down. He knows that less than two years after this picture was taken, Florence would no longer be a part of their lives. Avery hadn't been six months old when she left. Kelsey remembers following his frantic mother around the house, tugging on her skirt, and begging for a snack. She kept smacking his hand away and walking quickly from one room to the next, ignoring the loud television in the front room with Colton planted in front of it, and the screaming baby in the next room. She was gathering things and throwing them in a suitcase. Kelsey didn't know what this had meant at the time. All he knew was he was hungry and wanted a snack. Florence didn't even say goodbye or glance back at her children as she hurried out the front door. Kelsey sat by the door the rest of that day, waiting for her to come back so he could have a snack. The next face he saw come through the door was his father's.

Kelsey looks back to the photo of his parents dancing, his father's genuine joy. His mother's absent face. He wonders when it happened. When had she fallen out of love with Jonathan? From the look on his father's face, he hadn't fallen out of love with her.

At the bottom of the box, Kelsey finds more pictures of him and his brothers. There are over a hundred photos of the three of them running through the open field behind the house, chasing fireflies. Kelsey never knew his father took these photos. He smiles. He had spent every day after their mother's disappearance in that field with his brothers, up until he left for New York, left Colton and Avery and the field behind.

Kelsey wakes to a pounding behind his eyes. He groans and sits up, rubbing his forehead, realizing he had fallen asleep on the front room floor, scattered photos surrounding him. He wonders at the time, noticing bright light coming in from the kitchen window.

The pounding comes again, but it's the front door this time. Kelsey gets groggily to his feet and hustles to the door.

"Well, look at you!" says the woman on the other side. She looks to be in her late sixties, with wild silver hair, blue eyeshadow, and bright red lipstick. She's plump, wearing a tight blue dress and flat shoes. In her hands is a yellow baking dish covered in a layer of tin foil. "Kelsey Hurst, is that really you? You certainly have grown into a handsome young man, haven't you?"

Kelsey forces a smile. He suddenly knows who this is. Mrs. Dallas from three doors down, Ruthy Dallas. She had been his mother's best friend before Florence vanished out the front door, his father had told him. After that, Ruthy hung around his father, helping with house chores, and watching the young children when Jonathan had to work.

"Hello, Ruthy. It's nice to see you." Kelsey moves aside so Ruthy can enter. She walks circles around the front room, examining everything. She hands the baking dish to Kelsey.

"I made a casserole for you. I thought you'd be hungry."

"Thank you," Kelsey says, realizing he hasn't eaten anything since arriving at the airport yesterday morning.

"Oh!" Ruthy bends down, lifting one of the photos off the floor. She holds it up to the light, and Kelsey thinks he sees a tear in her eye. "Just look at them. They seem so happy, don't they?" She turns the photo around so Kelsey can see. He scoffs. It's the photo of his parents dancing.

"My father looks happy. I can't tell about my mother."

Ruthy nods. "Your mother was a free-spirited woman."

"That's for certain," Kelsey says, trying to fight back the anger bubbling in his chest. "So free she had to fly away."

Ruthy sighs and sets the photo down. "Your father loved her so much. She just... couldn't return the love, I guess. Last I heard, she's still living with that Mark fellow in Miami."

Kelsey's gaze snaps back to Ruthy. "What? You know where she is?"

"Well, not exactly. I was so mad at her for abandoning you guys, I never tried to stay in touch with her. After seeing what it did to your father, I just could never forgive her. I had no desire to look her up."

Ruthy wanders into the kitchen, Kelsey following, his hands and face feeling numb. It's the first thing he's heard about his mother's whereabouts since she left.

Ruthy's gaze finds the liquor bottles stacked on the counter.

She shakes her head at them. "Your poor father. I told him if he didn't give it up, it would be the end of him."

"He needed help and he refused. He needed therapy, though I doubt that would have helped him. He was always a drunk."

Ruthy turns to Kesley, eyebrows raised. "Not always. He never drank, not until your mother left. He grieved for her like she was dead. Probably would have been better for him if she'd actually died, no offense. He loved her so much. She was his whole world. When she left, he didn't know what to do. That's when he started drinking."

Ruthy steps closer to Kelsey and puts her hands on his shoulders. "Your father was a good man. I know there was bad blood between you, but you should know that he regretted it. He loved you. He told me how proud of you he was."

Kelsey reaches up and wipes away a tear. He sees the paper on the countertop behind Ruthy, not even remembering bringing it into the kitchen with him.

"When are services?"

"In two days. Thursday."

"I'll see you then." Ruthy gives him a kiss on the cheek then leaves.

———

Kelsey finds himself back in his father's bedroom after Ruthy leaves. He's still searching for something, though it's unclear to him what exactly that *something* is. With a sigh, he plops down on the foot of the bed. He gazes around the room as if lost, as if he'd never set eyes on it before. It's quiet; he's the only haunting presence in the room.

Kelsey feels a lump rise in the back of his throat. He tries to swallow it but instead coughs up a sob. He isn't sure why it's coming out now, why it waited. He wants to stifle it, shove it back down to where no sound can be heard, though his ears are the only ears capable of hearing it. *Maybe that's it*, he thinks, realizing the silence is what is getting to him. He stands abruptly, ready to run from the room, when his gaze is drawn once again to the open closet and a box he'd somehow missed on his first rummage through. It sits on the floor next to a pair of old boots, covered in dust. Kelsey reaches for it, seeing finger marks in the dust on the lid, knowing that it had recently been opened.

Kelsey's heart beats with frantic curiosity. He sits once again at the foot of the bed with the box in his lap. He pulls the lid off slowly and peers inside, almost afraid of what he'll find. His breath catches, and tears immediately spring to his eyes. He pulls out an article, clipped from the university newsletter. This was Kelsey's most recent article, a bit he wrote about how recent Covid regulations changed the daily routine on campus for the students. He rifles through the box again, finding all the articles and every story and poem he wrote that had been published in the NYU graduate newspapers and journals, and older stories and poems from his undergraduate years. His father had collected them all, had placed them like mementos in this box, had recently pulled the lid from the box and read some of them, just before the incident. His fingerprints on the dusty lid a ghostly touch of tenderness, of perhaps even pride for his son, the son who abandoned him so long ago, abandoned him just like Florence did. The box falls from Kelsey's fingertips as his body heaves.

He can't breathe. He opens his mouth and fills it with nothing. He runs from the room, runs through the kitchen to the outside field. The sun is bright and burning. His watery eyes ache in its heat. He stands beneath the blue sky on the green grass, and for the first time finds himself unsure of where he is. Unsure of what footsteps brought him here. Unsure of where to go from here. His thoughts whirlwind back to the paper he left inside, the one he's supposed to be writing. He suddenly thinks maybe he's forgotten how to write entirely.

The next day, Colton and Avery and their wives have all taken the day off work to come to the house. Two children, ages three and two, Colton and Avery's kids, chase each other down the halls and out the back door, through the field. The kitchen produces scents of roast and potatoes and pie. Colton and Avery's wives are cooking a big meal, while Colton, Avery, and Kelsey move through the house, packing things for donation into one box, and other things for keeping in other boxes. Kelsey is keeping most of his father's books. When he realized he didn't really want anything else, he decided maybe he'd give these 'easy reads' a try. Colton and Avery are shuffling through the photos. Kelsey keeps many of the photos of him and his brothers. He doesn't touch any picture portraying his mother.

After supper, they decide to take a break. Colton and Avery sit on the back porch, small glasses of whiskey in hands, chatting about work as they watch their kids run through the field. Amy, Colton's wife, pats Kelsey on the back as she hands him a glass of homemade lemonade. Her smile is pretty, and her eyes are sincere. "It's really good to see you again, Kelsey. The kids were so excited to see their uncle."

Kelsey watches Amy leave out the back door. Suddenly, Kelsey's father appears from the dark hallway. His face is shrouded in shadow, and he moves silently through the kitchen, following Amy. Kelsey follows his father, out the door, into the hot afternoon. He raises a hand to shield his eyes from the sun, and watches his father take a seat next to Colton. Kelsey walks around the chairs, standing near the steps of the porch, and stares at his father. His father's face is pale yet full of energy. He's smiling as he rocks in his porch chair. He's watching his grandkids running through the field. Kelsey wonders if he's thinking about the past, regretting not being more present for his family. Regretting letting the drink cloud his mind and make him forget that he had a family who loves him; three sons, two daughters-in-law, and two grandkids. Kelsey looks out to the field, to the kids, and sees the dusk sky darkening, sees little dots of light begin to emerge from the darkness. The kids squeal in delight and start smacking at the sky, at the floating bulbs above their heads, trying to catch the fireflies, like Kelsey and his brothers used to do as kids. Kelsey watches with a smile and with tears, realizing he too had forgotten he has a family that loves him.

He turns, looks for his father, but his father is gone now. Kelsey's lungs expand and gasp for a breath he can't take. He clutches his chest, then falls to his knees. Jonathan's disappearance has taken Kelsey's breath away. He chokes on a lump in his throat. Colton and Avery are suddenly beside him, holding him upright. They clutch his shoulders as he gasps in air. Their touches electrify him, makes his heart jolt.

"It's all right, big brother," Colton says. "You just let it out. We've got you."

Colton's words take Kelsey by surprise. He had abandoned them, and still they comfort him. He isn't sure he deserves this kindness, this sympathy. His tears soak into Colton's shirt sleeve, who suddenly wraps his arms around Kelsey. Avery does the same. And now they are weeping too. Kelsey clings to them, feeling a sudden strength in their embrace. Feeling a certainty he has lived without for so many years. His mind races back to the happy memories of the three of them captured by the photos, and he knows he doesn't ever want to let it go again. He wants to remember, not the whiskey or his father's drunken fits, not the nights he was roughed out of bed, but Colton as a young brother, following Kelsey around the house, asking annoying questions. Avery as a baby, standing up in his crib, about to flip over the side because he was too impatient to wait for someone to come get him. He wants to remember the cake batter on their faces and the frosting they licked off spoons. The fireflies they chased.

Kelsey sits alone at the kitchen counter. He can hear the TV in the next room. Colton and Avery sit with Amy and Heather and their kids watching a movie. They've turned the volume down so Kelsey can work. He stares at the paper in front of him. A few lines of jumbled thoughts he'd written staring back at him. He suddenly knows how to write the eulogy.

He turns the paper over, so the blank side is facing him. He's going to start over.

About that First Draft

Maggie Russell

When dull thoughts circle, or I'm thinking
in place, your work can echo,
voices ahead in the canyon, promising progress.

I don't need your draft to be perfect, to gleam.
A single line could stay with me,
a warming spell to chase away
isolation's too close embrace.

Do you know I tuck your words close to my heart,
tiny Milagros, bright in their shapes?
The whole of it matters less than
phrases, carrying me forward.

If a poem can hold a password,
an essay could crack a code, or
a story might make a map, then
a draft can be an invitation.

My Journey to Where I Belong

Daniel Yocom

I've been on the fringe of every group I have ever been a part of. It has been my choice. You see, I am transgender. I have understood this as a part of myself for as long as I can remember, even though I didn't have the words to explain how I felt. I know some readers at this point are not going to continue. My few short words to this point have probably angered some. Some who have known me for years may deny my claim, while others will say I am just following some trend that makes it popular to make such claims.

This is my story. It is a sixty-year journey, with almost all of it spent hiding the truth from others and myself.

I don't have any real memories of the first six or seven years of my life. Those memories are of pictures I've seen of myself and what others have told me I did. My years in kindergarten (two because my birthday is late in the calendar year, and we moved states) are brief flashes. My first solid memories start after my family moved to Utah in 1971, and I entered second grade.

The first few years of elementary school, I was lonely. My mom and I were practicing members of The Church of Jesus Christ of Latter Day Saints (LDS), but I was an outsider to my peers. They had known each other well before starting school. They had lived in the neighborhood together, while our house was on the edge of that community along a busy street. They attended church and grew up knowing each other in Sunday School, and I was the new kid. There was an after-school program, Primary, that happened at the church one day a week after school. All the active church-going children, or at least the children who had active parents, went. I sat by myself until other children were made to sit with me because we were in the same class. That is where I also started to learn about classism because my mom couldn't attend like other mothers due to her having a job. This level of separation became a standard I learned to accept as I grew older.

In school, I was segregated away from the other students when we would separate for English and Math. I had already done the text and workbooks they were starting. The teachers, the school, and even the district said they didn't know what to do because the policies at the time didn't allow for children to move ahead on a subject, and I wasn't considered a candidate for being advanced to the next class level—it might make me feel isolated. I learned on my own, and I also embraced that part of my life. But this is also when I started questioning other parts of myself.

I shared a bedroom with my two brothers, a makeshift room in an unfinished basement. I am the youngest of five siblings, and there is a gap in our ages. The next in line was four years older than me. He entered junior high school. My other brother is five years older than that, and he was in high school. My two sisters had bedrooms on the main floor of the house, eight and ten years older. I think I made my first inquiry in my bedroom about my feelings concerning my sexuality. If it wasn't the first, it was the first I remember.

"I want to be a girl." This was the simple statement I made one night while we were lying on our beds. I remember roughly what my brother told me.

"No, you don't. You're just confused because girls have it easier." This statement came from the eldest in the room. He then explained to me why girls have it better.

His explanation made my confusion bigger. He didn't give me any reason why I didn't want to be a girl but provided more justification.

Why not be a girl if girls had it easier? I didn't like what my life was like then. Any further discussion was cut off when I was told to just go to sleep and to stop thinking that way. I couldn't stop thinking that way. I learned quickly not to express my feelings and desires about how I saw myself and would rather be. I didn't have the words to explain how I felt. I did learn what others called it, and they weren't kind words.

My living on the edge of the groups at school continued. I wasn't athletic and was almost always one of the last people picked to be part of a team. In elementary school, I found plenty of time during recess to sit on the curb of the playground, wander the fence line, and watch the ants that lived at the corner of my curb. Those ants gave me inspiration. I found other ways to fill my time at school by getting involved with groups that were also on the mainstream fringe. My friends became those who were non-LDS or were part of inactive families. I started working in the lunchroom helping with the setting up, serving, and cleanup after the other students, and participated in activities like playing in the school band.

I set myself further apart from my peers by learning to play the flute. I was called a sissy, girly, fag, and other names because of my choice. That hurt, but I didn't stop. I wanted to play the flute. I couldn't explain why to those who questioned me. Not because I didn't know, but because I had already learned I couldn't tell them I wanted to be a girl and girls played flutes. This type of lesson or harassment—or what is now understood as bullying—continued through my years in elementary and junior high school. I was once called out to fight because I was carrying a flute on my way home from school.

During this same time, my lessons about my sexuality taught me other lessons.

It was in junior high when I met the first boy I understood as being gay. Neither of us were open about our sexuality. To be open then carried a huge risk of getting beat up. I saw this first-hand from my next older brother when a friend of his, his best friend, whom he had met in junior high and palled around with all through high school opened up about himself to my brother. They never talked again, and my brother threatened to kill him if he ever came around. He felt betrayed by his friend because they had partied together over the years. For me, this was another confusing point because my brother had never been sexually approached by his friend, yet it stirred that much anger and hatred.

This is not as extreme as what happened to my friend.

Our junior high fed into three different high schools. Many friends ended up in a different school. About halfway through my sophomore year (1980) I heard about an accident that took the life of my friend. Some of us who knew him got together to mourn the loss and talk. The official statement was he died from a freak acci-dent. There is no way we could prove it, but we believed he committed suicide because he was homosexual.

My time in high school allowed me to meet and become friends with more people living on the edge of what was consid-ered mainstream culture. We were those who were secure in hiding on the fringe of what was happening. We had learned different ways of hiding in plain sight. Our group included those who were sexually different, which wasn't expressed openly, and those who were punk, goth, and other groups that expressed their differences in how they presented themselves.

I first saw "The Rocky Horror Picture Show" when I was in high school. The movie gave me words to start describing myself and a way to explore and ask questions about my feelings and understand who I was, who I am. Those who know me understand that "The Rocky Horror Picture Show" is an important movie to me even if they never knew why.

This was the first time I saw something that didn't present a transgendered person as someone to laugh at or be scared of. It was intriguing.

Up until that time, and for many years after, the portrayal of transgender people, especially transgender women (men who see themselves as women) was done to portray them as unhealthy in some way or another. Before then, audiences were usually presented with drag performances considered funny. But they weren't transgender. They were men performing in costume. Their actions were usually for the humor of the situation, like in "Some Like it Hot." Those men were not considered bad.

Other stories used negative stereotypes of being transgender even when it was in the subtext. The movie and series "MASH" gave us Max Klinger, who was based on a real person from the military who wore dresses because it was considered a mental illness. I also remember the movie "Psycho" and how he was mentally ill and a murderer because he dressed in his mother's clothes. I heard people tie that to his fixation on his mother and wanting to be a woman. In later years, this was again the basis for one of the characters in "Silence of the Lambs."

But transgender women were also people to laugh at or to create a startling twist in a story. In "The World According to Garp," John Lithgow played Roberta Muldoon. She was an ex-football player and was used for additional comic relief because they pointed out the absurdity of such a masculine person wanting to be a woman. Jaye Davidson played Dil in "The Crying Game." The movie had a controversial nude scene with Dil. When I saw the movie in the theater, there were gasps throughout the audience when people saw the male genitalia, and some walked out. The other character, Furgus, in the scene became physically ill because of what they were shown.

Again and again, it was reinforced by what I had heard said

around me that men who want to be women, want to dress like a woman, want to be treated like other women are at best confused. Most likely they are mentally ill. They are perverts. They are predators. They are just evil.

They also justify the concept that because I see myself differently than they see me, this should give them the right to exclude me, hurt me, or hurt those I associate with. Some have gone so far to claim that my sense of sexuality is justification to kill me.

These are the fears I learned by the time I was ten or eleven years old. These fears kept me silent about myself for over fifty years of my life.

This treatment continued well beyond high school. I talked with representatives of the Gay/Lesbian Union when I started college. It wasn't called the LGBTQ+ community then. And even with those people who were more open about their homosexuality, the concept of being transgender was not very open and the stereotypes were strong. I don't hold it against the two people I talked to; I realized I knew more about the topic than they did back then. It did drive me further to the fringe.

My first marriage took a bad turn when I started to explore the topic of sexuality with my wife. We had met, and based on conversations, I was confident then and still am that she is bisexual. I thought we would be able to grow together. One day after some exploratory conversation and activity about the topic of sexuality we'd had the night before, she asked some very pointed questions.

My interior walls went up immediately, and I simply asked, "Why?"

With vitriol in her voice, she commented she was "afraid I was one of those perverts."

This was quite the turn in our relationship based on what we had previously discussed about her past. I won't go into other details about the short lifespan of the rest of that relationship. We parted ways and haven't seen each other or spoken for over thirty years.

For years after, I had to recover financially along with surviving the physical and mental abuse of that relationship. I decided I was destined to not have a close relationship. That was the case for almost ten years.

I met a woman who changed that. She was kind and welcoming. When I met her, she had friends in the queer community, and that wasn't just a veneer. I remained closed about my own sexuality because of my past. My friendships expanded to new people. People who are both part and not part of the community but were welcoming and involved in helping groups of the underprivileged, of any type, gain the respect they deserve from society.

From years past, I had heard how people threatened the family and friends of people who are transgender. I also had my own fear of losing someone I had found who had given new meaning to my life. After our marriage, I completed bachelor's and master's degrees and was pursuing dreams I never thought possible.

I had settled into my own mode of hiding, in part because I had not met anyone who identified like myself. I understand now how many, if not most, transgender people keep hidden because of the fear they hold because of the hatred they have heard during their lifetimes. Each of us is suffering in our own private ways.

After more than twenty years of marriage and reaching the latter half of my fifties, my life took a major change. First, I met people who were opening up about their sexuality and letting it be known they were transgender. Second, one of these people was my nephew's trans-son.

My great-nephew attempted suicide while in high school, and a big reason for that attempt was dealing with his own sexuality. The event took me back to my days in high school and the loss of my friend because he was homosexual. It hit me hard, and I decided I had to do something, say something.

I opened up to my wife first. To say I was scared is a gross understatement. I knew she was going to either leave or have me leave. She did neither. I then told my gaming group because this was where I interacted with my great nephew, his father, and some of his aunts and uncle along with some family friends. That also scared the hell out of me. Since then, the circle has been slowly growing as I face my fears with each new revelation.

It hasn't been easy for anyone. We have worked through issues of understanding and trust. I'm glad for that, because I had hidden a secret for so long from the woman, family, and friends I love and care about. Even now, while writing this essay about my life, I am concerned about how each one of those people will be treated because of what I heard growing up. I feel like I can now take the hate and violence that may be directed at me for how I see and define myself. Hurt, pain, and bigotry directed at the people I love because of who I am creates a feeling of protectiveness from me.

This journey of six decades has finally helped me to find my place and some peace (I still face fears daily).

I have lived on the fringes of the groups I have been involved with because of the fear I had of what people would do to me. I have existed on the fringe of a society that has expressed to me that because I see myself differently, I should not be a part of it, some going as far as saying the world would be better if I were dead. I have lost many years of truly living my life because of my hiding and running away from the truth of who I am and where I belong.

I belong where I am.

I belong where I am because of me. I have friends of all types. Some know who I am and accept me. Some have learned, and though they claim friendship have created a distance between us. Others don't yet know. They may read this. They may not. It no longer matters to me. Whether they accept me or not, it is their decision. If they accept me, we can create a stronger friendship. If they reject me, then I will miss them, but not the anger and hatred I recognize from earlier in my life.

I belong where I am because of others. I have helped others since I opened up about my sexuality. Not just those who have kept their feelings hidden but others who have never doubted their feelings. I have seen people explore their preconceived opinions. I have seen relationships grow and support for those who have struggled have gotten emotional support.

I belong on the fringe. That is where I grew up and lived for over fifty years. I see I belong there now to be a bridge between parts of our culture that are clashing because of misunderstanding and misinformation.

The fringe I am a part of is growing—not out of a fad as some misinformation claims. It is growing because some are tired of hiding, and others are tired of being hurt. I have seen more who are opening up about their differences because they are finding familiarity with others who have come forward—sharing a place of belonging with people willing to accept and support.

We all belong to the greater society.

SSH...I'M LISTENING

BRANDY WOOLLEY GREEN

I remember the exact moment I knew my little boy was different.

I was lying in bed, trying to fall asleep. It was a dreary October and we had various other issues on our minds. Our four-week-old daughter was underweight and having problems nursing and sleeping. Our eldest boy, aged six, had just skipped a grade when he kept having nightmares about the ghosts his classmates told him about. And our youngest son, Arthur, was learning the obedience that comes with being two and technically able to get out of bed whenever he wanted, as there were no chains deterring him, no crib barring him.

With three boys and one daughter all between the ages of six and one month, I was surviving on negative zero hours of sleep.

Yet still I laid awake in bed, tossing and turning, trying to fall asleep even when I knew I had maybe minutes before I would be called in for duty once again...for any of our children, really.

Except for our middle son.

My sweet almost-four-year-old, called Adam ("red earth") for his bright copper locks, never seemed to have any problems. Never really cried, never really threw tantrums, never really got out of bed or had nightmares or didn't eat enough food. I could rely on him to not have any problems. I could always count on him to stay in his bed, to not need anything in the night, unlike his three siblings. He was different.

And just as I closed my eyes, a voice whispered in my ear.

"You should look into autism."

It's one of those things that come completely out of the blue that makes your eyes shoot open, pauses your heart for several seconds, and leaves you utterly befuddled. Where did this thought come from? Who wrote it? And whose bright idea was it to put it into my head?

Of course I couldn't fall asleep after this ominous note. It will only take a few minutes, I thought. Just to quell my mind. Then I will for sure be asleep by eleven.

So, I Googled it. Signs of autism.

Christopher, older than Adam by almost two years, was the best older brother Adam could ask for. He was the one that taught Adam how to play pretend when Adam didn't know how. He showed Adam that when you crawl underneath the kitchen stools, you can make them scoot around the kitchen and pretend to be lawn mowers. And when Adam snuck into the fridge at night and pulled everything out of it, turning his bed into a nest of food because he was hungry, Christopher just giggled at him, patted his head, and said, "Silly brother!"

There was a moment, back in April of that year, that my husband and Christopher had been in a car accident on the way to school. After the car accident, Christopher and his father were both fine, thankfully, and just needed a chiropractic adjustment afterwards. However, my hubby got to talking with the good doctor about a few things Christopher had recently started doing, like needing to use the bathroom every seven minutes, crying a lot, having a hard time eating, etc. With all of these problems Christopher had, the doctor said we might want to look into diabetes.

Cue parenting freak out.

I didn't sleep, I didn't eat, I just researched "his condition" because I was already convinced he had it. That's what we worry-warts do, and what we excel at, amiright? Diabetes wasn't completely out of the blue. It runs in my family, and both of my younger brothers were hospitalized and falsely diagnosed for having it, so I know what it entails.

It turned out that Christopher didn't have diabetes...just anxiety and, heaven abroad, was I beyond relieved he didn't have it. I spent all that time and energy worrying for nothing. It turned out that the stress of the school year was just getting to my little big boy, and he needed a break to unwind, which came with summer.

So...that was all this is, I kept telling myself for weeks after-wards. Me just being a worrywart.

As it was, I was just being a worrywart again, just hallucinating with a sleep-deprived mind. Adam was a sweet child and far quieter as a baby than his older brother. He had been more than two weeks overdue, born in the Uintah Basin at home in a blizzard. Everyone thought he would need oxygen and we were all set up with it, but he surprised everyone by being perfectly healthy.

As a baby, my little Adam never cried. A lot of people said that none of our four children have ever really cried, they have just been so content and easy to take care of. But even compared to his easy siblings, Adam was even easier.

Different.

He was my only baby who didn't have some sort of problem with nursing. He loved playing by himself on the floor or in the crib, and the only time he ever really seemed to be upset was when his father held him upside-down (something all three of his siblings still giggle hilariously over when it is their turn).

He was my best one to nurse, my best to eat, my first to start signing by six months, my first to start crawling at eight months, my first to start walking at ten months, the first to even start talk-ing, perfectly and clearly. From the day he uttered his first word, Adam asked me most politely for everything.

Our worries abated. He was doing fine.

But in the back of our minds, we knew there was more to it.

When other children play, they smile and laugh. Adam didn't. He sat with his trains and spun the wheelsets with a concentrated pout. Sitting and spinning, sitting and spinning. When other children are overwhelmed, they pout and cry. Adam didn't. He spun his hands like he was turning invisible cogs as fast as he could. Sitting and spinning, sitting and spinning.

When I asked what he was doing, he'd say innocently, "I'm turning my spinners, Mother. Do you have spinners, Mother?"

As if everyone has hand spinners they turn.

Most children have the first instinct to demand or complain and have to be taught to ask nicely. I sometimes still have to remind both my other children to say "Mother, may I..." But not Adam. He used to say 'please' twice in every phrase he uttered.

"Mother, please may I to use the bathwoom, please?"

"Mother, please can I go to outside to play in the sandbox and to play with my digger twuck and use his scooper to dig fast, fast, fast like this I am doing with my spinners, please?"

My soft-spoken middle child couldn't *possibly* be autistic...right? He was different, yes, but not...*different*.

But in my heart, I already knew. Our middle child was different. Always has been. He wasn't behind in anything that we could really tell, besides potty-training—but millions of mothers have had a hard time training their sons to use the toilet, so he was hardly different in this regard.

So...yes. He was different. But...autistically so? It couldn't be.

But the more I looked into autism that night in October, the more I knew he was.

So, the next day, my husband and I found several different checklists from the DSM-5 and filled them out while we watched him around the house—separately so our answers would not just influence each other—and then we compared. He didn't meet every single criteria, but enough to convince us both that he was still on there.

Does your child have difficulty making eye contact for more than a few seconds? it said.

Yes, definitely. Adam had a very difficult time with eye contact. We would talk to him, and his eyes would flit all about the room. He hardly heard us when we raised our voices to get his attention.

"Is he near deaf?" I asked my husband. "Is he ignoring us?"

"No...he just doesn't understand we are talking to him."

Does your child have difficulty making facial gestures or knowing your tone of voice? it said.

He was very stoic for a four-year-old. He always had a really good poker face, and it was hard knowing if he liked something or not. So, I pretended I was sad and hurt, to test him. I buried my face in my arms and cried and said I was hurting.

Immediately, his brothers rushed to me and hugged me. Not Adam...he came closer and stared at me, his poker face still there. Not reciprocating sympathy or empathy. At least...not in a way that I understood.

Does your child have a hard time making friends? it said.

Yes, always has. He didn't have any friends at the daycare. He never talked to the other children, besides telling one or two what the rules were when he saw them being broken. Conversations with anyone other than those he was most familiar with were extremely hard to come by. And even when he did come up to ask for something when we were in a public, social setting, I almost always saw his arms were rigidly by his side, with his hands shaking back and forth in agitation, just turning his spinners.

At home, with his big brother, they were two peas in a pod. With everyone else, he clammed right up.

And I became convinced, just as I had been convinced his big brother was diabetic. Only this belief soon became a reality, and in January the following year, it became official.

Autism. Level two.

They call it high-functioning autism, but it used to be called Asperger syndrome.

His grandfather had Asperger syndrome.

Still, there were some things he did that didn't fit the stereotype. Like hating to be touched. Adam was the complete opposite with that. Every day he wrapped his little chubby arms around me, not letting go until after his brothers left. He grabbed my hand, petting it, sticking it in his neck, and wouldn't let go. He'd cuddle with me, making me ruffle his curly red hair, sticking his face in my neck. He'd lock and unlock our fingers in interdigitation as he'd tell me about his first day of school. Lock and unlock. Lock and unlock...

Lock and unlock.

About every other hour, Adam needed this physical touch from me. Or from his father once he came home, or from his brothers, though they weren't always happy to hug him back. They looked up at me from over his shoulder and gave me a fond, yet exasperated, grin when his hugs turned into ten-minute standing cuddles.

But there were other things Adam did that were eerily reminiscent of his diagnosis.

During a haircut, he couldn't stand any hair falling onto his skin where it shouldn't be. He would sit in his chair, crying, as we gently trimmed his fast-growing locks. Then he grew to where he would just sniffle quietly until it was done.

During fingernail trimming, it would sometimes take two people to hold him down and get the deed done. He seemed convinced that fingernails are a person's heart and soul and should never be parted from the body.

Or even taking a bath. He freaked out anytime water touched his face. But that child would still sit there, long after the water turned cold and the bubbles dissipated, for upwards of two hours if I let him. Just playing with the water, his fingers and toes as wrinkled as an old man's.

I'd go to him and asked if he wanted a fluffy, warm towel.

He'd say, "Shh...I'm listening."

In summer, he sat in the sandbox in one spot all morning long. His brothers flitted from tricycles to swings to slides and back again, but not Adam. His fingers sifted the sand, measuring it, watching it, feeling it, weighing it.

I'd go to him and asked if he wanted to come inside for lunch.

He'd say, "Shh...I'm listening."

In winter, he and his brothers would go outside for snow play. Five minutes later, tow-headed Arthur came back in, crying about cold fingers. Five minutes after that, quick-eyed Christopher came back in, complaining about cold toes. I waited for Adam. But he was still out there, an hour later, patting and molding the frozen snow.

I'd go to him and asked if he wanted to come inside for hot cocoa.

He'd say, "Shh...I'm listening."

Still, he was different during clay time, during puzzle time, during block time. His brothers would make something fun and then clean up afterwards, ready for the next activity. Not Adam. From lunchtime until dinner time, he would sit there, squishing the clay with his little hands. Or completing a puzzle, then messing it up, then doing it again, then messing it up again. Or making a firetruck with his blocks and then taking it apart, and then creating another one, and then taking it apart again. Feeling the cool, smooth plastic on his fingertips, setting each block on the top only to separate it once more, mesmerized at the power he held as he did this. For hours on end.

So yes.

My little boy had always been different. He had the patience to sit still when other children his age couldn't. He had the fortitude to be completely immersed in his work when, for other children, work was just a passing fancy.

And when I asked him if he wanted to be all done blowing

dandelion seeds and come inside for some food, he would just say "Shh...I'm listening."

"Listening?" I'd ask, sitting next to him. "To what?"

He handed me the dandelion seed. "To the dandelion talking."

I put my ear to it and listened too. To the dandelion seed as it talked. To the bath bubble as it popped. To the sand as it fell. To the snowflake as it melted. To the clay as it squished. To the puzzle pieces as they pieced together. To the blocks as they clicked into place.

Because my child is different.

He listens.

When nobody else does.

And back when he was three that dreary October when sleep-deprived me was trying to snatch a few snoozes, I listened too. To that still, small voice that told me to listen to my child. The one child that wasn't demanding any attention, that wasn't having any problems, that was doing everything he should.

I listened.

Now...are you listening too?

Railroad to the Creation

Wayne F. Gledhill

In the middle of the last century, when I was a boy, the Big Bang Theory was hardly a theory and was certainly not well known or widely accepted outside of university experimental physics departments. It would not appear in science books or physics classes for several years. The actors on the television show with the same name had not yet been born. Physicists tell us The Big Bang occurred between 13 and 14 billion years ago. Nobody was around to mark the exact date on some celestial calendar or give it any kind of cosmic recognition or even a cool name. Big Bang was its own description. Before the Big Bang there was nothing, not even time. Then, suddenly there was an explosion and in an instant there was everything. Stuff flying around in every which direction. You don't see something like that every day, but one summer night when I was ten, I experienced my own Big Bang explosion.

There are no nights better than summer nights and no summer nights better than those in August. August nights are not actually as long as those in June but in August, as the sun sets, time slows just a bit as do all other evening activities. Supper time is later, and sitting on the porch makes a bottle of Coke last longer.

For a ten-year old boy, growing up in a small, isolated desert corner of east central Utah, on the edge of the Colorado Plateau, an August night is the biggest part of the day. The crushing afternoon heat gives way to cool breezes creeping down out of the canyon and up from the river. The breeze freshens as it flows over newly irrigated melon and alfalfa fields. It smells like willows. Crickets are no longer tuning up in their wild May cacophony. They fiddle in unison now, all scratching out the same song, looking for a dance partner. It is too late in the evening for mosquitos. Twilight lingers late giving shadows a silvery edge. School is out for the summer. Reminders about bedtime have lost their meaning or are ignored. Night is the part of the day with no end. My whole universe, maybe the universe itself, is centered here. When I look at the night sky, my eyes search for its end but are always caught and drawn away by Orion with his great belt and sword. I search no further than his story.

Tonight is Thursday. Thursday is movie night. Benny and I were there in the front row of our town's small movie theater. Roy Rogers was the main attraction. Roy was in a gunfight. In the end, the West was made safe again. The newsreel tonight was about Korea and some famous general. One of my classmate's brothers is in Korea. In the army. My mom speaks in whispers when talking about him with her friends. Korea is too far away to think about.

Everything a ten-year old boy needs is here. I am comfortable with this being my place — my space — the center and whole of my universe. I have my friends and the complete freedom to discover whatever the town, the river, and the surrounding desert have to offer. However, this was the night when, for me, a greater universe exploded into view.

After the movie, Benny and I wandered to the drug store and watched Mr. Carroll clean up before closing. Mr. Carroll teaches seventh and eighth grade English and works part time behind the soda fountain. He is tall and single and wears fashionable clothes like the men in the Sears Roebuck catalog. His shirts fit tightly around his chest and upper arms. He never wears Levi's like the other men in town. He never wears boots or even oxfords like some men wear to church. He always wears loafers. Benny wondered if you could run in loafers. The eighth-grade girls are never late to his class and take their seats up front. At the drug store, Mr. Carroll is quiet and waits until you sit down on one of the stools at the counter before saying anything. "What's it today?" he always asks. He never asks about school like the other teachers. The soda fountain serves four kinds of ice cream: chocolate, strawberry, vanilla, and Neapolitan, if you can count that as another flavor. With those flavors and all the toppings, Mr. Carroll can make any kind of milkshake or ice cream soda you can describe. Even combinations of flavors. We scan the magazine rack for new comic books then decide to keep our dimes and leave.

Benny said we should ride our bikes over to the train station and watch the Zephyr go through. We usually watch trains from the hill south of the tracks, but the Zephyr's schedule brings it through town just before 10:00 pm. From the hill it is too dark to see anything but lights. Up close, the Zephyr is a long silver streak in the dark.

The California Zephyr is a thing of beauty. Its sleek silver design begins at the engine and flows all the way back to the last car. There is no clunky caboose hung on at the end.

The Zephyr is a single unit, whole and complete in itself. No rough edges. Gentle curves mold each car, giving each an appearance of speed and grace. Seen from a distance, the Zephyr seems to float in the heat waves above the ground, using the tracks only for guidance. Men in suits and women in hats sit high in the observation cars and sometimes wave at crossings. The Zephyr is the epitome of luxury and is advertised as such. When I dream, and dream of trains, this is the train.

At the station house we climbed onto the platform. The station is almost always closed except at night. At night it is open so mail can be picked up. Outgoing mail is placed in a large leather bag and hung from a tall pole next to the track at the end of the station platform. It is then snatched from its perch by a hook from the mail car as the night train speeds through town. Mail is sorted as the train carries it out of town, across the river on the old iron railroad bridge and out into the desert dark. Incoming mail is tossed onto the station platform in a similar leather bag.

Lights were on in the station. Benny and I pressed our noses against the glass to see anything inside that might be interesting. The stationmaster waved us in. He is a short man and to my knowledge has no name. He is nearly bald except for a ring of hair just above his ears. He doesn't scowl like some of the old ranchers who live across the river and from my perspective, he seems older even than most of the old-timers. But he smiled and continued to wave us in. We entered the waiting room which had two benches, wooden, back-to-back with each other. There was a desk with a sign on it that said Tickets. Behind the desk was a ticket window that opened up onto the station platform. A door next to the desk led into a back room. The station master motioned for us to follow him. Once inside, the back room seemed to be larger on the inside than the whole station on the outside. It was darker than the waiting room. There was another desk to the side of the door. A small lamp with a green shade sat on the desk but was only bright enough to light a few papers lying there. It was just bright enough so you wouldn't fall over anything. The room smelled clean and had the pleasant odor of the oiled sawdust used when sweeping. There were no windows. The stationmaster motioned to the far wall as he walked towards it. "Them's the trains," he said.

And in that instant, my understanding of the universe, of the size of things and possibilities I had never dreamed of, exploded. As big as I imagined my world was — as big as I imagined my place in the universe was — this dwarfed everything. A large panel filled the entire wall, almost from floor to ceiling. It was painted yellow, an old yellow, and had a gray cast to it that made it look like it had been cleaned too often. On the panel was an outline of the western

states, the whole of Nevada, Utah, and Colorado along with parts
of Idaho and Wyoming. Maybe Nebraska and Arizona and New
Mexico. Cities were labeled, both large and small, and each was
connected to its neighbor by long black lines. Peeking out through
small holes in the lines, every half inch or so, were long rows of
small clear light bulbs. Most of the bulbs were dark. Occasionally,
the ones which were lit would wink out and the bulb next to it
would begin to glow. The bulbs didn't give off much light. Light
was not their purpose. The purpose was to indicate place and time.
That map with its small bulbs drew me into an existence larger
than I had ever imagined.

"Them's the trains," the stationmaster repeated. Then,
pointing to one of the small lights which was lit up next to the spot
on the map marking our town, he said, "That's the Zephyr." He
took out his pocket watch, turning it to catch the light from the
desk lamp and said, "Should be coming through any minute now.
You can watch it all the way to Denver if you stay around long
enough."

This was no ordinary map. Maps were pages in books with
important places marked and countries, each with its own color.
Maps were for homework. But when you were through looking,
you closed those places up and put them back on the library shelf.
That's where they belonged. That was their home in the universe.
But this was a new world. A new universe. For me, it was newly
created out of nothing I had known before. This map was alive. It
showed not just the Zephyr which was about to come gliding in
out of the dark, but it seemed like every train on every track in
every state was here. Right here in the dark with Benny and me. It
showed a world larger than I had ever really thought about. I stared
and watched lights blink on and off in progression along the
various routes. There were trains everywhere, and they could go
anywhere.

The station master tapped me on the shoulder. We must have
been staring for a long time. "Trains's here," he said. I didn't move.

"You can come back," he said, "but I'm usually only here for the Zephyr. For the mail." On the platform we watched the Zephyr flow out of the darkness towards us. As it thundered past, its lights lit the platform. The mail bag on the pole at the end of platform suddenly disappeared. A thump signaled the arrival of new mail as a fat pouch came sliding across the platform towards the station house. And as quickly as it came, the Zephyr disappeared. I watched for a few long minutes, slowly realizing that while it had disappeared, it was not gone. It was going. Still going.

Benny and I jumped off the platform and walked back towards Main Street. I glanced up. The night sky was larger now. There were more stars. I looked for Orion and wondered which of its stars might be the furthest. The Milky Way had risen over the horizon. More stars. Maybe I would never travel to the stars. Traveling away from earth was still a Buck Rogers dream, but my mind was already exploring ways into my newly expanded universe. My place was no longer just where I stood. With my head back, gazing into the deepness of space, I could now see that those small dots of light were more than points in a constellation. They hinted of pathways. Orion no longer stood guard in the sky. He had raised his arm and was waving me to follow. To follow him anywhere. Everywhere. I stopped for a minute. It was still. The breeze from the river had blown itself out into the desert taking with it the last of the day's heat. I knew that this was my place, but I also knew that it was just one small lighted dot connected to others, all leading to where I would find the ever-expanding places of creation.

HELPING DORIS

SEPTEMBER ROBERTS

Holly

Holly went through her client's social history and home health order one more time before getting out of the car. Doris Peterson, 81, widow, lives with her grandson, still mobile, uses a walker. She needs help showering and will need light physical therapy while healing from hip replacement surgery.

Patients like her could be one of two things—a complete nightmare who hates everything about their recovery and all it entails and blames the people who try to help them, or a delight.

As she walked up the ramp to the front door, she hoped for wonderful, but braced for horrible. A handwritten note in shaky cursive greeted her. "Knock, then come in while you announce yourself."

"Mrs. Peterson? My name is Holly Campbell, your home health aide."

"Back here," a woman called out over the TV blaring in another room. "Head toward the light. Not in a *you're dying and should head toward the light* kind of way, although now that I think about it, that sounds kind of nice. Anything would be better than this ridiculous project I decided to start. Why is the eye of this needle so small?"

A smile tugged at the edges of Holly's mouth as she made her way down a hall, away from the loud TV.

Mrs. Peterson was clearly delightful.

"'Start a new hobby,' they said. 'It'll help you relax,' they said. Damn kids. They've been ruining my life since the sixties, why would they stop now?" She sat in a padded rolling chair while she scowled at a piece of needlework. A bright light had been bent over the workspace, shining through Mrs. Peterson's fluffy silver hair.

"Hi Mrs. Peterson, I'm Holly Campbell."

"Nonsense. Call me Doris." She turned her face up toward Holly and grimaced as she came face to face with the full force of the light. "This lamp is a bit much, isn't it? Could you move it away from me? My helpful offspring thought it needed to be close enough to my scalp to cause a sunburn. What am I, a lizard?"

A laugh escaped Holly's lips as she positioned the neck of the lamp so that it shined on the ceiling. "It's nice to meet you, Doris." She swerved around the walker by the door and held her hand out.

"Nice to meet you, Holly." Doris smiled wide and placed the hoop and fabric she'd been working on in Holly's open hand. "I've made a mess of that. Help a frail, old lady out, won't you?"

Holly squinted at it and frowned. Threads overlapped randomly, loose knots hung limply from both sides, and none of the colors made sense. "How about I take your vitals, instead?"

"If you must."

Holly pulled up a chair and opened the bag she carried her supplies in. While getting the blood pressure cuff in place, she glanced around the cluttered craft room with a sense of wonder. "Do you use all of this stuff?"

Doris nodded. "I dabble. I've been sewing most of my life. I taught my kids how, then my grandkids. Needlework is new." She scowled at the offensive hoop, which Holly had discarded nearby.

Holly couldn't imagine learning how to sew from her grandmother. They were practically strangers. Her parents didn't nurture relationships. Not even with her. But Doris was clearly the kind of grandma who would take the time to connect with the important people in her life. It was so foreign, she couldn't wrap her brain around it.

"Didi, why is the TV volume on max again? We've talked about this," a man called out from a room far away as the house went blissfully silent.

Holly froze, losing her count on Doris's pulse. That must be the grandson, who, for some reason, Holly had imagined as being a child. Not a grown man, as the rich voice implied.

"Speaking of grandkids," Doris said lifting an eyebrow.

"That TV was so loud my eardrums are bleeding," the man said, his voice getting louder.

"You big crybaby," Doris called out.

"*I'm* a crybaby? Who cried when I had to pull that needle out of your foot yesterday? If you hadn't been so careless with all your craft sh—" The man's voice cut off abruptly when he reached the open doorway to the room. His soft brown eyes locked on Holly's, and his mouth fell open.

Holly's back went straight, and her pulse quickened. The way he looked at her made her squirm. Like he was looking through her. And his lips looked so soft in contrast to his perfect teeth. A smattering of dirt covered part of his face. He must've been outside gardening. Probably shirtless and sweaty. Her eyes skittered down his chest to check.

Doris cleared her throat loudly, getting their attention. "Mason, meet Holly Campbell, my home health aide. Holly, meet my mouthy grandkid, Mason."

Their eyes met again. "Nice to meet you, Holly Campbell, home health aide."

"Nice to meet your mouth." She squeezed her eyes shut and willed the words back into her mouth, but to no avail. They hung there like little storm clouds waiting to ruin her day. "Mason. Nice to meet you, *Mason*." What was wrong with her?

Mason's eyes widened and his lips tugged up into a beautiful smile.

Doris chuckled. "Would you like me to leave the room? Give you two some privacy?"

"What? No. I need to finish taking your vitals." A bead of sweat slipped down Holly's temple.

"Is that what you've been doing for the past five minutes? I thought you just really wanted to hold my hand and you were trying to get up the courage to ask me on a date."

Holly looked down at her fingers pressed against Doris's wrist and released her grasp. "Sorry."

"Mason? Will you shake the nice lady's hand, then be a dear and make yourself scarce so she can get back to work?"

"Sure thing, Didi." He stepped into the room and extended his hand to Holly. She reached toward him and slid her palm against his. Delicious tingles worked their way up her arm. He squeezed her hand with the perfect pressure, gave her a quick smile, and left the room.

Funny. She'd greeted hundreds of people in her line of work, but none had left her so dazed as Mason just had.

Holly shook her head again and got back to work, focusing on recording Doris's vitals. "Sorry about that. Mason is very..."

"Distracting?"

That wasn't the word that came to mind, but sharing what came to her mind would be inappropriate. "Yeah. Distracting."

Mason

Mason paced the length of the front room, his feet creaking on the wood hidden under the carpet. Maybe he should go to the TV room and turn the TV back on to hide his anxious footfalls. But he could never get the volume button pressed in time and wasn't feeling up to being shocked by the sound. That left one option: listening to his steps and rabbity pulse.

Didi had warned him that a home health aide would be stopping by today. That whoever it was would be spending the next four weeks with his grandmother helping with showers, medication, and wound care. For some reason, he imagined a burly man in his fifties with a no-nonsense frown partially hidden by a walrusy mustache. Holly was nothing like that. She was soft and quiet and the most beautiful woman he'd ever seen.

"Be cool," he whispered to himself.

But maybe he didn't need to be cool. She'd said it was nice to meet his *mouth*. Maybe that meant she was just as affected by him as he was by her. Maybe. If he was lucky.

Mason glanced in the mirror hanging over the piano and noticed a smear of dirt running down the side of his nose and across his upper lip. That's when he decided he'd never been that lucky. He'd certainly not been lucky when Emily left him for another man. Or when she'd taken their house and dog and left him couch surfing like an absolute failure. At thirty-two he was supposed to have his life together.

He ducked into his room and wiped obsessively at his face. His afternoon spent weeding Didi's garden had just blown his first impression with Holly. Great. Putting his noise-canceling headphones in place, he leaned over his keyboard and got to work.

A while later, the overhead lights flickered, and Mason glanced at the door where Didi stood, leaning on her walker.

"What on earth are you listening to? I've been calling your name for two minutes," she said once he removed his headphones.

"Music. It helps me focus." She didn't need to know that it also helped to block out the sound of Holly's voice and his internal monologue about how embarrassing he was.

"Holly's gone."

"Oh?" His pulse picked up.

"She said to tell you goodbye." Didi's eyebrows rose. "She'll be back Thursday. Might I suggest you wash your face before talking to her again?"

"You're a pain in the ass, you know that?" Mason pressed his lips together.

Didi laughed, her thin shoulders shaking. "I'm funny."

"You *think* you're funny."

"Come on and make me dinner."

"I'm not your servant," he said as he obediently followed her into the kitchen, watching to be sure her feet were securely under her. It shocked him how well she was moving after having hip replacement surgery, but he still worried.

"That's for damn sure. If you were my servant, you'd be useful to me," she teased as she took a seat at the table. "What are you making?"

Mason glanced at the pile of veggies on the counter. "How does spaghetti sound?"

"I bet Holly likes spaghetti. I bet she'd like *your* spaghetti." Didi's eyebrows jumped suggestively.

Mason snorted his disapproval. "You're a troublemaker."

Didi grinned. "And you love me for it."

"I really do," he said with a laugh.

Holly

The next week, Holly checked the mirror in her car one more time before going in. She couldn't stop smiling. She would get to see Mason again. Every time she'd seen him over the past ten days, it got easier to talk to him without being a blubbering mess and mentioning his mouth.

"Doris?" she called out as she went through the front door.

"In my craft room again."

Holly smiled and walked quickly down the hall, resisting the temptation to look out the windows to the backyard to see if Mason was gardening again. He seemed to be outside working most mornings when she arrived. She was here to work. To be professional. Not to look for a disheveled man with auburn hair and the most beautiful golden-brown eyes.

"How are you today?"

Doris looked at her over the top of her glasses and scowled. "Worse than last time. Look at this mess."

For a split second, Holly's body coiled tight, ready to jump into action. Then she looked at what Doris was talking about. The needlepoint. With a sigh of relief, Holly relaxed.

"My hands are killing me, and I have nothing to show for it." The last bit was said with a pout.

"Let me help." Holly sat in the chair across from Doris and put her bag down.

Doris's pout disappeared. "You're going to take over my needlework project?"

Holly laughed. "No. But I will rub your hands." She took the hoop out of her fingers and put it down on a pile of embroidery thread.

"That sounds heavenly." Doris leaned back in her chair and held out her right hand.

Holly leaned forward and rubbed gentle circles across Doris's palm. "Have you been eating regularly and taking your medicine?"

"Yes, *mom*. Mason has alarms set for my medicine and forces me to eat. He's a bully."

Holly pressed her lips together. She loved the way Doris and Mason teased each other. It was a change from the snarling fights she usually equated with families. It made her happy knowing they could be that loving. If she hadn't seen it herself, she wouldn't believe it was possible.

"And you know he's a good cook."

"Yeah." Mason had been making her lunches for the last week

and a half. He was a fantastic cook. But that didn't matter. Why would that matter?

"He's also single."

Holly looked up and gave her a flat look.

"Are you single?" Doris's eyes twinkled.

"I know what you're trying to do."

"What is that?" Doris asked, all innocence and sweetness.

"Trying to get me to date your grandson. But it won't work. I don't date patients or their family members. Actually, I don't date at all." Relationships weren't worth it. It was easier to be alone.

"I'm not dying."

Holly frowned.

"You act like it's a done deal. I'm not on hospice. I just broke my hip. I'll be good as new before you know it."

"Especially if you keep doing your exercises." Holly tried with all her might to steer the conversation away from her dating life. Or lack thereof.

"Right. Which means your rule won't apply forever." Doris sighed and leaned back in her chair. "How do young people even meet these days? I met my husband at a singles dance."

If Holly played this right, she'd be able to keep Doris talking about her past instead of asking about Holly's future. "That sounds like fun. When was this?"

Just as Holly hoped, Doris started a story about the spring fling of 1960 and a dapper young man in a brown suit. It was love at first sight. They had moved into this very house two years later when she'd been pregnant with their first child. Every bit of the story was a stark contrast to Holly's childhood. Where Doris's family had enjoyed stability, Holly had moved every couple of years, the duration of each new location dependent upon how long her dad could keep a job. Drinking and working didn't mix.

"Let's switch hands," Holly said, interrupting the story for a moment and breaking out of her glum thoughts.

Doris sighed as Holly rubbed lotion onto her left hand and

then went on, talking about family trips and Sundays surrounded by extended family. The memories were filled with love, warmth, and humor. It wrapped around Holly like a hug.

"My hands feel so nice," Doris said with a smile. She closed her eyes, and within a matter of minutes, her breathing evened out.

Holly gently placed Doris's hand in her lap and tip-toed out of the craft room.

When she got to the kitchen, she found Mason busy getting ingredients ready for lunch. She hesitated for a moment, fighting with herself about whether she should offer to help. Yes, meal prep was part of her job, but she also liked spending time with him. In fact, she liked everything about this house.

"Doris is asleep, which means I can help you make lunch for once. Put me to work."

Mason

Mason smiled at Holly where she stood a few feet away grating parmesan for the pesto pasta they were making for lunch. Every time she came over, it was easier to be himself and not worry about trying to impress her. She seemed to like him for him. Then again, he was so out of practice, he might be misreading her.

The fresh bite of basil perfumed the air, but he could still smell a sweet scent that clung to Holly. That's how close she was.

They had been working side-by-side for a while when he finally said, "The basil is from Didi's garden. She grows it every year."

"I bet it's going to be great." She laughed and held up the grater. "Or should I say grate?"

Mason snorted. "You're funny."

"Not as funny as Doris."

"Don't tell her that, you'll give her a big head," he teased.

"You *really* love her." It wasn't a question.

"I do," He dropped his voice and leaned toward her, and added conspiratorially, "She's always been my favorite."

Holly pressed her lips together and mimicked locking them with a key. "I won't tell her that either."

"Can you imagine? She'd be insufferable." Mason smiled and shook off the water clinging to the basil leaves, placing them on a cutting board next to Holly's. "As the first grandkid, I practically grew up here. My favorite was Sunday dinner with Didi and Papa Larry. I still miss him."

"He sounds awesome. She was telling me about the day they met."

"The spring fling?"

"The one and only." Holly grinned and it lit up the room. Her smile did wonders to balance the melancholy he felt when he thought of his grandpa.

"I love that story." Mason sighed. "He's been gone for five years. Didi didn't do so well right after. We all took turns checking in on her, but she never missed a Sunday dinner."

"Everyone still comes?"

"Not everyone." Emily used to come, but that had stopped last year. Right before she left him. "Some people have moved away. But my folks come, and my aunt, and a couple of my cousins still live around here. I wouldn't miss it. How often do you see your family?"

"I don't."

"Ever?" His mouth hung open.

"We're not close. I thought that was normal until I started spending time here. You actually like each other. That's weird to me, but I'm learning it's a whole lot healthier than the mess of dysfunction I call family."

Mason shook his head and pulled the food processor from the highest shelf over the stove. "I can't imagine how hard that would be. My family is everything to me." When he turned around, he caught Holly looking at the strip of exposed skin between his shirt and pants. It had been happening more and more often, and he liked it.

"Smells good. What are we having for lunch?" Didi called from down the hall.

Holly smiled and turned toward her but didn't rush to coddle her. She just watched Didi's slow progress into the kitchen. "Your mobility is already better than last week. I'm impressed, Doris."

"I'm very impressive." Didi winked. "What have you two been up to? No good, I hope."

"Didi," Mason scolded.

"I was hoping I would have to avert my eyes. Finding you two *in flagrante delicto* would do my heart good."

Mason's entire body flushed. Not only from the embarrassment of what she had said, but because he often found himself daydreaming about being wrapped in Holly's arms. "I swear I'm going to push you down the stairs one of these days," he muttered.

"You and what army?" Didi asked with a laugh.

"Why don't I help you with a shower while Mason finishes making lunch?" Holly said, steering Didi's walker toward the bathroom.

"I'm not the one you should be trying to get naked." Didi's voice trailed down the hall followed by Holly's laugh.

Didi was going to be the death of him.

Holly

The third week, Doris insisted they change their schedule so Holly would come on Sunday at four. It was later than normal, but she was used to changing her work hours around her patients. Coming so late meant Doris would be her last patient for the day.

She helped Doris shower, then wash and set her hair. They tackled curlers, hairspray, and a hair dryer.

By the time they emerged from the bathroom, voices filled the kitchen.

"Sounds like the whole damn family is here," Doris said with a smile.

Holly froze. Was this why Doris wanted her to come over later than usual? She wouldn't put it past her to come up with a plan like this. Doris noticed Holly's panic.

"It's okay. They won't bite." She turned her twinkling eyes up at Holly. "Unless you ask nicely."

Holly laughed. She couldn't help it. She followed Doris down the hall and into the bustling kitchen. A half a dozen people filled the space, all laughing and teasing each other. Calls of greeting rang out, and each person took their turn kissing Doris's cheek or giving her a gentle hug.

"Give a woman some room, will you?" Doris used her cane to hobble her way into the TV room and sit down on the couch between two younger people.

Holly remained at the edge of the kitchen, unsure of what to do. She still needed to work with Doris on her exercises, but she didn't want to interrupt. If she did, someone would remind her of her place and tell her to get lost. They had been making enough progress that Doris had graduated from walker to cane. Missing a day of exercises could set her back.

"It's kind of a zoo, huh?" Mason asked, sidling up next to her.

Relief washed over her. Mason had that effect on her. He was the familiar face in a room of strangers. She knew he would go out of his way to make her feel welcome.

To prove her point, Mason said, "Let me introduce you to everyone."

He proceeded to say the names of his mom, dad, sister, aunt, and three cousins. One by one, the family members raised their hands and greeted her. The names went in one ear and out the other, but the warmth of their words stuck.

"There's a quiz after," Doris added with a chuckle.

Mason rolled his eyes. "Everyone, this is Holly Campbell, Didi's home health aide."

"It's nice to meet you all." Holly smiled and looked around the room.

Everyone got back to what they were doing before, chatting and laughing with each other as if a stranger in the middle of their family party was no big deal. The oddity of Doris and Mason's relationship extended to everyone. These people genuinely liked each other. No one said biting words that were meant to hurt others or gave fake smiles to cover them up.

"Give us a hand in the kitchen?" Mason asked, bumping his shoulder into hers.

"I should let you get on with your evening," Holly said, stuffing her hands into her pockets.

"I still have exercises to do," Doris called out from the TV room. "Will you give me a moment to rest, though? My energy levels aren't what they used to be."

"Aren't you curious about Sunday dinners at Didi's? You've heard the stories, now experience it for yourself," Mason said in a tour guide voice. It made Holly laugh.

An hour later, Holly stood over a massive bowl of mashed potatoes.

"Those look perfect, dear," Mason's mom said. "Will you please put them on the table? Everyone, dinner is ready."

"Oh, I should—"

"Sit down?" Doris cut Holly off as she walked past to the head of the table. "There's a spot set for you right there." She pointed to the open seat next to Mason, who flushed a bright pink.

"That's where I've been sitting since Emily left," one of the cousins protested from the couch.

"No arguments, or I'm cutting you out of the will." Doris winked at Holly while the family laughed.

"I shouldn't intrude," Holly tried to bow out one more time.

"I'm asking you to stay. Plus, you made the potatoes, which are my favorite. By default, *you're* my favorite." Doris sat down and leaned her cane against the edge of the table.

The conversation paused briefly for a prayer, then picked back up. They talked about everything and nothing. Even topics that would start an argument between her parents inspired jokes. Slowly but surely, Holly felt more at home around these people than she ever had around her family.

"Who's Emily?" Holly whispered, leaning slightly toward Mason.

He inhaled sharply and waited a while before answering in equally hushed tones, "My ex."

"Oh." Holly nodded and then spoke without thinking, "She must be pretty dense if she left you."

Mason's face lit up with a smile so big, everyone at the table noticed.

Mason

After dinner, Mason watched Holly working with Didi in the TV room. His cheeks hurt from smiling.

It had been a long time since he'd enjoyed a family dinner that much. He tried not to be too obvious about staring at Holly, but it was a monumental task. She'd been so hesitant at the beginning of the party, but it didn't take long for her to warm up. The second she was out of the room, Didi called him over, and he knew he'd been caught. He could tell by the look in her devious eyes. He stood in front of her and bent over so they could have a somewhat private conversation.

"She's a wonderful woman, Mason." Didi knew how to cut to the chase.

"I know."

"Have you asked her out?"

"Didi," Mason hung his head and laughed. He should expect her bluntness, but sometimes it still took him by surprise.

"Well? Have you?"

He looked up and met her eyes. They were gentle and loving and a little too pushy. "No. I haven't."

"But you want to, right?"

"Very much." He wanted Holly more than anything, but taking that step scared him.

As if Didi could read his mind, she said, "It must be frightening to put yourself back out there again. I'm not going to mince words. Holly likes you. You like her. Ask her out. She makes you happy and you deserve that. So does she."

"Didi," he said more softly, touched by her words.

"For a long time, you thought Emily was your person. Someone you could build a family of your own with. It's time for you to try again. Holly could be your person. You won't know until you ask. She's only here for one more week, so don't miss your chance."

Mason nodded. Yes, he could ask. He did deserve to be happy. And if the last few weeks were any indication, he knew he could make Holly happy too. "Okay. I'll do it."

"That's my boy. I was afraid I'd have to threaten you with my cane."

"You and what army?" Mason laughed.

Didi grinned up at him from her recliner. "Did I mention I want great-grand babies?"

"Okay, you can stop talking now." Mason straightened his back and shook his head. He could feel the heat on his cheeks spreading.

"As the eldest grandkid, you have certain responsibilities."

"Does anyone have a ball gag?" Mason said to the room at large.

Didi laughed but didn't stop talking. "I think I have a book somewhere that might help. It has diagrams."

The tips of his ears burned with embarrassment, which was when Holly came back into the room.

"Diagrams for what?" she asked, her packed medical bag hanging from the crook of her arm.

"Nothing," Mason said quickly, motioning to the door. "If you're ready to leave, I'll walk you out."

Holly

Holly smiled and nodded, trying to figure out why Mason was so flushed. "It was nice to meet everyone. Doris, I'll see you Tuesday."

"Don't threaten me with a good time," Doris said to the delight of everyone in the room.

When they were outside, Holly put her bag on the roof of her car. When she turned around, Mason bounced on the balls of his feet. She could feel his anxiety washing over him. What had she missed while she was packing up her supplies?

"What was Doris talking about?"

Mason stilled immediately. "She was just teasing me."

"She does that." Holly smiled. Everything about Doris and her entire family made her happy.

"Indeed. But she means well." Mason frowned. "I think."

Silence stretched between them, then they started talking at the same time.

"Mason, I—"

"I wanted to—"

They laughed and said, "You first." At the same time.

Mason touched her forearm, and the same electric tingles ignited, just like they had every time they touched. "You go first. Please." He didn't pull away from her.

Holly took a deep breath. The whole time she'd been packing up her bag in the bathroom, she'd been practicing what she wanted to say to him. "Mason, I've been thinking." She let out a long breath. She could do this. "Well, about you. And your family, and how nice they are and how comfortable I feel. You make me feel safe." She put her hand on top of his and their fingers melted together, like they belonged that way. She couldn't tear her eyes away. They fit together in so many ways. "This is all new to me. I mean, people have asked me out before, but I never wanted it, you know? I think I hide behind my no-dating-rule." She shook her head. "Not that you've made a move on me. I don't even know if you–" When she looked up, she saw the same need reflected back at her. "Oh."

"I want you more than you could possibly know." Mason stepped closer, and his voice got softer and deeper. "Tell me more about this no-dating-rule."

"It's just a stupid rule I made about not dating patients or their family because I'm too afraid to take a chance on people. Then I met you and your family, and for the first time, I'm not afraid." It was the truest and scariest thing she'd ever said out loud.

His beautiful mouth turned up at the corners. "That's good."

"I've wanted to kiss you since the first time we met," she admitted in a whisper.

"I seem to remember you saying it was nice to meet my mouth." Mason's body shook with laughter.

Holly smiled. "Why don't you shut up and kiss me already?"

"What about your no-dating-rule?" His breaths came quick and shallow, just like hers.

"It's just a kiss." She wasn't being totally honest. She'd been honest enough for one day. It was definitely more than a kiss, but it was best not to complicate things when her brain was short-circuiting.

"Does this mean I can't ask you out?" Mason leaned down and hovered his lips over hers.

"Ask me next week."

Finding Write Where I Belong

Debra Birdwell Winkler

I was asked recently when it was that I knew I wanted to be a writer. I immediately responded, "When I won a poetry award in fifth grade." I had been encouraged by my teacher to enter and was on top of the world. That was when I knew I wanted to be a writer!

In sixth grade, my teacher asked the class to write on a piece of paper what we wanted to be when we grew up. I proudly wrote AUTHOR and signed my name. Other students were praised for writing down doctor, nurse, judge, lawyer, scientist, teacher, and a slew of other professions. One girl wrote she wanted to be a housewife and a mother. The teacher said she could be more than that, but if she was sure she'd be happy, it was great.

When she came to my name, the teacher looked at me and said, "Debra, you'll never be a writer of anything because you don't read very well, and you can't write a lick!"

I was embarrassed and devastated, needless to say. She asked me what my second choice was, and I answered TEACHER.

I remembered she shook her head. "You know, Debra, I don't think you'll even be good at that."

I cried all the way home that afternoon because I was going to be a NOTHING.

Going through school, I carried the weight of that rejection. In high school, I found I could sing, and as a senior I auditioned for Juilliard and was accepted. I was on top of the world again but was shot down by my mother who informed me we couldn't afford the tuition. I was also accepted into a teacher's college, but my mother had pretty much the same reaction.

So, I was confirmed to be a NOTHING again.

After high school, I moved on to various clerical and secretarial positions, leaving my dream of being something other than a NOTHING behind me in the rearview mirror. After two failed marriages and three children later, I concentrated on making a home for my children and me, while earning enough money to make ends meet. For more than twenty years, I continued to work in office positions, taking care of my children, and slowly taking one college class at a time when I could afford to do so.

Finally, I met the man of my dreams who seemed to love me as well as my children. We dated for three years and, during that time, he encouraged me to finish college, encouraged my writing poetry and short stories, and encouraged me to never give up my writing dream. After we married, I finished college and became the teacher I yearned to be. But my writing dream was still not achieved. I did continue to write poetry and short stories, and created several plays for children (a couple were even performed in front of audiences). I began a novel when I was pregnant with my youngest. But I didn't know what to do with my writing, not until later.

Not until after I survived the next big changes in my life did my writing dream come to fruition. My husband died, my children moved out of the house, and I retired. Sounds rather sad and mundane, right? However, I had to do something with my time.

Finally, in February of 2020, I pulled out the box where I had stored most of my writing. Some handwritten, some typed out. I had a couple of these manuscripts on floppy disks, but I no longer had a computer that read those. I began organizing my creations and came across that first unfinished novel based on a particular time in my life. The story involved the murder of a not-so-nice antagonist who very few people in town liked. I set everything else aside and had the brilliant idea to finish it.

I retyped and rewrote and edited this novel. The villain stayed the same, but I added scenes which detailed his misdeeds, showed more details concerning the innocence of the wife and children, and changed the murderer. By the end of March 2020, it was finished. A 273-page manuscript of 84,551 words. A mystery. I was proud I had completed the story. My children were excited I had finally finished my first novel.

I felt a great deal of accomplishment but didn't know what to do then. That was the question. My family told me to continue writing. And that's when I realized my head was full of stories I wanted to put down on paper. When I mentioned my writing plans to a few friends and two of my sisters, they volunteered to read my stories and give their opinions.

It was easy to concentrate on writing because I'd hurt my right foot and was laid up with a boot for five months, using crutches, which injured my left shoulder, causing the need for rotator cuff surgery. COVID may have limited my access to the outside world, but I couldn't go anywhere anyway.

You know the old adage: "When God closes a door, He leaves a window open." I jumped through that "window" and began writing another novel and then another one and a third. I decided to search the Internet for classes and seminars to help me be a better writer. I found writing support, but each had a price tag I couldn't afford (at least the websites I reviewed).

My son checked out publishers and he received all kinds of information on how much it would cost to publish. One site promised it would only cost $5,000 to begin with for them to review my manuscripts and get me started on the way to publishing one of my novels, getting me out there in the writing world. That $5,000 didn't cover book covers, nor were they responsible for publicity. These guys would just put my novel on Amazon, but I would receive one printed copy for free. Another website promised I'd be a bestselling author in a year if I would just pay them oodles of money and they'd work with me. I didn't have the kind of money any of these sites wanted to charge. A friend of mine said I could have a book printed at the University of Utah for just $25 each, but they didn't provide editing services. The UofU was cheaper than the 'scammers' but I didn't think I could publish anything without a professional editor.

In my Internet research, I found out how to look for agents and read up on how to query and began investigating agents to see who would be right for me. By June 2020, I was armed with my three completed manuscripts. As I was working on another story, I began querying with lots of enthusiasm. However, by the middle of August, I had queried thirty-five agents and each one had rejected me with form letters. You know, "Thank you so much but your manuscript is just not for me." (We all know those letters).

Needless to say, I was feeling rather devastated again, but I refused to give up and, encouraged by my family and beta readers, I completed another romance. Looking for writing groups, I ran across the Utah branch of Romance Writers of America (RWA). I was ecstatic to call the point person to find out more information. She told me the RWA Utah Chapter was closing in December, but I could become a non-paying member until then. As requested, I sent the first chapter of one of my romances to be reviewed. I was told what I had was a good start and was given a few pointers, which I took to heart and edited this romance (which I was told was more a romantic suspense). I also now had access to the RWA website, where I found writing opportunities I never knew existed. Renewed with writing eagerness, I wrote another romance in September and October. Then, I found NaNoWriMo (National

Novel Writing Month) and wrote another novel during the month of November.

By January 2021, my querying still reaped only rejections, but I had finished my seventh novel and began on an eighth. I wrote something every day and searched various sites for submission opportunities. Finding Reedsy, Winning Writers, and Writer's Digest ended up being great because I submitted short stories tuned to writing contest specifications. I continued to be rejected by agents and contests, but then four of my short stories were printed online. I was in seventh heaven!

In May 2021, I joined a writing community of 600 writers from all over the world. With this online group, I learned a lot. We critiqued each other's manuscripts, met with editors and agents who offered advice, and received praise from each other. I was beginning to feel that my writing was getting better as I edited my manuscripts from what I was learning. I continued to query prospective agents through Query Tracker, Manuscript Wish List, and Association of American Literary Agents, as well as submitted to every Pitch War I could. In the summer of 2021, I attended the online Colorado and San Diego Writing Conferences, pitching a novel at each and was asked by two agents to submit a query letter and first three chapters of my romance. One agent rejected my novel, the other gave valuable feedback and requested that I resend it (I was rejected the second time).

In the meantime, I was getting unsolicited requests from editors to view my manuscripts who charged from $2,000 to $4,000 for a 50,000-word manuscript. I discovered Reedsy had editor recommendations, so I contacted three who were much more reasonable. I emailed all three but only one was encouraging and she's the one I went with. Although she couldn't work me into her schedule until November of 2021, she gave me ideas on where to search for more submissions. She also called me periodically to see how I was doing (and I do mean called).

Then, miracle of miracles, in September 2021, I found the

League of Utah Writers (LUW) and the Romance Chapter. I was elated. Liz Suggs and Virginia Babcock of the Romance Chapter were inviting and personal and supportive and passionate about my...MY...writing. I was cheered on by the group when one of my stories was published in an online publication (this story was nominated for the 2022 BEST OF THE NET NONFICTION AWARD). When we went over query letters in October, my letter was critiqued with positive suggestions rather than being told what I did wrong. I was invited to attend the Romance Chapter's 2022 Conference. I was also urged to pitch one of my novels at the Conference. This encouraged me to submit a short story to the Romance Chapter's open anthology call.

I did pitch one of my novels at the Conference in January 2022. The publisher asked to send my query letter and the first five chapters. The full manuscript was requested a couple of weeks later. By May, I had signed a contract and my romantic suspense, CYCLE OF COINCIDENCE, was published in November 2022. A short romance story was also published in the Romance Chapter's February 2022 publication, SECOND CHANCE, A Romance Anthology.

With the Romance Chapter's help and inspiration, I continued to submit manuscripts to various places. Then, another romance story was published in the 2023 Romance Anthology, SO WE MEET AGAIN, along with a short story in LUW's 2023 WE ARE DANGEROUS Anthology. I've attended several LUW Conferences and continued to be involved with the Romance Chapter's January conference for the last two years. In addition, I've had several of my stories published in other anthologies.

You know, Abraham Lincoln said, "The best way to predict the future, is to create it." I know that with the LUW Romance Chapter, I am creating a future. Liz and Virginia and this wonderful and caring writing group continue to stimulate me and others to be the best we can be with fabulous suggestions and support. Also, they have taught me to use their example of support and care for other writers.

Because of LUW and this magnificent group of LUW Romance writers, I know I am exactly WRITE WHERE I BELONG!

Thank you!

TAILS OF TIME

WMDAVID

"Man, if that ol' porch rocker could talk... What a tale of tails it could tell!"

Over seventy-five years' worth of tales, that's what. There's Arvie's arse and Cowboy's keister, Hank's heinie, Bill's bum, Carolyn's caboose, Cecil's stern, Sharon's cheeks, Freddie's fanny, both Ruby & Roy's rears... The list goes on.

Then, of course, there's Dave's derriere.

It might look like an old rockin' chair. By observation, you'd think it is mainly held together by a decades-old combination of paint and rust. But if you pick up this chair to move it, you realize it is heavy. And solid. Steel hardened by more than a century. If you were to try and peel back the layers of paint, you'd trace back through a lot of those years.

And you'd meet a lot of tails.

Mine is one tail that has seen every coat of paint since the original. If we could somehow reel the time together and my tail today could meet my 1965 tail, I don't know what they would say to each other. But tail-speak is another story entirely. And this one is about the chair.

Back when my tail and the chair first met, it sat on the front porch of my grandparents' home in Downtown Tibbee, Missis- sippi. You won't find that on a map. Pretty much if you don't already know where Tibbee is, neither this story nor a search of available maps will help much. (And callin' it "Downtown Tibbee" is an insider's joke, of sorts. It's where the only paved road and the railroad tracks crossed. Tibbee has neither a down nor a town.) So, let's just say Tibbee is *true* country. *Proud* country. Deep south. The kind o' country where folks didn't have air conditionin', so they sat out on they front porches of a warm summer's evenin' and rocked chairs like this one, in timin' with the heat-drone o' cicadas, their tails rockin' with the rhythm.

On such an evenin' half a century ago, my ten-year-old tail would have been relegated to the porch stairs. The rockin' chair would have been a place of honor for my elders. Next to our tails, there would have been half-downed glasses o' sweet tea left over from dinner with the sweat pourin' down the outsides of the glasses just the way it poured down our faces. And just maybe on this particular evenin' the tail in the old chair belonged to a man known to the community as "Cowboy." He was a carpenter by trade and a friendly face to all. He was also my grandfather.

The chair sat on the far end of the porch. In the grass just below (and within spittin' distance of the chair) was a huge cast-iron pot. More of a rusty cauldron than a pot. As a kid, I 'magined that we had somehow confiscated it from witches who had concocted their last brew. Just maybe, that was why a man called "Cowboy" now had it. I don't know. My grandfather died 'fore I was given the opportunity to glean much wisdom from him.

But on this partic'lar hot afternoon, my grandfather had taken me fishin' down to the pond, and this big pot was now swimmin' with bream. We would need to scale and clean 'em once the heat of the day abated. You see, the pot sat below the joined eaves of two tin roof sections and caught rainwater. From the rockin' chair on a rainy evenin' the splashin' in the pot would sound like a waterfall above the noise of the rain on the tin roof! Of course, we had a water pump and well-house, but this old pot worked as our water source for waterin' plants, rinsin' hands, or holdin' our bass, bream, or catfish 'til we cleaned 'em.

On evenin's when Cowboy sat on the porch, it was guaranteed that a passin' neighbor or two would stop by for a visit. And a glass of tea. Over the years, I developed the skill of scootin' my tail quickly through the open screen door to retrieve those glasses of tea. Those of us who dawdled learned that the stout spring on the door meant business when it slammed the door onto our young and skinny behinds. (Back then our tails were skinny, I assure you.)

Fast forward to the next paint job, and Cowboy is in our memories. I learned very young that friendliness and a larger-than-life persona are no match for cancer. His likeness remained for most of my life in one painting my Aunt Sharon left on the wall in the hallway of that old house in Tibbee when she later married and moved away.

The shadows of the years and the loss of my grandfather brought the need for my still-skinny tail to become the man of the house. Not that I deserved it... or even knew it for that matter. In high school and college, I was far from a man. But me and Joe from 'crost the railroad tracks and my younger brother Mark, well, I guess we paved our own paths toward manhood.

Probably just to keep us out of her way, or to keep us out of trouble, or to teach us things we'd never learn in college... hmm... In retrospect, it was probably for all these reasons (my grandmother was much smarter than I knew at the time). Any-hoo, my grandmother convinced us to build a log cabin usin' nothin' but hand tools. We picked a spot at the furthest corner of the property, on the highest hill in Tibbee, and overlookin' Trulove's Lake. (The cabin, like the tail-speak stories, is a different story.)

When you're fifteen years old and spendin' sixteen-hour days cuttin', skinnin', haulin', notchin', and stackin' logs, let me tell you— nobody's cookin' was as good at the end of a day as Grandma's! And whoever got to the front porch first after dinner got the steel rockin' chair! (We still didn't have air-conditionin'.) I can't recall much about the conversations on the front porch on those evenin's, 'cept for one common theme. As we thought of ourselves as true, frontier-mountain men (buildin' a log cabin by hand), we would always end up talkin' about how someday we'd end up livin' on a mountain out west. Heck, we might even buy us a mountain!

That summer gave way to a few others, and maybe another coat of paint for the old rocker, to find my tail gettin' older but not much wiser. I lived with my grandmother through college. I could try to make it sound noble and say that she needed a man around to help care for the place. But the real truth was that I needed my grandmother. My college education was more than most people got. It was farm life and gettin' my tail up early even on Saturday. It was goin' to class with purple thumbs from shellin' peas. (A tummy full o' peas 'n cornbread'll put a special smile on your face when your tail hits that chair on the front porch with a tall iced tea in your hand!)

Some things changed. Tibbee residents eventually ended up with "street water" that we had to pay for, and at one point at our old homeplace we added an air conditioner in one of the windows. (It was just for when we had comp'ny...) Other things didn't change as much. We still talked about how we'd end up on a mountain out west.

Someday.

You've certainly noticed that it is no longer the 1960s, even if you only do so through the larger shadow of my tail over time. That chair on the front porch saw a lot of family Fourth of July holidays, Thanksgivin's, and Christmases. It saw new paint and old tails. As I had children of my own, it held old tails and new tails at the same time! Heck, I can even remember my own father (bless his soul) sittin' on the porch and talkin' about mountains out west...

Tibbee, in its simplicity, taught us all a lot of important lessons. One of those lessons was to dream. Ironically, when you leave there, one of the things you dream about is Tibbee. And grandfathers that you have lost. And grandmothers that you have lost. And fathers that you have lost. And children that you have lost...

And then Tibbee, itself... is gone. You won't find *my* Tibbee on the map. My grandparents' house burned down. The porch burned down with it.

But not the chair. It just needed a new coat of paint.

If you have been kind enough to read this far, you might be wonderin' on the whereabouts of the old rocker. Well, I guess it held onto all those dreams and stories over and through the many years and coats of paint. It has found the mountain at last. Mount Ogden, Utah.

And this chair's story won't be complete 'til you visit, plant your tail, and add your story to it.

We'll have a tall glass of iced tea waitin'.

And if my glass holds instead some bourbon, you might hear another story or two... About ol' Tibbee Joe, who still lives across the tracks... About skinny-dippin' tails, 'n hand-hewn log cabins... And other tales that'll only lead to more. But then that's what rockin' chairs are all about. Tails n' stories. Life n' dreams.

FACING DRAGONS

BROOKE J LOSEE

A blade made of pure silver? That would attract thieves. Cornelias Quickslayer couldn't afford to deal with thieves right now, and honestly, I wasn't sure silver would improve performance anyway. And then there was the armor fashioned out of scales that glowed neon green and blue. That was bound to help with stealth.

Not.

It was all wrong.

With a frustrated groan, I pounded the delete key with my forefinger, giving the keyboard the kind of punch that should be reserved for a boxing ring. How many times had I rewritten this scene? It had to be approaching something close to infinity.

Because infinity was definitely approachable in my medieval fantasy land.

Getting the story right was quickly becoming the bane of my existence. At this rate, I'd fail to meet personal deadlines, or worse, fall into the pit of darkness. AKA: imposter syndrome. I would pull myself out eventually, but it would require time I didn't have and most likely more snacks than currently resided inside the pantry. One jumbo-sized bag of miniature candy bars had already succumbed to my ravenous stress eating.

Don't judge. A guy has to deal somehow.

I raked a hand through my hair and scrolled to the beginning of the chapter. Sometimes, a quick read of what I'd written the last few days would help me gain momentum. Sometimes, it wouldn't. Usually, I found joy in exploring the worlds that existed solely inside my head, but at times, the plot stumped me worse than a well-twisted Rubik cube.

Today, my story happened to be a Rubik cube on steroids, featuring several plot holes and a hero with a poor fashion sense— poor for fighting twin-headed dragons that were attracted to light, at least. He might do well battling a zombie bartender in a 70s-style nightclub, complete with disco ball. Maybe if I gave him sequined thigh guards, he could blind the undead with his dazzling wardrobe.

I shook my head to dash the mental image and focused my thoughts. It was time to tell my Elmer Fudd brain to give up the hunting because I'd gone down too many rabbit holes already today. Zombie bartenders didn't need to be anywhere on the radar of possible plot twists.

After another hour and a few hundred more words, I left my computer and shut off the light. It was almost 11 pm, and I needed to get some sleep for work tomorrow. By work, I meant my job as a lawyer—the way the bills were currently paid—not the writing and rewriting that awaited me after.

Snuggling under my covers, I unlocked my phone to do one last check for messages and emails. A lone text awaited me, the red number one hovering above the app beckoning me to take a peek, but I ignored it. I knew what it said, and I was far too exhausted to respond. Perhaps tomorrow I'd have more brain power. Then I'd know what to say, or rather *how* to say it.

I leaned back in my swivel chair with a satisfied smirk. Finishing a chapter always gave me the deepest satisfaction, especially when the completion was achieved with no regrets and the plot didn't look like a holey sponge. My hero had overcome the obstacles on his quest and arrived at the climax. He was even attired properly to face his twin-headed dragon.

This would be his most difficult fight yet, and my excitement at putting words to the page nearly had my fingers flying over the keyboard. But I stopped myself with a promise to begin the final battle this weekend when I could devote more than an hour or two to the cause. With an important meeting tomorrow at Eskrow and Eskrow Law, I'd likely be picking up a new case, and that meant the rest of the week would require late nights at the office. It wasn't a horrendous prospect. I liked my job, though the hours could be daunting. The weekend would still be mine, however.

And I knew exactly how I'd spend it.

I reached my arms high above my head, stretching toward the ceiling with a deep yawn. Building worlds was exhausting. Each time I won a case at the law firm, I felt a tremendous amount of pride, but there was something different about creating an entire world from scratch. I was in complete control of where my story went.

Unlike the real world where control was often nothing more than an illusion.

I had agency, of course, but I couldn't do anything about *other* peoples' choices. As if by instinct, I unlocked my phone and stared at the message app. There was a number two hovering there now, mocking my irritation—or maybe my hesitance. This afternoon, a second message had joined the first. I'd only read who it was from before shutting off the phone and ignoring it completely.

Curiosity pricked at me, but I didn't concede to its demands. I wasn't ready to face the words waiting for me, and if I put them off long enough, I would miss what I wagered was a request altogether. Eventually, I'd stop getting them.

Wouldn't I?

A mixture of guilt and disgust churned my stomach. When had I become such a coward? It was easier to come home and help my characters conquer dragons than to face the demons in my own life. Despite the mythical beasts and dark sorcerers, my fantasy worlds were safer than reality. I could slip away without fear of losing more than I already had, without worrying that the mistakes I'd made would follow me.

The problem was those mistakes were waiting when I came back. No matter how many dragons my hero slayed, he couldn't help me defeat the biggest one of all.

I tapped my finger against the edge of my phone, warring with my thoughts. Reading the messages wouldn't mean a commitment. At least I would know what kind of dragon I was up against. The smartest heroes took the time to strategize, didn't they?

I took a deep breath and tapped on the message app. The list popped up, and the sight of the name in bold lettering tightened my chest. Normally, I didn't have a problem answering texts from my mom, but this time of year was different. Every March I got the same invitation, one I knew would beckon me home.

Swallowing against the lump in my throat, I opened the thread between us.

MOM: Hey, Josh! Hope you're doing okay. We're getting tons of rain here and the mud must be six inches deep. It's like walking in quicksand.

A smile crossed my face. Mom always ranted about the weather via text. She ranted about it in person, too, but I wasn't privileged to have in-person conversations with her. Not anymore.

MOM: It hasn't stopped your dad from working on the lawn. We're planning his annual surprise party for Sunday night. Hope you can come.

Dad's annual surprise party wasn't actually a surprise. How could it be when Mom held it the Sunday following his birthday every year? I'd expected that to be the reason for her texts, but confirming it still made me nauseous. I hadn't spoken to Dad since last year. Since the last party, to be exact. The event was tainted with negativity and haunting memories now.

My finger hovered over the letters as I debated whether to respond. I'd tell her I couldn't come, and she would see right through whatever excuse I provided. It bothered me that no matter how I chose to word it, Mom would be disappointed. Hurt.

But I didn't know what else to do. A sharp sword of guilt stabbed at me, and not just because of Mom. The words spoken in anger had felt right at the time, but now? I wanted to take them back—to approach the situation differently.

Do-overs weren't a thing in the real world, though. When I didn't like where my stories headed, I could backtrack and rewrite them. Reality wasn't so forgiving. There was no editing my life; instead, each line written became a permanent fixture in my personal history.

I shut off the phone. Sleeping on my response wouldn't hurt. I had a few days before the party and would let Mom know well in advance that I couldn't make it. She'd have time to get over the disappointment and still enjoy the party. I might not be there, but my siblings would be, and they deserved to enjoy themselves even if I couldn't. They deserved to see Mom happy.

A quick shower relaxed my tense muscles, and my eyes fell closed as soon as my head hit the pillow, but rest remained elusive.

Several late nights at the office kept me from thinking too much about the text I'd yet to respond to. The longer I went, the more guilt wounded my insides. Mom had surely noticed the message had been read by now, but she hadn't sent another. I might have felt vindicated in my frustration and determination to avoid my parents if she pestered me about coming, but my mom had never been one to insert herself into her children's lives to an obnoxious level. She was kind and understanding, and therefore any justifica-tions I might have conceived for being a jerk flew out the window.

I needed to respond.

The entire drive home was dedicated to mulling over my words. What could I say that she didn't already know? The argu-ment with my father hadn't been a secret. She'd heard the entire thing. Anyone with ears in the vicinity had.

I was punishing my mother by not attending. I knew that. But I couldn't bring myself to face Dad. Regret might haunt me, but I wasn't the only one to blame for the incident. His words had been just as harsh. Just as infuriating. My temper had gotten the better of me, but that didn't mean that I was wrong to defend myself—to stand up for my dreams.

Becoming a lawyer was a point of pride in my family. Three generations proved that. I'd wanted to follow in Dad and my grandfather's footsteps for as long as I could remember, and so had my brothers. The celebration that followed each of us passing the LSAT was bigger than a presidential candidate's after winning an election, complete with kazoos and party poppers. The achieve-ment had forged a bond between us all that I thought could never be broken.

Until Dad discovered my secret hobby.

It had started with what I thought was curiosity. Dad asked questions after my oldest brother let it slip that I spent my evenings writing. The conversation shifted so quickly, with Dad scolding me for wasting my time and poking fun at my dream of one day publishing, that I barely had time to consider how my responses egged him on. It had all exploded in a matter of minutes, and I'd stormed off, angry and hurt.

And I'd bathed in those feelings ever since, refusing to step foot in my family home. For a year, I'd stayed away, despite living less than an hour away. For a year, I'd found a home in my story and lived there.

Maybe it was time to move on. I could let the argument go. If

Dad and I never discussed my *hobby* again, then we could make it work. Things might never be the same between us, but at least Mom wouldn't suffer for it.

I pulled into the garage and turned off the ignition. For several moments, I stared at the cement wall through the windshield, my pulse pounding in my ears. Could I do this? Could I agree to go and actually follow through? It wouldn't be easy, that much I knew for sure. The memories and feelings had festered for too long to simply rake them away like fall leaves.

But I could pretend. Just for one night. I missed Mom.

I missed Dad, too, but admitting that made the ache in my chest worse.

Reaching for my phone, I drew a fortifying breath. My fingers moved over the screen, and I hit send before I could second guess myself. The message was short. A simple, "I'll be there."

I couldn't decide whether I regretted the commitment or not.

Heavy footsteps carried me into the house, briefcase in hand. I needed a distraction from all the scenarios playing out in my head. I ordered a pizza and sat down on the leather couch, laptop positioned for a session of worldbuilding. Diving into the fantasy land I'd created calmed my nerves. Writing eased my concerns and frustrations. I'd started putting words to paper because of how it made me feel. It wasn't that I hated my life, but writing just did it for me —like how some people enjoyed snuggling their cats or exercising or skydiving. It was a rush. Something I could be proud of.

Something I wished my family could be proud of too.

I leaned back in my chair, once again happy with where my story had gone. Cornelias Quickslayer had achieved victory, defying certain death, with all limbs intact. The tension was good, the action believable. All that remained was to tie up the loose plot threads and write a satisfying conclusion.

Which I would do tomorrow after work. The rest of today would be spent at my parents' house.

Assuming everything went smoothly, at least. Maybe I was being optimistic, but hope was part of my plan to slay the beast of resentment sitting between me and Dad. Or put it to sleep, if nothing else. Back-up plans were always a good idea.

And if things didn't go well, I would have my story to escape to tomorrow.

The drive to my childhood home was shorter than I would have liked. Despite having a few days to prepare, I wasn't ready. What if the second I walked into the house, Dad berated me again? Did he even know I was coming? What if *he* didn't want me to come?

I tapped the steering wheel and tried to force the questions to the back of my mind. Whether my father wanted me there or not, I had to go. I couldn't continue to ignore Mom. At least if I showed up at the party, I would know for sure whether Dad wanted me around. And maybe, just maybe, we could put the past behind us.

There were two extra vehicles—Ash's red corvette and Kevin's sunshine yellow Lamborghini—in the long gravel driveway of my parents' country home, which meant my brothers had already arrived. Light chatter floated on a gentle breeze from the backyard, and the tantalizing scent of smoked short ribs assaulted me.

My stomach grumbled. I'd missed Dad's superb BBQ skills over the last year. Combine those with Mom's baking abilities, and I'd been one lucky kid growing up. After tonight, maybe I'd feel like a lucky adult.

I rounded the corner of the house at turtle speed, my heart beating so loud that it killed any chance of understanding the conversation ensuing on the back deck. Over the tall decorative flowers, I caught sight of my brothers laughing, an ease between them that made me jealous. I hadn't cut off ties with them, but since I never came around, I didn't see them as much as I used to. Mom wasn't the only one I'd punished because of an argument.

"Josh!" Kevin shouted, noticing me walking up the cement path between the pink peonies. "What are you doing here?"

I tried not to scowl. "The same thing you are, I'm guessing."

He descended the stairs leading up to the porch, blocking my path, and slapped me on the shoulder. "Obviously, but we didn't think you would come after..." His smile faltered, and he studied my face.

I stuffed my hands into my jeans' pockets. "Yeah."

What more could I say? It wasn't as though Dad and I had talked. I'd come for Mom, but I hoped to leave with the intent of coming back for *both* of them next time.

"Well, we're glad you're here," said Kevin. "Come on. Let's go inside. Dad just took the ribs off the smoker."

I swallowed and pasted on a smile as I followed him up the stairs to the door. Ash said nothing as the two of us passed him, but he did offer me a reassuring smile. Of the three of us, he was the most reserved. I envied his calm nature right now.

If the smell of food outside the house ignited my insides with anticipation, the aroma inside could have put me in a coma. Mom bustled around the island, side dishes in both hands, and added them to the bounty on the set table. I licked my lips without thought, my stomach doing a happy jig. It had been ages since I tasted Mom's treats.

She turned around, undoubtedly to fetch more food, but halted when her gaze settled on me. Her eyes seemed to glisten with her half smile, and before I could utter a word, she crossed the room and pulled me into her arms. I blinked back tears and hugged her, aware that both of my brothers were watching. We didn't cry in front of each other. Ever. But tonight, I would make an exception.

"I'm so glad you came," said Mom as she pulled away, her hands lingering on my shoulders.

"So am I," said a familiar deep tone.

My breath hitched at the sound of Dad's voice behind me.

Slowly, I turned to face him, Mom's hands sliding off my shoulders, taking their comfort with them. His eyes didn't hold an ounce of anger. I saw in them the same thing I saw every time I looked at my reflection—regret and hurt.

We stood there staring at one another for what seemed an eternity before I choked out a few words. "Happy birthday, Dad."

His face contorted slightly, but he didn't speak as he crossed the room. And then, just like with Mom, I was in his arms. Dad hugged me in a way he'd never hugged me before, as if he were afraid to let go. Even when I'd left the nest he hadn't expressed this much sentiment.

With an exhale, I returned his embrace. Everything inside me relaxed. Healed a little.

"I'm sorry," he whispered. "I didn't want you to leave the firm, to toss your degree aside. I thought... It doesn't matter. You're here." Dad pulled away. He wore a hesitant smile. "Thank you for coming. Maybe you could tell me more about this book of yours after dinner?"

There was a hopefulness in his voice that patched my wounded heart a little more.

"I'm sorry, too, and I'd like to tell you all about it. But, Dad, know that this doesn't mean I'm giving up my career. I still want to be a lawyer, I just..."

Dad gripped my shoulder. "I don't understand the writing thing, but that doesn't mean I can't appreciate it. Appreciate *you*. I'm proud of you, no matter what career, or hobby, you pursue."

I blinked back tears. "Thank you."

Dad and I both had dragons to face, and in that moment, I realized they weren't each other. I'd imagined having to defend my dreams again, but when it came down to it, the only thing that needed to be defeated was our own pride. We'd both made mistakes, and we'd both let them fester and keep us apart. The time lost pained me, but we could do better going forward.

I wanted to hug him again, but my family wasn't big on physical displays of affection. Well, besides Mom. Either way, I was hugged out, so I gave Dad my biggest smile instead. He returned it.

We ate dinner. We talked. We made memories. Things weren't perfect, but the storm that once raged inside me subsided. I faced a dragon today, and now I got to enjoy the results of my victory. Perhaps I'd been wrong. I could write my own story. I could choose which path I took to my future. Fantasy worlds were great places to escape. They were amazing to build and write. But they weren't where I belonged.

I belonged in reality with the people I loved and the ones who loved me.

HOT CHOCOLATE AND POPCORN

HYDEE CLAYTON

This week at the grocery store, surrounded by cardboard reindeer and jangling holiday tunes, I ran into Molly Murphy in the checkout line.

When we were children, Molly lived around the corner and down the street from me, and we were close pals until we got to junior high school. Then, somehow, we weren't together much. I assumed it was because she went to Catholic school, or maybe I got too busy to run and play around the neighborhood. But in the grocery store, even though we were now well past fifty, she had changed so little I recognized her easily. She sported the same "pixie" haircut she wore when we roller skated around the block together. Her voice still sounded cheerfully shrill. I looked at her and asked, "Molly Murphy?"

She didn't recognize me at all. I introduced myself, she put her hand on my arm, and we laughed. While the bag boy packed Molly's groceries into holly-print bags and loaded them into her cart, we caught up on the basics—marriage, children, divorce, disease. Then Molly said, "It's funny we'd run into each other at this time of year, because for my whole life, every Christmas I've thought about you and your family." Then she told me this surprising story.

"I don't know if you knew this, but my parents were alcoholics."

I didn't know. It never occurred to me. I never puzzled over why I hadn't seen the inside of her house. We played at my house, that's all. I had a big backyard and lots of room in the basement, so there was always a place to put on dress-up dramas, bounce on our pogo sticks, or pound on the tether ball. Everybody played at my house. And I didn't know what alcoholism was until long after Molly had disappeared from my world.

She went on, "At my house, Christmas was pretty much just an excuse to get drunk early in the day. I hated Christmas. Things were so—well, trust me, my house was not a place you wanted to be, especially on Christmas day. So, one year after the presents were opened and the brandy came out, I just left the house and came over to your place."

I had never wondered much about that, either, about why she showed up at my house in the middle of one random Christmas day.

Somewhere in the background "Deck the Halls" chimed from the grocery store speaker. The automatic doors let in a shock of cold air and then closed again. The scanner beeped rhythmically while canned soup and bagged rice slid by. Molly went on with her story.

"Your whole family was there. You were all playing Life, a brand-new board game, a Christmas present, I think. Everyone was on the floor around the coffee table in your living room. They all just said, 'Hi, Molly,' and scooted around to make room.

"I stayed all afternoon playing that game with you and your parents, your sisters and brother. I think we brought out some other games too. It was almost surreal, these parents playing board games with their kids, everybody making goofy jokes and laughing at each other. I don't think I'd ever spent much time with your brother before that, but I remember that he was really funny.

"One of the best parts was when your mother disappeared for a while and came back with hot chocolate and bowls of popcorn. It was like a real family. Like what I always pictured a family would be."

My own memory holds very little detail of that day. I always loved Christmas and looked forward to it, but no particular year stands out. All Christmases blend into one colorful event, where I competed with my sisters for the most creative gift wrappings and tried singing harmony when we gathered around our player piano. We picked out a tree together and decorated it together, always with the same decorations, and everybody opened new pajamas and slippers on Christmas Eve. A five-pound box of chocolates sat on the dining room sideboard for weeks, strictly rationed to one candy after dinner and sometimes one after school. Christmas dinner was ham and scalloped potatoes.

I always felt a little wistful lying on the floor by the tree after it was all over, thinking how sad that it always had to end, that the stack of gifts always had to disappear. Those colorful boxes with their bows and curled ribbons were almost always more interesting than whatever was inside. How sad that the lights and ornaments always had to go back into their boxes and down to the dank basement shelves.

Molly's memories must have been quite different. I didn't want to think about the details, and I guessed she didn't either. She managed her memories her own way, a brave enough way to make her comfortable talking to me about it now, all these years later. Molly continued her story without even a tremble.

"I always think about that day when the holidays come around. I decided right then that I'd make a family like that, too. I'd treat my children the way your parents treated you, and I'd make my house warm and welcoming like yours, make sure it was a good place to be. I've always worked hard at making Christmas wonderful."

I looked at the life-sized cutout Santa propped near the ATM, the tinsel adorning the case lot display, the relentless effort to make us all feel cheerful and enriched by the holiday, and I wondered: Have I always made my home warm and welcoming? Did I even notice what made a home feel that way? I always thought so, but the truth was, I'd never paid much attention to how my parents did it. Or even that they did it. By now, they had both been gone for too many years to count. But here was another reason to marvel at them, that they welcomed my friend into the middle of a family event without missing a beat, and that they undoubtedly knew why she was there, even though I didn't. I could only hope I had learned as much from them as Molly did.

My groceries were bagged by the time Molly finished her story, and my eyes were wet. I'm not sure if I managed much more response than, "Thank you. Thank you for telling me that." I squeezed her arm. We went our separate ways again.

Though not quite as separate as I once thought.

BLUE PINE SUMMER

C.W. ALLEN

I was *not* running away. At least, that's what I told Derrik as he helped me load the car. But like most little brothers, he had an annoying habit of seeing through my lies. Even the ones I told myself.

"Sure you're not." He tossed the last duffel bag into my beat-up old hatchback, folded his arms smugly across his Pearl Jam tee shirt, and smirked down at me. "You're packing all your crap and moving to a cabin in the woods because everything is going *great*."

I glared up at him. (Whoever gave younger brothers permission to get taller than their wiser, older sisters should be dunked in gravy and dangled over a hyena pit.) I spend a measly two semesters away at college, and the punk takes my absence as his cue to grow four inches and become the star of the high school lacrosse team.

"It's just a summer job," I argued. "It's not like I'm abandoning society and moving to Walden Pond."

Derrik looked at me like I was attempting to explain how numbers smell. I should have known a Thoreau reference wouldn't land with him, but there was no point explaining. He'd probably think the American Transcendentalists were some new indie rock band. Or better yet, an obscure *old* indie rock band. Then he'd get cool guy cred for having heard of them.

"There's plenty of summer jobs around here," he argued back. (It's a hobby of ours.) "You've spent, like, the last three summers working at the Dare-E-Freez stand, gossiping with your friends and testing weird ice cream flavor combos when you were supposed to be handing out waffle cones. You said it was the cushiest gig ever." He elbowed me in the ribs. "What, you spend a few months in the city and suddenly you're too good for us? Or did your fancy new college friends convince you to give up dairy?"

Just the opposite, actually. I had spent the last six months making midnight pilgrimages to the fridge, eating crusty pre-shredded cheese straight out of the bag like some kind of goblin raccoon. I even had the dark eye circles to match. And I couldn't say I'd made any friends.

The truth was... I couldn't stomach it. Any of it. Certainly not the prospect of spending all summer trapped in a plywood shack, slapping on a smile, and handing ice cream cones to my high school friends while they bragged about their fabulous internships or dating lives or sororities. Lying through clenched teeth when my friends' parents and parents' friends asked how school was going and what big plans I was making. Sprinkling their soft serve swirls with false hopes and socially acceptable life goals along with the rainbow jimmies. It was like having an open, festering wound and inviting everybody in town to poke at it. Dante couldn't dream up a more torturous version of Hell.

I couldn't tell Derrik any of that. My parents didn't know, for one thing. Derrik probably wouldn't snitch on me, but it didn't seem fair to burden him with my secret. I'd made such a big deal of getting into my first-choice college. Mom and Dad had canceled vacations and pushed back their retirement plan to pay my tuition. And I had absolutely nothing to show for it. I'd already switched majors twice, I was on academic probation, and I was hating every second of it.

So, no—I wasn't running away. I was just sparing everyone else the awkwardness of unearthing my pathetic reality.

I'd been scrolling morosely through the state's employment website, wondering what I'd do with my life if I flunked out of college, when serendipity dropped a ticket to freedom right in my lap.

Blue Pine Summer Camp. Counselors wanted. No experience necessary.

One Google later, I learned the camp was way across the state, on the far side of Blue Pine Lake. And after sifting through a bunch of passive-aggressive Yelp reviews, I discovered the campground was surrounded by forest so remote it didn't have cell service, let alone an internet connection.

No internet meant no emails from the university's various financial, scheduling, and eligibility departments, politely informing me how much time and money I was wasting on being a failure.

No cell service meant no phone conversations with my parents during which I'd have to cobble together imaginary plans for the fall.

It was perfect.

That's not what I told Derrik, of course. I handed him a bouquet of wilting excuses about the pay being good (lies) and the fringe benefits of peace, quiet, and fresh air (true enough, I guess, but not the point.)

Derrik chuckled ominously. "I bet that's what all the counselors at Camp Crystal Lake said, too."

"Make up your mind. Am I a stuck-up hipster, a forest hermit, or a nameless horror movie victim?"

I knew the sibling banter rules—Derrik *had* to make a last-ditch effort to win the argument. But he pulled it off in a way I never saw coming. He didn't sling more sarcasm or make fumbling attempts at a witty comeback. In fact, he didn't say anything at all.

He just... hugged me. Which shut me up more effectively than any obscure pop culture reference ever could have. *Punk.*

I hugged him back. "Don't get all sappy on me, bro. I'll see you in August."

My pals Taylor Swift and Dr. Pepper kept me company on the four-hour drive to Blue Pine Lake. I checked in at the office where the camp director tossed me the keys to the log cabin that would be my home for the next two months. At least, I assumed it was the camp director. The stocky middle-aged man behind the desk never actually introduced himself, but his official Blue Pine Summer Camp jacket sported a machine-embroidered patch that read *TODD.* No last name, no job title, just Todd. Once he'd checked my ID and made me sign a safety waiver, Todd went right back to what he'd been doing when I arrived. He kicked his hiking boots up on his desk, dunked a saltine cracker in his coffee, and popped the soggy square into his mouth, plastering his graying walrus mustache with gloppy crumbs.

I spent the next hour at my cabin getting unpacked. The other camp counselors stopped by to introduce themselves and make sure the newbie had remembered to bring all the necessary aerosol cans: mosquito spray, bear spray, sunscreen, and Easy Cheese. Unlike Todd, they all looked roughly my age, but their senses of humor had apparently gotten stuck in the seventh grade.

"Remember, the mosquito spray goes on *you*," Jake instructed.

"But the bear spray goes on the bear," added Ben. "Don't get those mixed up."

Bailey rolled her eyes. "Don't mind them. There aren't any bears out here anyway."

Jake let out a dark chuckle. "Not *anymore.*"

"What's that supposed to mean?" I asked.

Jake waggled his eyebrows ominously. "You'll see soon enough."

I didn't like the sound of that, but I didn't have too much time to worry, because just before dinner the first batch of campers arrived. It was time to get to work.

The job wasn't hard. The canteen made all the meals, so it's not like I had to figure out how to survive on foraged pinecones and centipedes. And the camp nurse kept track of all the campers' poison ivy cream and asthma inhalers, so I didn't really need to know much about taking care of kids, either. Any time a kid asked if the mushroom or berry they'd found growing down by the lake was edible, the answer was always "No." And any time a kid grumbled that they couldn't figure out how to light kindling with only a flint and steel or tie a double half hitch knot, the answer was always, "Keep trying! You'll learn best by doing." It didn't matter that I couldn't tell a wild raspberry from a nightshade berry or a double half hitch from a bowline knot. The campers assumed I had things under control simply because I had an official Blue Pine Camp Counselor tee shirt and a shiny silver whistle on a lanyard.

If only faking my way through college was this easy.

I wasn't fooling the camp director, of course. Todd saw right through my "you'll never learn if I do it for you" routine. He just didn't care. Lack of initiative was exactly what Todd wanted from a rookie camp counselor. The activities roster hadn't changed in forty years. It wasn't my job to dream up fresh ways for the campers to embrace their unplugged, outdoor summer. All I had to do was keep them from wandering off or throwing rocks at each other.

Something else that hadn't changed in forty years? The campfire stories. Ben and Jake had been Blue Pine counselors for three years running, and Bailey had been a Blue Pine camper herself a decade ago, so they were eager to initiate the latest batch of kids into the camp's traditions. They only gave the kids a week to get settled in before gathering everyone at the fire pit after dinner for a lesson on proper marshmallow toasting technique. At least, that's what they claimed we'd be doing. But once they finished setting up a herd of preteens with pointy sticks, open flames, and enough sugar to give hummingbirds the jitters, they had a captive audience for their *real* plan—telling the scariest stories possible.

I had some reservations about this plan. The camp nurse was great about dealing with runny noses and puke and wiggly teeth, which give me the willies—mostly the teeth—but I was pretty sure she'd claim bedwetting and night terrors weren't her department. Putting three dozen kids into a sugar coma right after making them sit through a horror story competition didn't strike me as a recipe for a stress-free night at work. Why, exactly, were we making our own jobs harder?

"We're making memories," Ben insisted.

I didn't doubt that. Might be creating a few new phobias, too. But whatever else the kids got out of this, it was sure to be memorable.

Jake went first. He had this heavy metal flashlight big enough to swat a baseball with, which he held directly under his chin as he delivered a fairly standard rendition of the old hook-handed hitch-hiker urban legend. Then he passed the flashlight to Bailey for her take on Bloody Mary. And by the time the marshmallows were gone, and all the kids were primed with sticky faces and jumpy nerves, it was Ben's turn to recite Blue Pine's signature ghost story: The Ghost of Blue Pine Lake.

I had to admit Ben was a good storyteller. He leaned forward and dropped his voice to a mysterious murmur, like he was letting the listeners in on a secret. Instinctively, all the kids leaned forward too. The flashlight beam etched deep shadows into his eye sockets and cheekbones. His teeth looked different, somehow, in the glaring spotlight. Bigger. Brighter. Sharper.

Many years ago, Ben claimed, there was a counselor at Blue Pine Summer Camp who went out hiking in the spring, checking the trails for fallen trees blocking the path. He came around a bend in the trail and found himself face to face with an enormous bear, ravenous with hunger after its winter hibernation. One swipe of the grizzly's massive claws, and the counselor was dead. When he didn't return to camp, the forest service was called in to search for him. The rangers followed the bloody trail to the cave where the bear had dragged the camp counselor's mangled corpse. The bear reared up to its full height and roared until their ears nearly bled, but luckily one of the rangers had brought along a shotgun. A single bullet through the heart, and the bear was dead too.

"To this very day," Ben whispered, "the spirits of the counselor and the bear roam the woods around Blue Pine Lake seeking revenge on their killers. They say if you're out stargazing past midnight, you might see their ghosts glowing an unearthly blue among the trees as they wander for eternity, stalking each other—or anyone else who might get in their way."

"That's not funny." Todd emerged from the shadows, which made all the kids jump. "Show some respect. Old Hal was the camp director here when I was a kid."

This was all part of the plan, Jake had explained at dinner that evening—Todd had his lines memorized.

Naturally, the kids took the bait.

"Wait, this story is *true*?" asked a freckle faced girl in braided pigtails. "A camp counselor actually died here?"

"Yup." Todd stuck to his usual deadpan manner, which really sealed the deal for the kids—they didn't know he *had* a sense of humor. "Back in '87. Hal wasn't just a Blue Pine counselor; he lived here year-round as the facilities manager. Camp season hadn't started yet, so none of the kids saw anything, but the news made all the papers. And when I came back that summer, Hal's cabin was empty."

With that, Todd pointed at one of the staff cabins. *My* cabin, as a matter of fact.

"Enough about that. Let's lighten the mood a bit, shall we?" Todd held up an old guitar. "It's time we taught you the official Blue Pine anthem."

All the kids shuffled closer together on their log bench to make room for Todd to sit. He stretched his legs toward the fire and strummed a few bouncy intro chords, then belted out the first verse:

When you're feeling blue and mopey
and you've run all out of hope, be
full of cheer
never fear
there's a place

Where the water's clear and shining
and the pine boughs are entwining
and the breeze
through the trees
is soft and sweet.

Bailey, Jake, Ben, and the handful of kids who had come to camp last summer joined him in the chorus:

Bluuuue Pine! Calling me home—
No place on earth is as fine.
Bluuuue Pine! Wherever I roam
you'll always be there when I pine.

Not exactly poetic genius, but whatever—I'm no music critic. There were like six more verses, which I couldn't keep straight, but after the second round, I was able to jump in for the chorus. Everybody seemed to love this camp so much, I had a feeling this song was going to come up again. Might as well get on board and learn it.

When the song was over, Todd declared it was bedtime and sent everyone off to their bunks. But the night wasn't over, apparently. My fellow counselors had one more plot in the works.

We met at the canteen. I arrived in time to hold the door open for Ben and Bailey, who were dragging in the ugly brown shag rug from Todd's office. Jake emerged from the janitor's closet with an empty spray bottle and a soda can. He popped the can open and poured the clear, fizzing contents into the spray bottle. Then he screwed the top back on and started spritzing the rug.

"Anybody gonna tell me what's going on?" I asked.

Ben pulled three tiny flashlights from his hoodie pocket, then passed two of them off to me and Bailey. "Tonic water," he explained with a nod at the spray bottle. "It glows under a blacklight."

"Amazing what you can buy online." Bailey laughed and clicked her flashlight on. It glowed a dim purple, barely visible under the canteen's humming fluorescent lights.

She didn't have to explain any further. I knew exactly where this was going. One of the guys was going to drape the rug over his shoulders like a cape and stomp around the campground making bear noises while the rest of us trained our flashlights on him. The tonic-soaked rug would reflect the UV rays. Boom—instant ghost bear.

I played along. We'd come this far already, and the plan would go ahead with or without me. We heard some whispers and clunks at the bunkhouse windows, so at least a few of the kids must have gathered to see what was going on. To my surprise, the tonic water trick actually worked pretty well—the rug saddled on Jake's back glowed electric blue. It wasn't exactly bear-shaped, but I wagered the ghost story was still fresh enough on the kids' minds to nudge their imaginations in the right direction.

And maybe... not just the kids. Fifteen minutes later, we called it quits and returned the rug to Todd's office. And as I traced the moonlit path back to my cabin, I could have sworn I saw something glowing in the trees.

I bolted the door behind me, flipped up the light switch, and scanned the single-room cabin. Everything was just as I'd left it. I let out a slow breath, flooded with the sheepish realization that I'd let a goofy prank—which I *knew* was only a prank because I'd helped pull it off—jangle my nerves.

Then, the lights flicked off again. And leaning back in the cracked leather armchair next to the bed, one foot propped up lazily on his knee, was the blue, glowing figure of a man.

I shrieked and turned the lights back on.

The chair was empty.

The lights turned themselves off again.

The man was back.

He just sat there, offering an apologetic lopsided grin from under a bushy mustache. He looked older than me, but not *old* old—mid-fifties, if the spidery creases around his eyes were any indication. Actually, aside from the glowing, he reminded me of the flannel-clad lumberjack mascot from that one brand of paper towels.

I guess my staring in slack-jawed horror wasn't doing much to kick off the conversation, so he got things rolling himself. "They got a bunch of the details wrong, you know. In the campfire story."

"Hal?" I whispered.

He nodded. "The bear isn't the ghost of Blue Pine Lake—I am."

"I can't believe it," I mumbled. "Derrik was right. I'm gonna get murdered by a summer camp ghost."

"Simmer down," said the ghost. "This isn't Camp Crystal Lake."

"*Simmer down*?" I repeated. "There's a strange man in my cabin. A *dead* strange man. A dead strange man who's mansplaining movie references he shouldn't even know about."

"First off," he argued, "it's *my* cabin. This was my home for more than twenty years before I died, and even longer since. And before you ask, no—I haven't been hanging around all week spying on you. I leave the cabin alone when it's occupied. Secondly, I died in 1987, and there's a movie theater in the next town over. Of course, I saw *Friday the 13th*. Hiding hockey masks in unexpected places was basically the camp counselors' only form of entertainment, back in my day. And third, if I was here to kill you—which I'm not—how would you suggest I pull that off? I can't even touch anything." To prove his point, he waved his hand through the chair, revealing that he wasn't actually sitting on it—just floating as close as possible to the seat.

"Why are you here, then?"

"Bored, mostly. And I wanted to set the story straight. And... I'm not sure, actually. You seem like you could use somebody to talk to."

I wasn't eager to blab all my secret anxieties to a total stranger, let alone a phantom intruder, but I figured letting him get his ghostly business off his transparent chest might convince him to go away. So instead of taking him up on his offer, I plopped down on the end of the bed and let him do the talking.

Turns out Todd had been right. In addition to running the summer camp, Hal was the campground's winter caretaker, so he lived at Blue Pine year-round. And since camp was only in session during June and July, that meant he mostly lived alone. But his run-in with the bear hadn't been in the spring. It was early fall, just after the campers went home. And the bear hadn't wanted to turn him into a post-hibernation snack. She'd been protecting her cubs.

"Wasn't her fault," Hal insisted. "We came around a bend in the trail, going opposite directions, and surprised each other. She only did what came natural. The forest service had to put her down, of course. Couldn't have a killer bear hanging around a kids' camp. But they didn't shoot her. It was more humane than that. And from what I heard, the cubs got sent to a wildlife sanctuary until they were old enough to be released in a remote corner of a national forest."

"But what about the ghost story?" I asked. "Is the bear's spirit still here?"

Hal's mustache twitched thoughtfully. "She did hang around for a bit," he admitted. "I caught glimpses of her now and then, trundling through the woods—searching for her cubs, I think. But she didn't stay more than a few months. When their scent wore off..." He shrugged. "Moved on, I suppose."

I could see how Todd and Ben might have gotten the story mixed up. And Hal's explanation made sense. But there was one nagging detail left. "So, if you're not mad the bear killed you," I asked, "and the bear's not even here anymore, why are *you* still here?"

Hal laughed. It wasn't a sinister, spectral laugh like in the movies. It was just... normal. Like he was a totally regular guy who just happened to be see-through.

"People get a one-track mind sometimes, you know? They can't imagine any 'unfinished business' besides revenge."

And with that, still laughing, Hal vanished.

The next morning, I jolted awake before my alarm even went off. I put the extra minutes to good use by staring at the ceiling, attempting to convince myself that my midnight visitor was nothing more than a marshmallow overload-induced dream. But I couldn't.

I had enough lies in my life at the moment. I might not be ready to level with everyone else, but there was no point gaslighting myself in the process.

True to his word, Hal kept his distance from the cabin. I spent the next two nights expecting him to make an encore appearance and resolve the cliffhanger he'd left our conversation on, but he never showed. And for some reason, that annoyed me. Strangely enough, I found myself disappointed that my house *wasn't* haunted. And that's when I decided I didn't have to put up with getting ghosted. I could go find Hal myself.

I didn't have any gadgets for reading spectral energy or any clue what I was doing, for that matter. But if Hal knew we'd gotten his story wrong, then he must have been hanging around while we told it. Maybe, I figured, he had a list of favorite haunts. So that night, when the campers were snug in their bunks and the last of the staff cabins finally put out its lights, I crept outside and fumbled through the darkness to the fire pit.

Todd always made sure the fire was thoroughly extinguished before he went to bed, so there weren't even glowing embers to keep me company as I settled onto one of the log benches to wait. I leaned back and watched the constellations slowly rotate across the inky sky. And just about the time Ursa Major came into view, I caught a faint blue light in the corner of my vision.

"It's really a bear, you know." Hal had flickered into existence on the next bench over. He pointed up at the cluster of stars I'd been staring at. "Most people call it the Big Dipper. Supposed to look like an old-fashioned drinking ladle. But the ancients used the stars to tell stories, and that story was about a bear."

I didn't ambush him with questions right away—I just let him talk. When Hal finished comparing the Greek star bear legend to the Iroquois version, the conversation drifted to how my counselor duties were going. Apparently, even a dead guy could tell I was faking my way through this outdoorsy stuff. Before I knew it, I was spilling my guts about the rest of my life, too.

Hal nodded sympathetically. "That sounds familiar. I suppose I was running away too. Not the college and expectations bit, just... I dunno. Got sick of all the people, I guess. The busyness.

Running around, frantically scraping together enough money to afford doing it all over again the next day. But out here, I never needed to impress anyone. My house came free with the job. I just woke up every morning and took care of the place. It was simpler, being alone."

"So, you never went back?" I asked. "You just noped off to the woods and never saw anyone again?"

Hal laughed. "I wasn't a total hermit, you know. Forest rangers came by at least once a week. And this place was as busy as an anthill in the summers, crawling with campers. But if you mean people from before, from my old life... I suppose that's true. My mom had already passed. Dad and I never really got on. My city friends were doing well enough without me." He shrugged. "I guess there wasn't anyone I particularly cared to see again. Or maybe I didn't think they cared to see me."

I wanted to commiserate. I wanted to send a high-five straight through his wispy hand and cheer, "Yeah! Who needs 'em? Loners for life!" (Afterlife, I guess, in his case.) But I was shocked to realize I couldn't relate. I might be drowning in other people's expectations, but that was only because I knew how much they cared about me. Everyone in my life wanted me to be successful and happy, and I couldn't bear to let them down by admitting I was neither. Not having anyone left to disappoint just sounded... sad.

What started as an experiment became a nightly ritual. While the rest of the camp slept, Hal and I met at the fire pit to watch the stars and talk. I shared stories about my childhood shenanigans with Derrik and all the trouble we got into. Hal finally taught me how to tie a double half hitch knot and how to tell poison oak leaves from harmless sumac.

When a week of gossip sessions passed without drawing any attention from the rest of the camp, Hal decided it was safe to show off his ghostly party trick. Somehow, he could spark a dim purple flare in the fire pit. The flames were as cold and lifeless as a gutted trout—I could pass my hand right through them without feeling anything at all—but the shifting light gave off comforting campfire vibes.

It was time. We were friends now. I *had* to know. If it wasn't about avenging his death or tasks left undone, why was Hal's spirit still here? The ghost bear was able to move on, so there must be someplace to go.

Hal tried to deflect with a joke. "My singing voice isn't good enough for the angel choir," he chuckled, "and I doubt my harp skills would be any better." But when I didn't laugh along, he gave in.

"The truth?" he asked.

I nodded.

Hal leaned back with a sigh and gazed up through the pine boughs. "Maybe the way people talk about heaven, with all the harps and pearly gates and sitting on clouds, is just another type of ghost story. One of these days, I might get the urge to go adventuring and see what else is out there, but so far I haven't felt the need. Whatever is supposed to come next, I'm not convinced it could be quite as nice as this."

Without explanation, he pulled his second trick of the night— a misty ghost guitar materialized in his hands. He stared into the crackling flames and began strumming the camp anthem.

Hal was right about his singing voice. The gruff tenor was far from angelic. But there was something captivating about his performance all the same. This wasn't the jaunty tempo Todd used to convince the kids to sing along. Hal's rendition was slower, gentler. And by the time he made it to the chorus, I understood.

"*Blue Pine, calling me home. No place on earth is as fine. Blue Pine—wherever I roam, you'll always be there when I pine.*"

It wasn't an anthem. It was a love song.

Hal was already home, in the only place he had ever felt he

belonged. If I stayed a hundred summers, I would never feel the way Hal did about this place.

This wasn't exactly an encouraging revelation. But the longer Hal sang, the more a hopeful possibility began to sprout. Maybe when I was ready to move on, I could build the life that felt like home for me. And I was already surrounded by people eager to help me pull it off.

Two months and three batches of campers later, my Blue Pine summer came to an end. Thanks to Hal's nightly tutoring, I had grown into a pretty proficient camp counselor, if I said so myself. I didn't have to, actually—Todd said it for me.

He offered me a handshake as I loaded up the car. "I know it's a bit early to plan for next summer. But if you want, there will always be a place for you at Blue Pine."

I appreciated the offer, but I had to turn him down.

It was time to go home.

In the Right Place but Wishing
I Were Anywhere Else

Steve Capone, Jr.

"Keep coming back," the choral response went. "You're in the right place."

I'd heard this before, but I wasn't sure where. In early 1999, Sandra Bullock's film *28 Days* (not *28 Days Later*, mind you—a *very* different film), popularizing some of the rehab and recovery tropes we've come to know and hate, wouldn't be released for another two years. I was a kid, so I didn't know any of the old gems like Michael Keaton's *Clean and Sober* (1988). Maybe *The Basketball Diaries* had scenes from twelve-step meetings? (Did a literal shudder pass through your body's involuntary systems when you read the words *The Basketball Diaries* like it did mine? If you've seen it, your autonomic response will indicate whether or not you are of my people.)

These people—people who had lost husbands, wives, and children, who had been to prison, shot cocaine and heroin "speedballs" into their arms, between their toes, and—it happens—sometimes into their penises—these *addicts* were responding to me. I had said the words, but I was not like them.

"I'm an addict," I had said. Not "I'm an abuser" or "I might have a problem," but "I'm an addict." The others had leaned in to hear the [barely] fifteen-year-old who *might be getting it*.

I think I even believed those words. I had tried to stop a sickening number of times. Part of me wanted to stop. But a bigger part of me—the part driven by a confused survival instinct—didn't want to stop. Not for a second. I wanted nothing else than to *keep going*. I wanted to run you over with a truck (were I old enough to drive and well-off enough to come by a half-ton pickup) to get more. I would have flushed the whole fucking meeting down a toilet in exchange for more.

But first, I wanted her to notice me. I don't remember much about that first meeting, other than a desire to be literally anywhere else and a desire to scoot my chair over even closer to a girl whose nickname was "Skittles." You see, in intensive outpatient the week prior to that meeting, I'd discovered that she liked Skittles. So, I brought some of the candy one night to group. From then on, she was "Skittles." Pretty cringeworthy, looking back. But what is addiction—or our teenage years, for that matter—but a series of godawful cringeworthy moments? I wonder if the girl is now a woman or if she died young. Most of the people I knew back then in the context of addiction, rehab, and early recovery have died. Some have not.

So, I went to this meeting with the girl whose nickname I won't repeat because remembering I invented it makes me feel ashamed. Actually, "went with" pays "we each got a ride from our terrified parents" a bit too much credit. I went to that first meeting because I wanted the girl from rehab. I wanted her bad. Bad enough to go to a twelve-step meeting. I don't know what I wanted from her. I assume I wanted sex (a barrier I wouldn't break with anyone for literally years). But there was more to it. I wanted attention. I needed her to tell me that she wanted to be around me. That she wanted to touch me. I wanted to be held, and I craved that attention from the opposite sex, primarily.

Some months later, my sponsor told me, "Before you love a

woman, you've got to learn to love a man." The implication here—do I need to spell it out? It's kind of like poking fun at the impossibility of me being gay, which I daresay we maybe shouldn't have dismissed so quickly. But I digress.

After those addicts told me, "keep coming back" and "you're right where you belong" those first times, I figured out eventually that I had a captive audience in twelve-step meetings. Their whole deal was to sit quietly and listen while I shared what was on my mind. And if I sounded fairly put together, people would hang over me, telling me that it was oh so great I was getting my life together at such a tender age. Or they'd tell me that they'd spilled more beer than I'd drunk (I'm certain this was true) and tried pushing me out of the meetings. There were no other people under twenty-five years of age or so, which to my fifteen-year-old mush puddle of a mind was a ripe old age indeed.

Because I was seeing only the differences between me and these people, I developed few genuine connections. I captured center stage every time I shared at a meeting, and I relished those moments. Some people have trouble speaking in front of other people, but after my mind cleared from inebriation and withdrawal, I never had that problem. Huge crowds frighten me, sure, but a roomful of people—ahem, addicts—over whom I've convinced myself I lord as smarter and better situated for success? No problem. I held court (in my own mind). I orated (they told me to "keep coming back"). I bragged. I dug myself a hole, in short.

The thing about looking like I had it all together was that as things fell apart (things always fall apart), I had nowhere to turn with that shameful truth (it had only become shameful because of my own perception). I had no one whom I trusted with the bad along with the good. I was launching dishware off the back deck down to the road and valley below. I was tossing billiards tables in fits of rage, breaking friends' bones (okay, one friend, one arm, but still—really?), and generally living completely out of control, clean or not. And I trusted no one with the truth of even the general state of things.

Even if you've never been in or known anyone in recovery, a scenario that becomes less and less likely as the years pass, you're probably asking yourself, "Did you have a sponsor? Someone you were supposed to go to with this stuff?" The answer is yes, I had a sponsor. That was essential to looking the part. I didn't see it as a disguise, but that is what the sponsorship thing turned out to be, for a good long while. I didn't tell him when I wanted to use. I only told him what I was figuring out. What I thought I was figuring out. He was a part of the court I oversaw, if an elevated member of it. I was different, even from him.

When I wanted to get fucked up, though, there were few barriers in my path. I hadn't dropped the old people, places, and things. I hadn't dropped my guard against uncomfortable but potentially lifesaving changes, hadn't let go of the reserve with which I treated all things "recovery" (scare quotes required at this stage). I had surrendered, as they say in those meetings, yet the surrender had been conditional.

Around the time of that first meeting and through my first stint in rehab, I stayed clean for all of twelve days. After that, I might have admitted failing, and I might not have. But then five days were all I could hold out. And then two. And then zero. Soon, I'd stopped trying. Eventually, I left rehab. I have to assume I didn't leave that place with clean urines and that I couldn't stay clean because I wound up in another evening outpatient program for teens. I think the first rehab was somehow less intensive and the second more so.

I have to shrug at these early memories—thinking back to them is a lot like trying to remember what it was like to be a four-year old. Details about my circumstances were hazy then, and they're hazier now. The emotional heaviness, on the other hand— that is crystal clear, even a quarter century later.

When I say that I couldn't stay clean, here is what I mean. I'd wake up three days, maybe four days without getting high, and I'd get ready for school. I'd smoke essentially continuously throughout the day—at one point, I boasted that I was killing a pack a day in school and a pack a day out of it—and I'd see old friends. I'd see the kids who sold me bunk acid, fake opium, or whatever, and I'd be jonesing.

I'm not using the word "jonesing" here in the way that heroin users do—I was not sick in the sense they were sick. But a rattling box of jitter-creatures lived in my body, threatening at every moment to explode from crotch to chin. The only thing that would make me feel better—leagues better, said the creatures—the difference between dying and surviving—was to buy, beg, or barter for something more and to ingest it. The muscles would release only when I put it in my body. What was it? It didn't fucking matter. A pill. A toke. LSD. Whatever. I would put it under my tongue, into my nose, or sucked it deep into my lungs like a last breath, and the pain would go away. The agony of existence. *That's* what I'm talking about when I talk about jonesing.

I'd be feeling this command—this reminder like a knife in my head—telling me that I had to get to school because that's where the shit is. And I'd get there and see those people who could, maybe, possibly, perhaps have something that would stop the incessant noise in my head. I hated that noise. I couldn't stop looking at other people looking at me. I couldn't stop worrying that I was about to have a heart attack, or that other people could see that I had *wasted my life* to that point.

Oh, I worried about normal shit, too. I hoped someone would go to homecoming with me (one poor soul did, and ever since, I'm sure she's regretted offering me the opportunity to ditch her to get high with my friends). I worried that I was failing my classes—all of them—because I was. I became convinced that I was a literal moron, and I had scant evidence to the contrary.

All of this angst would—*poof*—go away, if only I put something in my body that contained the magic I needed.

Not being able to make it at the big high school, I attended an intensive outpatient behavioral program at a psychiatric ward, spending all school hours in the ward and getting to go home each evening. While I was there, I met a guy who would later be busted for selling L to an undercover on Duquesne University's campus. That is to say, I met a new connection. He could drive, even. He was super nice about it, too, driving whatever I wanted to my house. This was especially important because my parents were keeping me home at all hours I wasn't in that hospital, uselessly trying to save me from myself.

The psychiatric hospital didn't do the job. Then, I was doing school at a remote location, one-on-one, in the city hall's library, for a matter of weeks or months. I would show up stoned or drunk. They refused to let me come back after a few of those missteps.

Did you ever find yourself thinking that you could *run off* a high—as in, walk quickly—and then get in your parents' car totally sober a few minutes later? I talked myself into that one more than once.

I spent Easter—a religious holiday that meant fuck-all to me, but which had a significance just because I *couldn't get out*—in an inpatient facility for young people with drug problems. One kid bragged about how many cars he'd stolen. Another talked about getting addicted to pain meds after a brown recluse bite. Mostly, they were just all a lot more badass than I was. They called me "dictionary." No shitting around.

About four days into this inpatient rehab thing, the fog began lifting, and the tiles on the bathroom floor stopped undulating every time I sat down to take a shit—which was itself an unpredictable and confusing experience in that home full of strangers. I came to. I woke up, coming around to the fact that I wasn't leaving anytime soon, that my depressive troubles were the same as they were back in school, that I carried a constantly pulsating nuclear payload of anxiety that was showing up more and more frequently, and that—most importantly—no one in this place could get me fucked up. No one could fix me up the way I needed.

So, I did what many addicts do in this situation. I called my parents and cried. I begged them to come back to retrieve me. Told them I'd go to meetings every day and rehab every night. Promised them the world, told them that I couldn't hack it, that I could stay clean at home with them if they'd *just come and pick me up.* By some miracle of personal strength, they refused.

I then threatened to run. Staff informed me of the consequences if I were to do that, beyond the obvious ones involving exposure to the elements during winter in the middle of nowhere, Pennsyltucky. I was under eighteen, and all runaways must be reported to the state police out there in the sticks. I'd be picked up and detained until either my parents were willing to come get me out of juvie or I was entered into the state system of care for indigent children.

I cried more. Harder. I hated my parents with all of my being. I went to my cot in that room of twelve or fifteen cots, and I cried on my bed. Others either pretended I wasn't crying or told me that they did the same thing and that it'd pass.

By week three of that month in central Pennsylvania, at the house meeting where we read the rules & regs every afternoon, when a guest speaker said, "Maybe two of you will be clean in a year," I was looking around wondering who the other guy was going to be. I was a changed man. Child. I believed.

I returned home. I did not stay clean. Lasted a few weeks, maybe. My mother called the rehab asking for help. The large Black man who had been my scary (yes, the suburban white kid was raised to be afraid of all Black men) shoulder to cry on while I was inside told me to buck up and go to meetings and keep going to aftercare. Every weekday evening, I attended an aftercare evening group session, and for whatever reason, they didn't kick me out. I got serious. The date was 5/25/1999. It was the first date

I remember because it was the first time I stayed clean for more than a few days at a time.

No, I didn't stay clean from that point on. But here's where the story turns in an important way. I began going to meetings every single day. Four days after my latest clean date, I attended a twelve-step retreat.

I rode out there with a guy clean for about fourteen years—a millennium, from my view—who drove an old pickup truck with roll-up windows. He didn't tell me to stop smoking cigarettes. He just wanted me to stay clean, and he welcomed me to what I perceived to be the cool kids' club. It was there I met a future best friend. That future best friend loved the Grateful Dead, too. He and I stayed up all night, sans chemical assistance, and went fishing at sunrise. We annoyed all of the old folks around us by talking and joking through the darkest hours.

On Saturday night of the retreat, everyone attended the main speaker meeting. When the group there did a clean time countdown, saving the folks with the fewest days clean for last, I stood up when they got to "four days." People of all ages and backgrounds came together to support me, and I felt it: they cheered, hooted, and shouted encouragement. They told me to keep coming back. I wanted to come back to the retreat in 2000. I wanted to be the one standing up with a year clean next time around.

On Sunday, when we broke down our campsite and packed up to leave, the older guy with the Ford pickup told me he expected me to be back next year. I nearly cried at the thought of such a good and distant thing being possible.

That weekend, I realized something that saved my life. I could have a blast, could socialize, and could get through a weekend of camping without getting high. I also learned these twelve-step people—these *addicts*—were my people. They understood what I was going through, even if I believed (for a reason that is beyond my understanding today) they couldn't relate to me as a teenager. They could empathize with me, an addict in pain.

That weekend was not the beginning of my long-term abstinence and recovery. It was, in a way, prerequisite to it, though. By the time my life fell apart to a greater extent than it had earlier that year, in September and October of 1999, I knew to whom I'd turn.

I turned to my people, and I got honest about my decrepitude and desperation. I stopped holding court and started asking for—and accepting, often enough—help. When the sharing came around to me during a meeting, I told people I couldn't stay clean, didn't know where I was going to sleep that night, and hadn't eaten all day. They fed me pizza, gave me a ride to wherever I was staying, offered to put me up on their couches (I refused), and told me to come back clean. Eventually, I did.

Besides the sayings we know from rehab movies and television episodes, there's another one oft repeated in twelve-step meetings: "When I was beaten, I became willing." That happened to me, and the desperation was a gift. My sponsor became not my disguise but my brother in recovery—I am godfather to his daughter, and our families vacation together. My sponsees and friends in recovery are welcomed to family dinners in my home. My wife, a woman whose vulnerability has taught me the lessons from that first year all over again, is in recovery—between us, we've been working to better ourselves for over forty years.

These days, it is I who am welcoming people new to recovery, hoping that they'll stay and accept us as their lifeline. Attending meetings in my twenty-fifth year clean and recovering, whether on the other side of the world or in my hometown, to step over the threshold of those church basements (this movie trope is true) is to know that I am exactly where I need to be.

TOSSING AN EIGHT

DAVID RODEBACK

I'd never been in this wing of my new school, Lakeside High, but I leaned against a cinder block wall and waited. I knew I had the right door when girls who looked like dancers started trickling out with gym bags. I didn't know anyone yet, except my cousin, and I didn't know her very well. She was two years older – and my ride home.

"Are you waiting for somebody?"

I turned and saw a burly girl almost as tall as me, with a round face, blonde hair, and a very long gym bag. She'd walked past me and then come back. At first I thought she was a teacher, but she had some acne, so probably not. She wasn't smiling, but she didn't look mean. She seemed confident, like she knew she belonged – like I did, sort of, at my old school, where I played sophomore lacrosse. Lakeside didn't have lacrosse.

Be friendly, Mom had said.

"Uh, yeah. Waiting. Is that okay?"

She shrugged. "Boys usually don't come down this hall, but I don't think there's a rule or anything."

Girls I didn't already know, I couldn't really talk to. But I tried. "Do you know if... I mean is, uh, Emily Bates still in there?"

"Em? She'll be out soon. Are you that cousin from Mesa who just moved here?"

"Cousin. Yes. Em's... my ride home."

She switched her bag to her other hand. "Welcome to Lakeside High. You have a name?"

I nodded. "Yeah."

She watched me for a few seconds. "Which is?"

"Uh, Rick."

"Short for, uh, Richard?"

"Short for Jerrick." I sounded nervous just saying my name.

Her eyebrows went up. "Is that one of those made-up Mormon names?"

"Yeah." Someday I'd like it, my parents said.

"I'm Jane. Classic name, and I'm not Mormon. But this is Utah, so I know a lot of you."

Ask questions, Mom had said. Whatever comes to mind. You'll never feel like you belong until you know people and people know you.

"What's in your bag?" I half-pointed.

"Practice flags, rifle, saber." She finally smiled, but faintly. "Hey, uh-Rick, relax a little. They're not real weapons."

"So that's... color guard... stuff?" I was doing better. At least the words were coming out in the right order.

"I'm in the color guard," she said.

"Are you... manager or... something?"

She tilted her head slightly. "I'm *in* the color guard."

She sounded patient or maybe restrained, which should have been a clue. Later, my excuse for what I said next was that I was new, she was a girl, and my brain got messed up. "Thought you had to be... a dancer... to do that."

She pressed the corners of her mouth together, like she was trying not to frown. "Dancing is one of the things we do. What's your point?"

"You don't... look like... a dancer."

She hefted the bag. "What do I look like, uh-Rick from Arizona?"

Knowing I was in trouble didn't help. "Shot-putter?"

She shook her head and looked tired or something.

The glancing slap to the top of my head came from nowhere. Actually, it came from Em's hand, which came from nowhere. I hadn't heard her behind me, but apparently she'd heard me.

I stepped away from the blow and turned.

Em looked like a dancer – an angry dancer. "You can be a real Rick sometimes, you know that, Rick?" Each time she said my name, she snarled.

I didn't say anything. I watched in case she tried to hit me again.

"Jane, my cousin Rick is a sophomore in every bad sense of the word. but today I'm his ride." Her eyes flashed. "As soon as I decide where to dump the body."

She looked at Jane but talked to me. "Jane Van Allen is Weapons Captain of the best high school color guard in the state and a champion shot-putter. She knows several ways to hurt you, but she's a lot nicer than I am, and hurting you is my job now. And my new hobby," she added cheerfully. She slapped me, another glancing blow to my head, and her voice went cold again. "Pretty bad day you're having, Rick."

Her voice softened, but not for me. She put her free hand on Jane's arm. "I apologize for my cousin. He'll never bother you again. And we'll shorten 'Jerrick' to 'Jerk.'"

Jane said nothing, and I couldn't look at her. My head was spinning, and I expected Em's hand to come flying at me again.

"Sophmo-Rick, it's time to apologize to the nice senior."

Okay, apologizing made sense. When I looked up, Jane looked hurt, and her earlier confidence was gone.

"I'm sorry," I said, and I meant it.

Jane just looked at me with somber eyes.

"That'll have to do for now, I guess," Em said. "I'll call you, J. You come with me, dorkwad."

I outweighed Em by at least fifty pounds. But when she pulled you away, you went away.

When I was sitting in her car, half-angry, half-scared, and half-embarrassed, before she even put the key in the ignition, Em turned on me. "Wow, are you stupid! You don't say anything about a girl's body unless it's a compliment. Even then, you'll think twice if you're smart, because a lot of things boys think are compliments don't sound that way to girls."

"I'm sorry, okay?" I sounded whiny and upset, and I hated that. I was whiny and upset, and I hated that too. I wanted to tell her I hadn't said anything so badly wrong, but I remembered the look in Jane's eyes. I hadn't meant to hurt her.

We were halfway home before either of us spoke again.

Ask questions, Mom had said.

"What's a weapons captain?" At least I could talk to Em. She was more my cousin than she was a girl.

"She's one of our captains. Works super hard. She's an amazing leader, and she tosses rifle and saber like nobody in the state. She has scholarship offers for that. She's also the kindest girl you'll ever meet."

"She's not Mormon."

"Methodist. So what?"

"I don't know. She just told me."

"She's a far better Christian than me," Em said.

"Yeah, that's obvious," I said with completely stupid honesty, because Em called me names and made my head hurt.

She slammed on the brakes and parked at the side of the road. I thought she was going to hit me again, but she used words instead. "You know that saying, 'Blood is thicker than water'? In your case blood is dumber than a box of rocks. You don't learn quickly, do you?"

Now I was mostly angry. "I'm not stupid. What am I supposed to learn? That some senior girls are violent?"

"What you're supposed to learn is, until you have something positive to say, just shut your piehole."

"I didn't mean to hurt her." I should have stopped there. "And I didn't hurt you."

"Jane's my best friend, the most amazing person I know. But she's sensitive about a few things, and she might be crying right now because of you. What you said to her is what you did to me."

"I didn't mean—"

"I believe you. You're just tall, blond, and stupid. Let's go home."

She was short, brunette, and mean, and for the rest of the short trip I bounced between anger and shame. In front of my house, before I got out, it was shame. "What can I do to apologize to Jane?"

"I've been thinking about that. Saturday is state, and now you're going with my parents. While you sit and watch some really good color guards, Mom and Dad will teach you how amazing we are and how hard we work to be that way. When we perform, you're going to watch us, especially Jane, because she'll do something unbelievable."

I didn't like her telling me what to do, especially with my Saturday. "Color guard is your thing, not mine."

"I'm making it your thing. Plan on watching the shows, not your phone. And after we win, or even if we don't, you're walking up to Jane and telling her how sorry you are and that she was completely amazing."

"What if I have other plans for Saturday?" Like finding the right box and unpacking my PlayStation, but I didn't say that part.

"You just changed them."

"What if I don't want to change them?"

"I'll talk to Uncle Pete and Aunt Mimi, and they'll change

them for you." She cocked her head. "Maybe they'll come too. That would be cool."

The color guard finals were in a community college gym. Most of the people sat up high, probably so they could see the whole floor at once. We sat down low.

It wasn't terrible. Color guard girls are pretty, most of them. There were a few color guard boys too, but I watched them less.

I tried to be bitter about losing my Saturday, but it got harder and harder. Swinging the big, colorful flags around so quickly and in unison couldn't be easy. My favorite part was when they tossed rifles or sabers high into the air, then caught them, usually, when they came down.

Aunt Susan turned to me. "At the end of our show, Jane tosses her rifle really high, probably an eight, which you just don't see in high school. That's eight rotations before she catches it. She'll spin 360 degrees while it's in the air, and then she'll catch it and flip it back up into a six, probably. When it comes down, she'll be on one knee – or maybe both, I forget – and she'll catch it and hold it above her head, and we'll all go nuts."

Half an hour and a couple of schools later, I gathered the courage to ask Uncle Jim, "Did Em tell you what I did?"

He shook his head. "She just said you wanted to come and watch, and we should explain things to you. And break your knees if you try to leave, or your phone if you watch it instead. What did you do?"

"I accidentally offended her friend Jane."

"We love Jane. She's amazing." Something in the show we were watching caught his attention, and after that he must have forgotten to ask how I offended Jane.

During the show before ours, I saw our color guard waiting inside the doors at one end of the gym, on the other side. I couldn't pick out Em, but I couldn't miss Jane. I watched her go to each of the others and give them a hug, and I thought she said something too. I couldn't see their faces clearly, but they stood straighter and looked more confident when she was done.

About the time they ran out and started setting their flags and things at the edge of the floor, before the show started, I stopped trying to feel bitter and just watched.

Maybe I was biased, but our color guard seemed more energetic than the others, and more precise too. At the end Jane tossed her eight, which apparently was perfect, and so was the six after it. I'd seen enough rifle tosses to appreciate how much higher hers were than everyone else's, including the guys I saw who were really good. The cheers all around me were the loudest so far, including from my aunt and uncle. I cheered too, but mostly I thought how hard it must be to do what she'd just done, especially with everybody watching. Just catching a falling, spinning rifle seemed superhuman.

I was nervous as they announced the awards. It wasn't so much that Lakeside High was my new school or Em was my cousin or Jane was her friend. I was nervous about apologizing to Jane. In my head I practiced things to say.

All the color guards lined up on the floor for the awards. They announced the lower places first, with their numeric scores. When Lakeside didn't get third or second place, my aunt and uncle still had calm, matching smiles. When the announcer said we'd won first place, they jumped up and cheered. I stood up too.

When I thought it was over and time to find Jane, my aunt said it wasn't. "The winners repeat their show as an exhibition. Jane might try eight and eight this time, or at least eight and seven. Em says she's been practicing."

I knew what to watch for now, and I knew from trying that I couldn't count how many times a rifle spun. But her eight looked just like before, and everybody cheered. When she flipped it right back up for the six – or seven or eight – I thought I heard her cry out above the cheers.

It was higher than a six, maybe, but it wasn't spinning right, and she just stood there instead of kneeling. She'd caught it with her right hand before, above her head, but she didn't even lift her right arm this time. She tried to catch it with her left hand, not as high, and I thought I saw the rifle butt hit her face on its way to the hardwood floor. I heard her gasp, then the crowd, and she slumped to the floor.

The others held their final positions until, one by one, they saw Jane and gathered around her.

Some adults, probably coaches, pushed their way through and backed everyone else away, except Em wouldn't go. I only saw Jane clearly for a moment. She was sitting, curled up, holding her arm or shoulder with her other arm.

A lead weight formed in my gut.

I couldn't see her face. She rocked back and forth, and there was blood on the floor, and even more on a towel they held against one side of her face.

The rest of the guard had backed up a few feet, but they hadn't left her. They looked miserable, and at least some of them were crying. Em knelt beside Jane, rubbing her back. I could see Em's face pretty well, because her hair was back in a tight bun. She looked miserable too.

They let our team stay but quietly ushered everyone else to the exits. I saw two paramedics rolling a stretcher in, and I tried to imagine what Jane's injuries might be, besides a bad cut or something. I knew from TV the kinds of things that happened to football players, but not color guard people.

I waited in the hall with my uncle and aunt and a lot of other people who talked in hushed voices. Finally Em appeared, wearing gray sweats with "Lakeside High" in big red letters.

She was breathless and wide-eyed, and I saw tears. "Mom, Dad, I'm going with Jane's parents to the hospital."

"Of course," said Uncle Jim. "What happened? How is she?"

Em's voice shook. "It's bad. They think she severed a muscle or tendon on her last throw. Then her rifle gashed her cheek and maybe broke her cheekbone. It broke her collarbone too." Her voice caught. "A piece of bone is sticking out."

I didn't notice how pale Em was until I felt myself turn pale.

Uncle Joe gave her a hug. "Call if you need a ride."

Aunt Susan hugged her too. "Do you want us at the hospital?"

"No. The whole team wants to go, but Coach says it's too many people. Kate and I are going."

I didn't say much on the way home, but I remembered to thank my aunt and uncle for the ride. I kept seeing Em's pale, tearful face in my mind, and Jane too, and the blood. I hadn't seen the bone sticking out, but I saw that in my mind too.

Mom and Dad were furniture shopping. Their note said they'd be back late. I found my PlayStation and set it up, but I couldn't concentrate on a game. I thought about texting Em. I thought for a long time, to make certain it wasn't a dumb idea.

I still wasn't sure, but I sent, "How's Jane?"

It was half an hour before she replied. "In surgery. Collarbone broken, dislocated. Cheekbone not broken, just stitches, and she really did tear a muscle off her shoulder. Seems like she hurt it shot-putting before and thought it was better, but it wasn't, so now it's a lot worse. She'll be here at least a few days. Can't use either arm for a couple of months."

I was stunned by all the damage, too shaken to smile at such a long message from the cousin who didn't like me.

"I'm sorry," I replied. "You still at the hospital?"

"Yeah."

"Thanks for telling me all that," I wrote. "I hope it goes okay."

"You're welcome."

A few minutes later she added, "Thanks." Em was a pretty like-able cousin, when she wasn't mean.

I hesitated, then sent, "Are you okay?"

"No."

"Sorry. But I'm glad you won state."

She sent me a thumbs-up. "So is Jane."

I should have put my phone down. Instead, I looked through my message threads from all my friends from my old school. Not one of them had texted me since I moved.

How was I supposed to fit in anywhere, especially without lacrosse? I didn't know anybody, and everybody else at Lakeside already had a cozy circle of friends. Even the friends I had forgot me as soon as I moved away, so I hadn't really fit in there either.

Fitting in with Em and Jane might have been good, but they were seniors, plus I'd already messed that up.

A new school and a new city would get easier, Mom and Dad had said as recently as yesterday. They hadn't said when or how.

They also said, if you break it, you fix it – about people stuff especially.

Em hadn't been angry when I texted her. That might not last, but fixing it with Jane might fix it with Em too.

If I could fix it with Jane.

I knew when I walked into the hospital the next morning, wearing my white shirt and tie for church, that I didn't fit in there either. I must have looked as lost as I was. An old lady at a desk asked if she could help.

I was better at following directions than fitting in. Soon I was a quiet hallway, staring at the partly closed door of Room 337. I couldn't see in far enough to see Jane, but a TV was playing.

I knocked softly, but she probably couldn't hear over the TV. I took a deep breath and knocked louder.

The TV stopped, but I still barely heard her. "Come in."

I pushed the door open and slowly stepped into the room until I could see her and she could see me. She was pale. I saw bandages but no blood, and an IV stuck in her arm.

Her voice was flat and tired. "Hi, um, Rick, is it?"

I nodded. "You can call me Sophmo-Rick... if you want to... like Em said."

The side of her face that wasn't bandaged got part way to a smile, maybe, but her voice didn't change. "Never heard her talk about dumping a body before. What are you doing here? You're dressed for church, I guess."

"I'm... I'm sorry."

She looked puzzled and tired – or sad. Maybe remembering me made her sad again.

I could barely talk, but I had to. "Sorry for... for what I said at school." My face was hot. "I'm not good at... I'm bad at... talking... and thinking... first. Sorry I hurt you."

She nodded slowly. "I kind of forgot about that. Bigger prob —" She gasped softly and winced.

"I'm sorry about that too." The words came a little easier. "I was there. You were really good. You were the best... weapons person I saw."

"You were there?" her face brightened a little.

"Em threatened me."

Jane took a slow breath. "Em. My head's blurry. Let me see. Thanks for being there anyway, and the nice compliment. Oh, and the apology. Want to sit?"

I didn't know if she was just being polite or wanted me to stay, but I saw a couple of chairs against the wall opposite the bed. I sat in the nearest one, kind of on the front edge.

"Not there. Pull... pull your chair over here, so I don't have to talk so loud." She pointed with one finger of her IV hand.

The space beside her bed didn't look much wider than the

chair, and it wasn't. I tried to be careful, but I banged the chair against the metal bed frame. "Sorry," I said. "Did that hurt?"

"No. Did Em make you come here too?"

"I... came on my own."

"That's nice."

I shrugged – something Jane couldn't do for a while. "I wanted to apologize."

"Which you did. What else shall we talk about?"

This was dangerous. Maybe a question about her would be good.

"How can you do eights, when no one else can?"

Her expression didn't change. "I'm bigger, as you pointed out the other day." She continued before I could apologize again. "Weight training for shot put helped a lot."

"How long did you have to practice?"

"To get to eight? About five years, at least four days a week." She closed her eyes, winced again, and her breaths were louder – but none of that was my fault, probably.

"Is there... anything... I can... do for you?"

She nodded without opening her eyes. "Would you hold my water cup so I can get a drink?"

She opened her eyes again, and I saw them up close while she drank. They were pretty and brown. Her needing that much help made me sad.

"What?" she whispered, looking up at me. "Am I pathetic?"

"I'm really sorry you're hurt."

She nodded slightly but winced. Her brown eyes watched me. "Just say it already. Whatever else you're not saying."

I sensed danger again. "Not sure I should."

"Is it nice?"

"Can't always tell."

"I'm harder to offend than Em thinks. That was just a bad day."

I blurted it out. "You have pretty eyes."

Her expression didn't change, and she hesitated. "You think so?"

"Was it okay to say that?"

"Yeah."

She winced again, her breath got louder, and her eyes grew dull.

I thought of another question. "Which part hurts most?"

"Right now, my face, and the bone isn't even broken. Usually my arm. Sometimes my collarbone. Could we talk about something else?"

I heard a click. She had a thing with a button in her hand. "Morphine works fast," she said, and her face relaxed.

"Should I go now?"

"I don't mind the company."

We were silent again. I tried to think of anything to talk about besides her pain.

"So, Rick," she said, "do you have your eyes on a college?"

"No. I mean, I don't know which one... or what to major in."

"No rush. Mission first, right?"

"Yeah."

"Two years is a long time to pause your life."

"I guess."

"So many of you do it. Em's thinking about it. I really admire that."

"Thanks. I mean, I'm not going yet."

"But you want to, right?"

"Planning to. Not sure I want to."

Something about her eyes softened. I hadn't heard another morphine click.

"Most guys won't admit that to a non-Mormon," she said. "You believe in Jesus, right?"

"Yeah."

"Why wouldn't you want to help him save other people?"

"It's just... I'm really bad at talking to people."

"I was really bad at tossing a rifle. I just kept doing it."

"That's different."

"Maybe, but you're already doing better than you did before."

"I'm not trying to... tell you about my church."

"So try. Ask me if I want to learn about your church. You're even dressed like a missionary."

"Do you?"

"Don't be lazy. Ask the whole question."

It still wasn't easy. "Do you... want to learn... about my church?"

"Not today, thanks. I'm not feeling well, and I'm kind of drugged."

I had an idea. "How about another day, when you feel better?"

"No, thank you. I like my own church."

I just stared. I hadn't expected immediate rejection. We were practicing.

I sort of heard a smile in her voice. "I just rejected you twice, and you didn't die or anything. You can do it."

She probably was a great color guard captain, like Em said.

I thought of something else. "Does this mess up your scholarships? Em said..."

She stared out the window at a wall. "The muscle could be a year. They'd hold the scholarships, but I wasn't taking them anyway."

"But you're so good. I mean, I don't know anything, but everybody says."

"It's not what I want to do with my life. I just wanted to be really good while I was doing it. Ow." She slowly turned back to me. "I keep forgetting. No deep breaths for a couple of days."

I didn't know what to say.

"I wanted one pair of perfect eights with an audience," she said. "Should have been happy with what I had. Could you help me with another drink before you go?"

I knew that last part was a hint. "Sure, uh, let me put my chair back... first."

Her brown eyes watched me while she sipped through the straw.

"Thanks for coming," she said. "I'll put in a good word for you with Em."

"I could use that."

"You could use what?" said Em's voice from behind me. "What are you doing here?" She sounded a lot less mean than the other day.

Jane's voice was tired and weak. "We've been talking. He was okay."

"You already forgave him, didn't you? You're too nice."

"He apologized. And you know what Jesus said. 'Forgive us our trespasses, as we forgive the dumb things boys say after guard practice.'" Her voice sounded dreamy.

"Did he bring these flowers?"

I hadn't seen the vase of flowers in the window. I should have brought something.

"They're from Connor."

Something twisted in my gut. I looked at Em, then Jane. "I should, you know, get to church."

"How'd you get here?" Em asked.

"Walked."

"Two miles?"

"Less than an hour."

Em turned to Jane. "I brought you some things. I'll come back after church. Sorry." To me she said, "I'll give you a ride. Meet me in the waiting room down the hall."

"Thanks," I said, and my brain went blank, except for noticing Em's dress. It was lots of colors in a complicated pattern I couldn't figure out. She looked nice.

She caught my eye. Did she know I was admiring her dress? "That means you should leave us alone for a minute," she said.

Sitting in Em's car again brought back fresh, unpleasant memories, but Em was different this morning.

"Jane says you were nice. You told her she has pretty eyes?"

I blushed.

"Do you have a crush on her? You do! Look at your face."

"I like her, but not... not like that."

"There might be hope for you yet. Not with her. As a human, I mean."

"Don't take this wrong," I said, "but is Connor her boyfriend? I hope he's nice."

"He's really nice. Not sure they have a future though. Six months from now, he'll be wearing a nametag."

"They can write to each other."

"Trust me," Em said with a distant look. "Missionary e-mails aren't much of a substitute for the actual boy."

I was afraid to ask what popped into my head, so neither of us said anything for a minute. I watched her as she drove. She looked unhappy, and I didn't think it was with me. Jane would know how to cheer her up.

I asked my question anyway. "What's your missionary's name?"

"I still don't like you enough to tell you that." She sounded tired, and she kept her eyes on the road.

"I said I'm sorry. For the other day."

"And I didn't kill you and bury the body. We're even."

We were silent until we parked at the church, so it could have been a lot worse. Em turned off the engine and stared straight ahead.

"His name is Brandon," she said, and I stared in surprise that she would tell me. "He's in freaking Madagascar, which may or may not explain why I haven't had an e-mail from him in two weeks. Again. The internet there sucks."

She turned to me. "I miss him, okay?"

I nodded.

"Supposedly, it's hard to be a good missionary when you really miss somebody you left at home. It's pretty hard to be left behind too. I'm only telling you so you'll appreciate it later, if there happens to be a girl who misses you."

"If I go. Missionaries have to be good at talking to people. I'm not, obviously."

"You have to talk to people to do most things. So practice. Visit Jane again. A lot of us will, or she'll go out of her mind."

"Would that be okay?"

"Be a friend to make a friend. You did okay this morning."

"She makes me feel like I belong here."

"Maybe you do." Em brightened. "Sometimes I ask myself, WWJD?"

"What Would Jesus Do? How is that about Jane?"

Em looked like the same cousin as before, but she was already being nice, and now she actually smiled at me. "It's not that. It's What Would Jane Do? Hey, we should go in. I'll introduce you to some of the guys. You're on your own with the girls."

Home

Nicole Dvorak Klunder

What does it mean
To belong?

Finding connection
through community support
Such an amazing discovery
All on its own

Realizing you're
Not alone
Shared interests

Exploring, journeying, living
Connected through words
Words...such a craving

What does it mean
To belong?

I sip the hot tea
Sitting before me
Ginger spice
Elderberry, how nice

I tap the pencil top,
White screen silently
Screaming at me
My fingers land
Lightly on the keyboard

Home?

The heart of the bustling city
The dazzling lights that fill the streets
Row by Row

The chaos and mayhem
Cars, horns, music, crowds
Graffiti chaos

Color splashes, Art
Expression
Freedom

The tall, white wedding chapels, or
A row of chapels
Nestled between whites
And colorful flowers

Home

The comfort of your bed
And safety
The twinkling lights, vast view
Across the city, only minutes away

Home?

Opportunity awaits
Dreams, ambition, courage
Instincts, connections, memories
Perspective, diversity
Life

What does it mean
To belong?

I close my laptop
Stare out into the dark
blue sky
Taking a cleansing breath
Thinking...
I'm right where
I need to be...

HOME

You Belong

C.R. Langille

The aroma of stale coffee, cheap air fresheners, and body odor assaults my nostrils as soon as I walk into the place. I don't want to be here. I don't want to go into the tiny little Mom and Pop gas station to go to the restroom, especially in the middle of nowhere, USA. But when Mother Nature calls, don't you dare ignore Her.

A group of middle-aged men stop their conversation mid-sentence as soon as I walk in. While I can't hear exactly what they are saying, their whispers speak volumes, and the weight of their stares could drag a whale to the bottom of the sea.

I'll just get in, do my business, and get out. I'll even skip my personal rule about buying something to justify my use of the facilities because the quicker I can leave, the better.

Pulling my pink sweater tighter around my body (as if that would help stave off the attention), I search for said facilities but ultimately come up short.

Yay! (Imaginary jazz hands...)

It means I'll have to talk with the guy behind the counter. The one who stares at me like he is trying to figure out if he wants to fuck me or fight me. In short, gross.

I hurry over to the counter and the sneer that Dave (so sayeth the official nametag he sports on his grubby shirt) gives me answers the last question.

"Is there a restroom here?"

Dave looks me up and down, that crooked sneer setting harder into the corners of his mouth.

A giggle comes from the group of men, and I caution a glance their way. I wish I hadn't.

Young men, three of them wearing construction safety vests. Maybe highway workers or maybe building something nearby. It doesn't matter. They giggle even harder when I shoot them a look.

The jingle of metal across the counter pulls me back to Dave. The keys to the restroom lay in front of me, attached to a large wooden plank that somebody painted the word MEN on in large white letters.

Heat flushes through my cheeks. Seems like all my misgivings about Dave were valid. Bonus points for me.

"Uh, the women's please?" I say, trying to sound as kind and lovely as possible, although I'm pretty sure even Dave can read between the lines.

Dave either snorts or growls as he snatches the key away and throws another set. This time, the keys are attached to a hairbrush with several colors of hair stuck between the bristles. I am too slow to catch them and they clatter to the floor, eliciting another round of giggles and whispers from the construction team in the back. Maybe I should look into becoming a stand-up comedian.

I crouch down and snatch them up, wishing I could just run back to my car and get the hell out of here, but my pride stops me. It's just a bathroom, these are just immature morons, and I. HAVE. TO. GO!

I take two steps before I realize I still don't know where the bathrooms are.

With a deep sigh, I turn back to Dave. "Where are they?"

Dave points outside to a small concrete building maybe fifty feet away.

Of course. Nothing like a trek through the dark to the restroom.

"Thank you, Dave."

I'm pretty sure the way I just said his name could freeze the sun, but I don't care anymore. With the yucky hairbrush-keys in tow, I step back outside. The sour smells of the store are replaced with the acrid cut of gasoline mixed with a scent that only happens in humid places after a rain. Not petrichor, but something else. Kind of musty... industrial even.

The muggy night air coats my skin like plastic wrap, and I'm assaulted by a squadron of mosquitoes. But you know what? As much as I hate humidity (and hate bugs even more), I'll take this over Dave and the Construction Gang of Gigglefucks any day of the week. Even Mondays.

As I make my way to the restrooms, the clack of my boots echoes across the concrete. The only other sounds are the buzz of the dull yellow light flickering on the tiny building's wall and the drone of insects. It is kind of nice in a this-might-drive-me-crazy-if-I-listen-to-it-for-too-long kind of way.

Just around the corner, there's an overflowing dumpster and a raccoon hoping for an effortless meal. As soon as the trash panda sees me, it scurries off into the darkness. Apparently, I'm appalling to everything around these parts.

Lucky me.

Next to the dumpster are the doors to the restrooms, one labeled MEN and one affectionately labeled, WHORES. Someone thought themselves quite the artist and had painted over WOMEN and replaced it with the lovely new moniker.

If something like that had taken place back home, someone would have fixed it within a day. The faded paint indicated that this had been here for some time.

Another struggling light positioned between the two doors fights to stay lit, just like its sibling.

Just get in, do my business, get out.

Easy-peasy.

I hurry over and put the key in. The lightbulb pops. I stifle a scream, and the normally fun sensation of a scare washes through my entire body and starts me trembling something fierce.

With the buzz from the light gone, I am blanketed with silence. Even the bugs have stopped singing their hymns. Probably a coincidence.

Sure. A coincidence... and I am the Queen of Costco. Horror movies are part of my DNA, and I know what comes next.

I try to turn the key to unlock the door, but it's jammed.

"Come on!"

I jiggle it, hoping maybe that will fix the issue, but it holds on tight. The thought of having to go back in there and let Dave know about the lock is not a pleasant one.

As I continue to force the key, being careful not to bust the damn thing, the thud of footsteps fills the air.

Hopefully, it's not Dave or one of those construction workers, but I can't think of who else it could be.

The footsteps pick up speed, getting louder the closer they get. A cold pit forms in my stomach, and I want to throw up. I don't dare look, because if I see someone running at me in the dark, I know I'll freeze up.

Just. Got. To. Open.

Any moment now, whoever is coming over will turn the corner and see me.

Frustration and desperation make wonderful dance partners. Part of me wants to scream as I jiggle the keys and turn. Part of me wants to run—a big part.

Just as the footsteps near the building, the key finally turns. The insects take up their cries again, and I throw the door open. I don't wait to see who it is as I slam the door shut behind me and engage the deadbolt.

For a moment, I do nothing but try to catch my breath, resting my forehead against the cool metal door. It's dark in here, so I feel around for the switch and flip it on as soon as my fingers brush up against it.

Just as I do, the door handle wiggles.

Someone is trying to get in.

I take a step back, holding my breath. My phone is in my purse, and I try to dig it out with shaky hands. As I yank it out, the edge catches on the inside of the purse, and I lose my grip. It falls to the floor with a clatter.

"Shit."

The handle wiggling picks up in intensity.

BANG!

Someone kicks the door with enough force to rattle the crappy aluminum bathroom stalls. I grab my phone and find a large crack has spider-webbed across the screen.

Should have splurged the extra $50 for a protective case. The screen lights up, but it is unreadable.

BANG!

I let out a scream and drop the phone again.

"Leave me the fuck alone! I'm calling the police!"

They try the handle again a few more times, then it all stops. For what feels like hours, I sit on the yucky restroom floor staring at the door, halfway expecting someone to bust in at any moment. But nobody does.

My stomach gurgles, reminding me why I came here in the first place. I don't want to go out there right now. Hell, I don't want to go out at all. Who knows if those pricks are waiting for me?

I do my business, continuing to listen and jumping at every little creak and groan in the building. Hopefully, my little fib about calling the police scared them off. They don't know my phone is broken.

Still on edge and thinking someone will kick the door down, my heart jumps out of my chest when a woman's soft cries come from the stall next to me. I stifle a scream and try not to make any noise. Kind of silly though when I think about it. Anyone who was in here before me would have heard the racket.

But wasn't it dark when I came in?

Was someone just sitting alone with the lights off?

The thought of it makes me uneasy. Perhaps they were also hiding. But how would they have gotten inside without the key? I need to chill. Maybe there is a spare...

"Hello?"

I don't like how meek my voice sounds. It also cracks, dropping back into my old pitch and tone for just a moment.

The crying continues, but nobody answers. They are probably scared out of their mind. I know I am.

"It's okay, I'm just here to use the bathroom," I say.

Again, no answer, just some sniffling. It was past time for me to get out of Dodge. I finish up and wash my hands, all the while eyeing the stall next to where I was. The door is closed.

"Do you need me to take you somewhere or call someone? Are you hurt?"

The crying stops.

Thoughts of whether I should stay and help this stranger or just go race around in my mind. Ultimately, I decide I can't leave without ensuring the person is okay. Besides, those goons could still be waiting outside, and a few more minutes could be the difference.

"Hello?"

I shuffle a little closer to the stall. The crying starts up again.

I knock on the stall door, and it pops open. Not enough to see inside yet. (Please don't be a monster. Please don't be a monster. Please don't be a...)

"It's okay, I'm here to help," I say and push the door all the way open.

There's nobody in there. The lights flicker and then I'm bathed in darkness.

(No. No. No. No. This can't be happening!)

My nerves are alive, screaming for me to run. I can't see anything, let alone process what just happened.

The crying comes from right behind me, and I swear something brushes a hand through my hair.

I scream again as I tumble forward and slam my knee into the side of the toilet. Pain shoots up my leg. I ping-pong between the wall and the toilet before finally hitting the ground.

The darkness is heavy, and it moves. Slithers like a snake in the tall grass.

The click-clack of something far away echoes through the tiny bathroom. The sound is distorted, farther away than it should be. I mean, this place isn't that big, but the echoes sound like they are down a long hallway.

I fumble for my phone. The screen lights up, but everything is warped from the cracked glass. Working from muscle memory, I try to navigate to where my flashlight setting would be. Amazingly, I find it, and my phone's light cuts through the darkness.

I'm in the stall and the door is closed. My light illuminates not-so-ancient pictographs drawn onto the door in Sharpie. From the looks of it, the crude drawings depict a mating ritual of some sort. As much as I'd like to stay and study the moronic art, the train departing Bullshit Creepy Bathroom leaves now.

I stand, grimacing in pain when I put weight on my bashed knee. Blood trickles down onto my shin, soaking through my dress. I will probably need stitches or something.

When I limp out of the stall, my heart drops into my boots.

This isn't where I was before. I was in a small restroom with two stalls. This building stretches as far as my phone's light shines. The facilities were dirty and uncared for before, but now they are something else entirely. Smooth tiles cover the walls. Maybe they were once white, but now they are covered in grime and a black moldy substance. The sinks, dozens of them, line the wall along with a mirror that seems to stretch on forever.

The tarnish on the mirror makes it nearly impossible to see my reflection. A rusty looking coating creeps across it. From off in the distance comes the echo of dripping water.

"Nope."

I turn to leave, willing to face the horrors of the real world instead of this twisted nightmare. However, there isn't a door. Just a blank bit of tile where it should have been.

This can't be happening. Did Dave drug me? Am I tripping right now?!

There comes a clicking buzz as an EXIT sign flickers to life down the endless hallway. I fight back tears again as the impossibility of it all burrows its way through my thoughts. Maybe I hit my head when I fell and this is all a delusion, or perhaps I'm in a coma.

Maybe I'm dead.

I refuse to believe that. It has to be something else, a psychotic break or something. If I can just get out of here, then maybe it will go back to normal. I limp down the aisle between the sinks and the stalls. All the doors are shut, and here and there I can hear more crying and sobbing. Sometimes, the doors shake as if someone is trying to get out.

The radiating buzz of the EXIT sign gets louder as I near. A bathroom stall door hangs haphazardly from one hinge just below the sign, blanketed by the menacing ruby-red glow. I shine my light into the stall and find it's a doorway into another room.

There comes another click-clacking echo, like someone walking with heels across the tile floor. It's off somehow though, more clicks than there should be. Maybe a group of people.

"Hello?"

It's like I'm in a cave. The echo of my voice bounces around the room and back down the hallway.

"Is someone there? I'm trying to get out of here."

The click-clacks stop.

"Please, I just want to get out of here."

The click-clacks turn into a scurry, causing a shudder to wriggle up my spine. I don't want to see what it is, so moving farther into the room is the only option.

Rusted lockers line the walls with a few decrepit wooden benches strewn about. The floor is wet with brackish water pooling from a drain in the middle of the floor. I do my best to walk around the puddle.

Once past the lockers, I come across the shower room. It's arranged like an old school shower with a column in the middle of the floor and multiple shower heads attached all around it. The kind of place men would joke about not dropping the soap.

Words scrawled in a brownish paint (maybe blood?) cover the walls.

Help me
I want to go home
No! Please just let me go
Help
I belong
Help
I don't deserve this
Help
Help

My hands are trembling as I read. I feel like my heart is going to punch through my ribcage and fall onto the floor, and I can't shake the feeling that the room would eat it.

BANG!

My breath catches in my throat. The noise comes from back where the toilets are. It sounds like someone slammed one of the stall doors.

BANG!

BANG! BANG!

More and getting closer. I don't want to meet whoever is doing that, so I limp farther into the locker room. There must be another exit. At least, I hope there is.

After navigating through the locker room, I find another doorway. The door isn't like the others. This one is wooden, with heavy oak planks held together with iron hinges that are blacker than hot tar. Instead of a knob, a metal ring hangs in the center of it.

I pull and nearly yank my shoulder out of socket, but it budges just a little. I put my phone in my mouth, grab the metal ring with both hands, plant my feet, and pull as hard as I can.

Little by little by little, the door creaks open, hinges screaming in protest the entire time. Finally, it is wide enough for me to fit through. The darkness I find on the other side is so thick, my flashlight doesn't make a dent at all.

Click-clack.

I spin around, shining the light all over, but there isn't anything there. Just the lockers.

As I turned to look through the door again, more click-clacking comes. This time from the shower room.

"Hello?"

I'm not sure why I kept trying to talk to whatever it is. It never answ—

"*You belong.*"

I freeze as its cold voice pierces my ears. It sounds like a woman, though they are whispering, making it difficult to hear clearly.

"What?"

I take an involuntary step back, one foot crossing the threshold into the darkness. There comes a slow clicking, and then a pale hand appears from around the corner of the shower room. Long slender fingers with fake acrylic nails on the end. One nail broken. The rest are different shades and lengths, as if the person couldn't decide what color to use, so they just grabbed whatever was in front of them.

"Are you okay?" I ask.

"You belong."

I belong? I really didn't like where this was going.

"Look, I'm just trying to get out of here. I made a mistake. I never should have stopped here."

Click.

Clack.

Click.

A young woman pokes her head out from behind the corner. Her skin is pale, almost translucent, like her hand. She has long black hair that drags across the ground. It is all clumpy and stringy, like she just got out of the shower. Dark black streaks stain her cheeks. Her mascara has run—she was the one who had been crying before!

Some of the fear dissipates. It's just another scared woman, like me.

"It's okay, you can come with me. I'll get you out of here and to somewhere safe," I say as I reach out a hand.

Her eyes are full of fear. Fear and something else I can't place. They dart from me to behind me where the darkness waits.

"Come with. You?"

"Yeah, honey. It's going to be okay. Come with me."

She smiles. Not a warm smile, but the kind of smile a hyena gives its prey.

Click.

Clack.

Click.

A long, bony leg stretches out from where the girl stands. Longer than it should be and jointed like a spider's. But it isn't a leg... and that isn't a foot attached to the spindly limb. It is another hand, and several plastic bracelets sit upon its wrist. When it *steps* on the floor, the bracelets smack together—*click, clack.*

I watch in horror as more of the appendages stretch out, pulling the deformed mass of the thing into view. Eight legs attached to a fleshy body made from dozens of other unfortunate women smash together as if they were some horrific clay amalgamation. A patchwork of horror.

The thing crawls out, its plethora of cheap jewelry clicking and clacking with each step. A different woman's head, this one blonde with an undercut and a tattoo of a hedgehog driving a riding lawnmower across her temple, lolls to one side as the thing moves. The woman's mouth opens and closes, and I can't tell if she is gasping for breath or trying to speak. Several other heads have grown from the creature's body like horrible polyps.

All words and sounds die in my throat.

"You belong."

When the creature speaks, all the mouths speak.

Its voice is many voices. The voices of all women who have been killed, violated, beaten, and discarded across the vast wasteland of restrooms throughout the world coalesce into one desperate sound.

Tears run down my face as the thing smiles, revealing a maw filled with three rows of glassy, needle-like teeth.

It rushes toward me, and I run through the door. The pressure changes, and my ears pop as I step through the threshold fully.

I fall to the ground screaming, arms up to block an attack I'm sure is about to come. When I open my eyes, I'm back in the dingy little restroom, the sterile florescent light doing its absolute best to keep things lit.

I scramble to my feet, looking all around for that thing, that monster. But it's just me. Oh my God, the door back outside is there again!

I rush over and fling it open, desperate to get back to the humid night air and the hungry mosquitos only to reveal the dark locker room again.

Click.

Clack.

The sound comes from behind me. I turn and find her looming over me with a monstrous smile.

"You belong."

Dave cranks up the radio, absentmindedly nodding along with the music. The group of construction workers bring over a case of beer and put it up on the counter.

"Did that tranny come out of the bathroom yet?" one asks.

Dave chuckles and glances over to the restrooms.

"Not yet. Gonna give that snowflake another minute to stew in his own fear, then I'm gonna take the master key and drag him out of there. Teach him what we do to degenerates and perverts around these parts."

The front door slides open and a second later the bell chimes letting Dave know someone just walked in. He looks over and finds the snowflake in question standing there. They are missing one boot, and their hair is wet, covering most of their face.

"Awww, did you fall in?" one worker says with a chuckle.

This gets the group laughing, but Dave doesn't like this. Something isn't right.

"You get the fuck out here. Don't come back, you hear!?" Dave shouts.

The lights in the gas station flicker. The radio warbles, static overtaking the music. Or is that people screaming and crying?

A voice crackles through the radio's noise.

You do NOT belong.

The lights go out followed by the click-clack of *something* walking through the door.

THE RED LINE

MICHELLE LEE

I'm not a soldier anymore! Only, my lizard brain doesn't seem to remember that. It still hosts all the aggravations associated with living the military life.

My heart thunders, my breathing is choppy, as I search with wild eyes for a parking space to abandon my Subaru. It's been decades since my last visit to this sprawling VA Medical Center, located in downtown Salt Lake City. I'd come then to visit my Vietnam-era uncle, admitted for some malady I've long since forgotten, before adulthood. Still, it's eerily familiar.

I dart into an empty space in the new multitiered parking terrace; tires screech as I apply the brakes. Dread clenches my gut. A hospital. A military hospital. God help me.

I'm not a nurse anymore either, I remind myself, but my anxiety begins ratcheting higher anyway. I've avoided hospitals for years now, preferring a desk to the bedside. Too many tragedies and irredeemable losses.

I don't belong here. I'm a writer, dammit! And for good reason. Not because I want to bury my head in the sand, forgetting the traumas of the past, but because I want a better life. The life of my dreams. That's not in the forefront of my mind, however. Just a haunting echo of an echo.

I leap from the car, scooping up my purse on the fly. Did I lock it? Who cares!

I'm dashing to the front door, heart in my mouth, glancing up to verify I've reached Building 1. Double doors whoosh open. I hurdle into the lobby and halt. Kiosks with gloves and hand cleaner stand sentry before a bank of hastily erected folding tables and plexiglass barriers.

I'm instantly reminded of Covid restrictions and resign myself to yet one more delay.

Three weeks before, I'd retired, escaping my life as a pediatric nurse case manager—as giddily as I'd once escaped the Army—to pursue my true passion; writing. Steering toward this glimmering dream has sustained me through many of life's most turbulent storms. I'm supposed to be settling into retirement, pen in hand. Only a few remaining hurdles, I'd promised myself, and then... fully immerse in the dream of capturing on paper that which my writerly brain is constantly conjuring—ideas, visions, sentences, scenes, all crafted with only the choicest words. But now, the dream of writerly-me flounders. Right then, the only thing that matters is arriving here—reaching Dad.

Behind the first plexiglass barrier is a wiry gentleman, grizzled silver beard protruding around the edges of his disposable yellow mask. I snag one from the kiosk and don it with trembling fingers before taking another step. The fit is familiar, as is the scent—ever present reminders of not only the pandemic, but my profession—past profession that is. The grizzled man stands at attention, watching.

He follows my progress to his station where he grips a clipboard and pen as firmly as he might once have gripped his AR-15. His rheumy hazel eyes lock on mine. Nerves tingle my fingertips as I wait for him to cue me on what comes next.

"Last four?"

I blink in confusion. *Waaaa?*

I step aside, waving the next person in line to move ahead while I send out a choppy text to my sibling. I learn *last four* refers to the final digits of a social security number. Shouldn't I have been able to deduce that? No... It's been a quarter century since I last thought of myself as a number. Thank God. A lifetime since I left the Army to become a civilian nurse. Also, I've never had a reason to know Dad's SSN.

Standing before the grizzled man again, lips trembling, I sniffle, grateful for the required mask, secretly wishing for the safety and comfort, of my cozy home office. My writerly hideaway... but... more so, for Dad to be healthy once more.

And still alive.

I read the numbers from the screen of my phone when I reach grizzly-man.

"Name?"

I state my name. He wrinkles his brow, scanning a printed list, then looks at me with a glint of suspicion. It hits me—he holds a list of people scheduled to be seen in VA clinics, or former soldiers currently hospitalized. Of course.

"Oh, not me," I tell him. "I'm a visitor. I'm here to see my Dad."

Grizzles makes a call. They're going to permit me to enter as a visitor, even though, he informs me, it's Covid and there's a strict limit as to how many family members are supposed to be allowed in. A chill trickles down my spine; that's not good. It means they think Dad's about to pass. Squaring my shoulders, I blink away tears.

Writerly-me shudders and sinks beneath the surface of my

mind, treading water now, as she has since my first proud authorial attempt—a book of poems I painstakingly penned on fancy cardstock and bound with masking tape at age ten.

Grizzle's demeanor softens as he swooshes his hand toward the rear of the lobby indicating a path through the bank of workers anchored behind plexiglass, processing other supplicants. "Follow the red line. It'll take you to the elevators. When you leave, follow it back to the lobby. Have a nice day, ma'am."

My eyebrows quirk. Red line? I march on, scanning the horizon, pondering "red line." I should have clarified, but there's no turning back. Possible "red line" meanings surface then drift away in my anxiety-riddled brain as I continue through the lobby.

Writerly-me: red lines through the words of my first painstakingly crafted eighth grade essay (including the comment: *you didn't write this!*)

Soldier-me: the *thin* red line... the point of no return.

Nurse-me: hot red lines streaking along a vein, or the Red Line —the train I formerly rode from home to work and back.

What did he mean?

Where?

My mind is swirling in a hurricane of fear and guilt, given all the delays in my journey to arrive here. The last days have become a waking nightmare. Ironically, the horror of it all is not lost on writerly-me. If only I could pretend that this too is simply story fodder and deny the real purpose of my visit. Put my worries on hold for just a moment and ignore the reality of Dad's sudden, mysterious illness which I'm about to confront.

———

Nearly three weeks earlier, with the blessing of my husband and teenage son, I worked my last shift as a pediatric nurse case manager in my cozy home office, originally thrown together for Covid's work-from-home scenario. I've decorated with framed

NaNoWriMo posters collected over the last twenty years of intermittent rough drafts. Also, one cherished poster of Earnest Hemingway, titled *Endurance*. Beside my desk, I've shelved my life-long collection of novels, including college texts, like nursing (the greatest art), and cherished picture books which I've narrated innumerable times for each of my four children. I've made it my writerly paradise, in anticipation of no longer finding myself caught in the corporate net which has become *Healthcare*. At 5:00 pm, I snap the lid of my laptop down, done checking boxes, ready to pick up the pen and begin. I sigh deeply with satisfaction, soaking in the quietude.

But before I truly launch my new chosen profession, I have to help pack up the contents of my daughter's storage unit near Sacramento, California, and make the long drive to Florida, helping her through yet another move in her decade-long saga toward her pediatric residency.

As we sort and pack, I receive the first call; something is going on with Dad. He's feeling out of sorts. Weak. There in the echoey hallway of the storage complex, my Doctor Daughter coaches her grandparents, convincing them to call an ambulance. She disconnects the call, round eyed. *Could* be a stroke, she murmurs.

I've arranged for a giant moving truck. As we reverse-Jenga her curated belongings into the eight-by-eight-foot space we're allotted, we're both antsy to get moving. We'll drive straight home, unload cherished possessions which won't be making the trip to the East Coast, then make a quick side-trip to check on Dad in the ultra-rural community which is Dry Fork, Utah. When we're sure he's stable, we'll set off. But characteristic of my unfailingly willful father, before we reach Salt Lake, he's discharged from the ICU where he's been treated for a mere stomach bug. His blood pressure is finally normal. All is well. Still, we make that side trip. And he is feeling better. Just weak. His ICU stint and the strange malady, which took such a toll on my normally thriving eighty-year-old father, seems to have resolved. As we drive away, waving from our open windows, he's back on his tractor. All is well.

Only it's not. Dad's downward spiral has only begun.

Three days into the journey, jetting along in my daughter's Forrester, loaded to the gills, having traversed Utah and New Mexico and half of Texas, we discover something's going wrong. Dad's becoming weaker. He's readmitted to the hospital. Then as we brave a (literal) tropical storm landing on the coast near Baton Rouge, Louisiana, Dad can barely stand or feed himself. His admitting physician is struggling to determine a diagnosis. As we reach Orlando, he's rushed via ambulance from his tiny community hospital to the Salt Lake City's VA Medical Center.

The red line, I discover, is a red linoleum stripe, painstakingly laid between polished oatmeal-colored linoleum tiles, dividing the shiny river of never-ending hallway like the slice of a surgeon's scalpel. It disappears into the gloom.

I follow the red line as grizzly-man ordered. It leads me into the bowels of the brooding beast that is the VA. If I were writing this scene, my protagonist would have just stepped into another dimension, helplessly caught, whirling through time and space into the unknown. Finally, the red line jogs left. Silver elevator doors lurk in the shadowy foyer. It's Sunday—I suppose they dim the lights to conserve energy. I wait, clawing my palms with my fingernails, watching the numbers above the two banks of doors— 5, 4, 3, 2, 1, G. The doors on the right trundle open. I'm reminded of the gaping maw of a catfish. Or a shark.

I step in and jab three.

My stomach sinks as the elevator ascends. I don't need to be frightened, I remind my nurse-self. It's just a hospital, like every other hospital you've practiced nursing in over the last thirty years, smelling of floor polish and rubbing alcohol and ghosts. No different, except it's the VA, filled with veterans of all shapes and ages, rather than tiny beings who fit in the crook of my arm. Anyway, I tell myself, you're a veteran too. No big deal. So what if everything about your surroundings screams military? Being here prompts memories of the day I signed my officer's commission and took the oath. But my fear isn't about being surrounded by flags and posters of smiling female veterans that say *I am not invisible.* The ultimate fear is... did I make it in time.

The elevator dings, and I'm released into a foyer identical to the one below. This entrance has a gatekeeper too.

I pluck my father's *last four* from my memory bank.

"That way," he says in his dark rumble, beetle brows bunched above kind brown eyes. I barely register his concern. Instead, I'm trying to imagine what the next few minutes will hold. Am I in time? Is Dad still here, or is there just a husk lying in that bed?

On floor three, there's no red line to follow. I simply keep walking and arrive at a nurse's station. There's more "last four" and signing in.

"No, not your name," says the woman wearing nondescript navy scrubs and the standard yellow mask, after handing me a clipboard. "His name. Who are you visiting?"

I tell her.

Pity softens her face. She points in the direction of Dad's room. Another river of oatmeal-colored tile, Sunday lighting, shadows lurking. Then, there he is. Dad. Frozen in his hospital bed beneath white sheets. Mom on one side, sister on the other. Brother at the foot, pinching Dad's toe. Can he even feel that?

My sister holds Dad's hand, limp in her strong grasp. Mom turns, and I pull her into a hug. She's shorter than me now, which makes her less than her lifelong five-foot-two. Her shoulders are fragile, her eyes red with recent tears.

Finally, I'm told that Dad has contracted a rare disorder, Guillain-Barre' in which something triggers his body to make antibodies against itself. These antibodies are eroding the specialized covering of his motor nerves, the myelin sheath. Each electrical signal he sends below his neck gets lost before reaching the muscle he needs to recruit. And it's progressing.

In dashes a tall dark-haired women with boundless energy and a sharply pointed nose. Even with the mask over her face, this is evident. Her brown eyes sparkle with fierce determination. I like her immediately. Now here's something, someone, I can relate to. The disconnected feeling of being in the wrong place at the wrong time begins to evaporate. I'm not doing what I intended, but writing can wait. For a little longer. As soon as Dad begins healing —which we're informed is likely—I'll start writing in earnest. For now, I plan to remain glued to his bedside. I'm already wearing my mental nurse case manager hat. I've got this.

Days later, Dad—in the massive reclining wheelchair which dwarfs him—and I prowl the VA's hallways. I'm almost stoned, wasted with fear and exhaustion.

It's once again a ghostly Sunday. Shadows loom in every corner. It's been a week since my return from Orlando where I'd flown to be with my daughter at her remote graduation-via-screen, compliments of Covid. My brief departure meant the rest of the family was burdened with overseeing Dad's care instead of me, the family nurse. But now I'm back, entrenched here on the third floor with him, and everyone but me has gone back to work—'cause I don't work now, do I?

Mom's hanging on by a thread. She's returned home to load her suitcase with a few belongings, find someone to watch the cat and chickens and goats and change the water on the alfalfa... and to take a much-needed break.

So, Dad and I mark time, exploring to keep his extremely agile mind engaged. We find an outdoor courtyard and begin listening to Ed Abby's *Desert Solitaire*.

I'm scared sick the disease will continue to rob him—steal his ability to speak, or breathe, or he'll develop some unpredictable complication, such as pneumonia or blood clot—but I'm hiding it well. Every day, I juggle to buoy the flagging spirits of extended family as I hover over him. I've in essence abandoned my teenage son, husband, and two dogs to be *the one*. We've started a text chain with the five remaining siblings of Dad's tribe, which once numbered eight, and all their children. Sharing pictures proving he is still living is tricky. Sunk into his once robust frame, he barely looks himself. Deeply tanned and calloused farmer's hands lay limp against white sheets. Mostly, we're sharing all the upbeat deets, of course.

Dad is trying not to think about the next treatment. His *blood scrub*, he calls it. Hours in literal hell. But it is the only thing keeping the proteins from chewing his motor neurons' myelin to pieces. For some reason, the pain my father feels while undergoing something very much like dialysis is unheard of. It shouldn't be but it is. For him it's bones shattering like shards of glass.

Just that morning, I'd demanded a change in his treatment plan with the aid of his tall, dark-haired avenging angel-nurse. I say to the medical team "pain is what the patient says it is." Yes, he'll die without the treatments, but seeing him scream and writhe in pain is intolerable.

He whispers, *"Can't you put me in a medical coma. If not that, what about medically assisted death?"* He means, put him down. Pull the plug. (But true to his nature, my eloquently spoken father says, "medically assisted death.") This is unthinkable. He'd never before have considered such a thing. But that was before he knew the feeling of the blood scrub. And there's at least seven more to come.

A pain specialist, a nurse like me, but with specialized training and extra initials behind her name, has promised to come up with a solution.

That afternoon as a plasmapheresis specialist hooks Dad up to a US Postal-mailbox-sized machine for the dreaded *blood scrub*, a middle-aged former Army medic, masked but still managing to project joviality, bounds into Dad's room. I try to imagine what the lower half of his face looks like. His smile must be spectacular.

"Time for vitals, Mr. H. Do you need to use the urinal?"

Dad nods, barely. I move aside, giving him privacy, an almost nonexistent commodity. Stepping out of his room also gives me time to breathe and think. I glance up and down the hall. I'm alone. I close my eyes. I pray the nurses and assistants, who are forming bonds with him, remain. With their help, we might get through this rabidly progressive disease. I don't think to pray that I will one day find a time and place to write. Writerly-me is fully submerged and holding her breath.

Seven weeks since I "retired," and I note while helping him with oral care that he didn't gag (he's extra sensitive to gagging). That means his body attacked the nerves enabling him to swallow. He's been made NPO, meaning, all his nutrition from here on will be via the tube while we pray the damage to his nerves finally stops. The next thing to go, I'm told, is his breathing. At his age, weaning from a ventilator might prove impossible.

Treatments have nearly ended. The pain specialist, thank God, *did* come through with a new drug. Dad sleeps through most of his remaining blood-scrubs, until near the end. I can't imagine how relieved he is. His nurse and I brush tears from our eyes and sigh, filled with thankfulness following the last.

And then... a miracle. That evening after his final treatment, my paralyzed father wiggles his thumb, and I capture it on video.

Later, surrounded by a team of doctors, a pharmacist, and two nurse practitioners, I break down and hug the pain specialist, much to her embarrassment. It is nearly impossible to be professional—a self-appointed nurse case-manager—when my father's life hangs in the balance. I suppose, underneath the layers of soldier, nurse, and writer... foremost... I am a daughter.

Treatments are long over, and we're marking time, hoping for another miracle. Trying more chemical options to spur healing along. To break the monotony, we are spending every unoccupied hour outside, in the gardens. This one is called the Gem Court. A garden built for veterans, by veterans, surrounded by a tall brick wall.

In the center stands a century old oak, thicker than a wagon wheel at its base. Squirrels and hummingbirds play in the trumpet vines, wending through a wooden pergola near the lush green stretch of grass. Rose bushes are in bloom. A fountain gurgles nearby, spilling into a small pond with floating lily pads and giant goldfish lazing below. We've already made the full circuit of walking paths. Fifty yards away, another similar garden boasts a sweat lodge.

I'm curious about the sweat lodge. Would they allow my father to enter and participate? Something about that idea appeals to both of us I think. We are drawing closer to some spiritual center. A spring of hope. I am open to everything which might prolong my father's life and prevent or reverse the disease's progress.

Mom and I pluck cherry tomatoes from plants in the raised beds and pop them into our mouths. I munch and they spurt tart juice across my tongue. Dad's dark-haired nurse, still at his side, plucks wild sage and offers the minty green leaves to his olfactory nerves. Anything to bring him joy, to distract him from the reality of what is.

I eyeball a bistro table, hidden beneath the pergola draped in trumpet vine. Writer me pokes her brow and nose above the surface of my consciousness, *hmmmms*. I feel the tug of longing to jot down my thoughts, or better yet, fully submerge into that delicious creative mental space, like the goldfish lazing beneath the lily-pads. I should be taking notes, recording these images and sensations. But I've quit carrying a notepad. My laptop is abandoned on my lonely desktop, at home. The lack of these has left a vacancy in my middle. It is time to remedy that... but how? Every minute is devoted to him, and to Mom, and to kindling connections with my husband and son.

But it has to happen. I can't let go of that, else, what were all those years of dreaming, and efforts to learn the craft—not to mention abandoning my livelihood—for?

―――――――

Weeks later, I hit save and click my laptop shut, tuck it into my backpack, and prepare to depart. Dad's spent hours staring at the ceiling. Months into his illness, we are in a step-down facility, still wearing masks, still seeking places to wait out the hours. Longing for the VA, I approach the nurses' station to find my father's assigned caregivers, noses pointed at their screens.

"My father needs help with a shower and toileting."

Eye rolls are suppressed. "We'll call his aide."

I'm thankful for my mask once again. It hides the rictus of rage twisting my unsmiling mouth. Wait, can't nurses help him with these tasks? Yes. They can. And if they won't, this nurse will.

Though this place is supposedly primo, a *specialty hospital*, it most definitely is not. Unlike the VA, he's just a body here. Not someone of value. Someone who risked his life fighting for his country in Vietnam. Just an old, helpless man with a perpetually grumpy expression. God, what I would do to get back to the VA. We're told before he can return there though, he must be showing some gains. In other words, healing. Regrowing the myelin sheath around his nerves. Acute inpatient rehab isn't an option until then.

This hospital's only redeeming feature is the stream running through a giant campus of posh, now vacant office buildings. And silence. It's the one thing I love best about the time of Covid. The minor traffic issues. Empty parking lots. Privacy for mourning and healing and striving to find ways to keep my father afloat. On our way to the stream, the sidewalk is uneven. He feels every bump, startling, as though I'd let him fall from his wheelchair. We roll into position beside the stream, beneath the trees, and I begin reading. Hemingway's *A Moveable Feast*. My French pronunciation of street names is laughable to say the least.

Start French lessons. Duolingo. Dad's been studying Portuguese, Japanese, and Spanish. He gives me a half smile. He's worried I'm spending too much of my life at his side instead of with my son and husband. I probably should be with them more, but nights have to be all, for now. I can't leave Dad here. Not alone. We can't keep him in this situation much longer. I have to get him out of here. He's spiraling into deep depression.

"Yeah." I smile back. "Great idea." So, of course, I do.

And late that evening when I return home, my desk is quietly welcoming. Words flow onto the page. Writer me smiles and swims in her lily padded dream of words and stories and emotions.

The next day, I call the VA. "Please help us," I beg. "Please. If he has to stay here, he will die from neglect and despair."

We are back at the VA. Therapy here is vigorous. From my perch beside Dad, I glance up from my laptop and watch him with his OT as he manipulates a spoon. Then, off to the PT gym, where my laptop perches on my knees, as Dad precariously balances for the first time in months. Finally, something is working. We're getting through. Getting somewhere, even if we don't yet know where.

It's been six months. We are in a meeting of the entire medical team, negotiating Dad's ongoing care with case managers, neurologists, rehab doctors and nurses, dietitian, PT, OT, social-work, and speech therapy. Mother. Did I forget any?

I ask, "If myelin grows only one millimeter per day... when will this end?"

No one knows. His recovery is slower than expected. But he has survived. This old guy who survived a war is fighting another. We need to get him home. *I* need to get him home.

November 11, 2021, Veterans Day, a van has been called to take Dad home to the farm. To Mom.

The entire staff has gathered, clustering in the hall, seeing him off. He's mastered the use of his highly technical motorized wheelchair. Swallowing and breathing functions are intact. We have all the tools we'll need to care for him, compliments of the VA, including a ramp and his very own ceiling-mounted lift, installed in the newly remodeled downstairs bedroom and bath.

I spread a blanket over his lap and tuck it in around his thighs to begin our triumphant walk to the double bank of elevators, when suddenly his chair jerks ahead, ramming into a custodial cart.

Everyone gasps and jumps to intervene. Dad chuckles. I'd tossed the tail of his blanket over the joystick controller in my haste to meet the schedule which has been set for us. It's entirely my mistake.

Then we're home. Mom's on the porch, hands clasped. Sister's guiding Dad in off-ramping, marshaling air-traffic as usual. Relieved, I'm filming, hiding my tears behind the lens of my cell phone. We are home. Finally.

Meanwhile... I'm like a weather balloon—bombasted in gale-force winds for months—abruptly cut loose, drifting into a calm blue sky. I'm rising, higher, lighter, faster. Back to my own life.

And... I write. I bury myself in it, find healing in it, ensconced in the curated writing space where once I practiced nursing, calling on the help of literary angels to guide me back to where I belong. My desk. My screen. Ensconced in my office, in my make-believe world. It's safe there. And there's a story to write.

November 11th arrives, 2022. *What is it* about this day? In the VA lobby, boxes of cards wait to be distributed to vets receiving care. I gather two from the box. We follow the red line back to the bank of elevators. We read the thank you notes written anonymously by kids in schools around the valley. One for Dad. And mine. I'm a vet after all. We shed tears of thankfulness, and I stick by his side. Assure his care. Turns out I'm still a nurse.

Am I still a *writer*? Of course, I am.

Dad's biannual two-week stint of therapy is coming to a close. It's November 11, 2023. VA Medical Center. Yes, it's Veteran's Day! I carry my computer, opening it often. It doesn't matter where I am. What I'm doing. I practice my profession of writing. Traveling

back to the family farm again and again. Daily life with a growing
son, a forgiving husband. I write while Dad discovers adaptations
in the outpatient therapy clinic. And each day is like a homecoming. People, once strangers behind masks, greet us with bright
smiles in well-lit hallways. *Mr. H! Wow. You're doing so well.
Congratulations*! I'm mesmerized by their faces—the lower halves
—of these wonderful, kind people we've come to know so well.

Dad's been in appointments—therapy and dermatology—
practicing independence. I'm practicing not being a helicopter
daughter. My laptop is open in front of me, the screen glows, my
fingers tap complex rhythms, conjuring magic. A sweet girl, the
cashier with her bubbly disposition, says, "Ma'am I'm sorry... may
I clean your table?" I glance up. Time's flown.

The young girl's smile is kind and understanding. She's seen
me in here plenty, typing away, passing the time, but also focusing
on caring for myself. And this feels like the right place to do it. In
the bowels of the VA hospital, down a long dark tunnel they say
was once the setting for a horror movie. To the cantina (cafeteria to
civilian mortals) sipping bad coffee, eating my lunch from a sack.
Waiting. Typing. Immersed to the gills in creative energy.

I scan the room. The bustle, laughter, bangs of pots and pans,
murmuring of nurses and doctors, patients and soldiers, has
accompanied me for hours. But now, I'm the solitary lunch strag-
gler. I feel a stab of worry. Dad hasn't called. However, he has his
motorized wheelchair and a phone. A tablet. He's become very
handy at communicating via both. He knows where I am.

I stand to gather my things and realize... I'd happily stay. It's
not my office, but I'm comfortable here. As I walk out of the
cantina, I glance into the tiny general store with its veterans' t-
shirts, hats, and nearly everything else you could ever want—
including haute couture perfume on sale for Christmas—and I
realize, I've become very comfortable here on this sprawling
medical campus. His daughter, still a writer... writing, amongst our
people. Soldiers. Caregivers. I *follow the red line* at Dad's side,

through the sliding doors toward the parking terrace. My Doctor Daughter is chatting with Dad on his tablet.

"Happy Veterans Day, Grandpa!"

Grizzly-man winks. He knows I'll be back.

And yes, I'll be writing.

Writing... right where I belong.

The Hindering Hue

Samantha R. Christensen

On a plot of land, in a garden so small,
lived a pink hopper who was lonely and all.
Lilah Lilac, that was her name,
and her hue mismatched their green range.

The other grasshoppers would make fun and jeer
Then point out her color with so snide a sneer.
The "normal" grasshoppers would blend into the shrubs,
While Lilah popped out like bright lights from a hub.

One windy strewn day, with the sun nice and bright,
the gardener came out in happy delight.
With a shovel in hand and a pocket filled with seeds,
the gardener pulled up dead grass and snatched out the weeds.

With a careful hand and lots of care, the gardener planted some
seeds in patches,
With a few here and even more over there.
The days lingered on, but in just a few nights,
sprouts came up to all the grasshoppers' delight.

Seeds took root, and a shrub sprang up from the ground
bearing pink blossoms that really did astound.
"How weird," said the other grasshoppers. "How silly," they all
said.
Instead of green leaves, the bush was practically pink instead.

In less than a day, Lilah Lilac soon found
she was not so solo in the garden sound.
Other pink hoppers all went searching and knew
where the safe-haven pink bush blossomed and grew.

Not all too different, Lilah finally had friends
who were similar to her since they could also blend.
With the new arrivals, all the green grasshoppers decided
to be more kind to all so that they were not so divided.
And Lilah Lilac, although pink, was no longer shunned.
From then on, she was loved, adored, and even welcomed.

About the Authors

C.W. Allen is a Midwestern transplant to rural Utah where she serves as the President-Elect of the League of Utah Writers. She writes long stories for children and short stories for former children. She is also a frequent guest presenter at writing conferences, which helps her procrastinate knuckling down to any actual writing. Her award-winning middle grade fantasy series *The Falinnheim Chronicles* is out now, with many more stories waiting in the wings. Follow her latest projects at cwallenbooks.com.

After forty years in finance, **Linda Allison** enjoys life as a writer, photographer, and explorer. Her essays and poetry have appeared or are forthcoming in *MoonPark Review, Bright Flash Literary Review, The Bluebird Word, Dark Winter Lit,* and others. Her photography has appeared or is forthcoming in *Burningword Literary Journal, The Sunlight Press, and Persimmon Tree.* Linda was awarded first place in the League of Utah Writers 2022 Olive Woolley Burt New Writer Contest.

Rachael Bush published her fourth book, *Love on Location,* with The Wild Rose Press in 2018 under her pen name, September Roberts. As September, she writes romance that's smoking hot and always happy ever after. As Rachael, she writes the *Botany for Everyone* series, because everyone should know the basics of botany. You can find out more at botanyforeveryone.com. When she's not writing, she volunteers as the President of the League of Utah Writers, serves on the Blue Quill Chapter anthology team, and helps build the app for their conferences. For nerdy science and art, follow Rachael on Instagram @botanyforeveryone

A multi-genre, Utah-based writer hailing from the Rust Belt, **Steve Capone, Jr.** can often be found tossing a pizza or haunting a local library. He released *Max in the Capital of Spies: A Max Fredericks Story*—a YA historical fiction / espionage story—in 2024. Look for another of Steve's young adult Cold War novels, *Jimmy vs. Communism* (Gibbs Smith), in 2026. He's won awards for his nonfiction and fiction alike, and his short fiction appears in anthologies like *We Are Dangerous* (LUW Press), *Darkness 102* (Collective Tales Publishing), and *This Isn't the Place* (Timber Ghost Press). Steve is a pizza advocate, dog rescuer, and proud member of the League of Utah Writers and the Horror Writers Association.

Though the furthest thing from a scientist in real life, **Samantha Ruth Christensen** is an alchemist with words and experiments to find a happy medium. She is a sucker for happily ever afters and enjoys reading anything from fantasy to historical fiction. Samantha is from a small town in Utah where she draws, runs, writes, and cherishes the small moments with friends and family. She can be reached at https://linktr.ee/christensensamantha or christensen.sam.r@gmail.com.

Now retired, **Hydee Clayton** spent most of her professional career as a technical writer who, like so many in that field, dreamed of becoming a real writer one day. She writes memoir, short stories, essays, novels, and screenplays. She belongs to two critique groups of aspiring writers and attends writing workshops and seminars as often as possible. Other things that delight her: spending time with family and friends, reading, caring for her cottage-style garden, learning to tap dance, making pretty things with fabric and thread.

Robyn Dabney is an author, copyeditor, and outdoor adventure enthusiast. She describes her stories as having something for everyone—a sprinkle of suspense, a dash of adventure, and a whole lot of good versus evil. She lives in Germany and maintains a home base in Moab, Utah. When she isn't writing, Robyn chats about books as a co-host of the Tipsy Nerds Book Club podcast and plays in the great outdoors.

Wayne Gledhill is new to writing and has had one short story published. He is still looking to have his first novel published. In addition to writing he builds scale model wooden ships.

Brandy Woolley Green is a traveler, both in time and out of it, has lived in over twenty different places, runs a daycare, and is also the mother to six children. When she isn't taking care of her kids and others, she is escaping to find nature wherever it can be found around the "Ogre" (Oquirrh) Mountains. She won eleven Olive Woolley Burt awards for her stories and poems in the space of one night, and has several publications in anthologies. She's written works for children and adults. You will most likely find her on a mountain talking to God.

Alexis Hansen lives in rural Utah and writes sci-fi and fantasy except for when she accidentally writes other stuff. Her favorite hobbies include drawing, sewing, serving as a jungle gym for her many kids in the form of goat yoga, being overrun by piglets, and hiking. She also enjoys going on walks with her dog and fulfilling her honorable duty as a cat bed for her feline overlords. You can find her on Twitter @goatlextales

Melissa Lee Holmes recently graduated with her BA from Weber State University. Her short stories, "Neptune's Landing" and "Eulogy", were published in the literary journal, *Metaphor*, where she won 1st place for short fiction 2019, and 1st place for flash fiction, 2023. She is the author of the dark fantasy series, *The Watchers*. Melissa lives in Northern Utah with her husband and two kids. When she is not writing or deleting what she's recently written, she is usually in the mountains hiking or trail running, or passed out on her paddle board on some lake somewhere.

Lorraine Jeffery has won numerous prizes and published over 150 poems in journals including *Westward Quarterly, Ibbetson St., Clockhouse, Orchard Press, Naugatuck River Review, Halcyone* and *Tahoma*. Her first book, *When the Universe Brings Us Back* was published in 2022. Her chapbook, *Tethers*, was published by Kelsay Books in 2023 and they will also publish *Saltwater Soul* in 2024.

Nicole Dvorak Klunder, originally from Long Island, New York, decided to head west in 2007 with her husband of 18 years to embark on a sunny west coast adventure. If she is not working as a hairdresser, freelancing as a makeup artist, getting lost in the mountains with her husband, or participating in her many other talents, she's falling in love with her new passion: writing. Some of Nicole's poems have been published in anthologies. She has a quarterly newsletter as well as nine blogs posted which are listed on Instagram and Linktree -- you can read them here: klunder | Instagram | Linktree

C.R. Langille spent many a Saturday afternoon watching monster movies with her mom. It wasn't long before she started crafting nightmares to share with her readers. She is a retired, disabled veteran with a deep love for weird and creepy tales. This prompted her to form Timber Ghost Press in January of 2021. She is an affiliate member of the Horror Writers Association, the DEI Chair for the League of Utah Writers, and she received her MFA:

Writing Popular Fiction from Seton Hill University in 2014. Follow her here: https://link.heropost.io/crlangille

Caryn Larrinaga is an internationally best-selling mystery and horror author. Her award-winning works include novels and short stories, as well as content for RPGs, newspapers, and zines, with adaptations for film and audio. In 2021, the League of Utah Writers named her Writer of the Year. Watching scary movies through split fingers terrified Caryn as a child, and those night-mares inspire her to write now. Exploring her fears through writing makes her feel less foolish for wanting a buddy to accompany her into the tool shed. Visit www.carynlarrinaga.com for free short fiction and true tales of haunted places.

Michelle Lee quit her day job, a long and illustrious profession in which she cared for ailing humans, to write. You'll find her happily immersed in words on as many days as life allows, steeped in YA magical realism, adult romantic fiction, or the occasional creative essay. When not writing she spends time dancing in the kitchen to the music of Jazz greats, hiking in the beauty of Utah with the company of her canine companions, or celebrating life with her husband and their four fantastic offspring, always with a story in mind.

C. H. Lindsay (Charlie) is an award-winning poet & writer, housewife, and book-lover—not necessarily in that order. She currently has short stories and poems in over forty anthologies and magazines including *Amazing Stories, Fantasy Magazine, Moonletters, Space and Time Magazine, Strange Horizons*, and *Utah's Best Poetry and Prose*. She is currently working on five novels, six short stories, and at least two dozen poems (although the numbers are always in flux). In 2018 she became Al Carlisle's literary executor. She now publishes his true crime under Carlisle Legacy Books, LLC. She is a member of SFWA, HWA, SFPA, LUW, and is a founding member of the Utah Chapter of the Horror Writers Association. Mostly blind, she lives in Utah with her "seeing-eye husband," library of books, and a bossy cat. You can learn more about her at www.chlindsay.net.

Brooke Losee lives with her husband and three children in central Utah where she enjoys fishing, exploring, and gathering as many rocks as her pockets can hold. Brooke obtained a BS in Geology at Southern Utah University but has always had a passion for all things books. Brooke began her journey to authorhood in 2020 with the notion of publishing one novel. That book turned into a series of seven, and the Pandora's box of ideas was unleashed. Her works range from fantasy to historical, all featuring a sweet and clean romance. To follow her writing journey and keep informed about upcoming stories visit http://www.brookejlosee.com.

Benjamin Martin was a technical writer during his engineering career. Now retired, he enjoys writing creative nonfiction. At age 80, he keeps active by swimming, hiking, and playing racquetball. His wife and he are empty-nesters living in northern Utah.

Pat Partridge writes across genres. He is the author of the mystery *Fragile Memories*, the sequel, *Buried at Bears Ears*, and the humorous road-trip novel *Fast on Fifty*. His book of political humor is now in its third edition. Over the past two years he has won nine awards from the League of Utah Writers for his short fiction and novel first chapters. Recently, his short fiction has appeared in *Remington Review, The Haven, Fabula Argentea, Ariel Chart, Litro,* and multiple anthologies. He is pleased others find his writing worth reading.

David Rodeback came to American Fork, Utah, in 1998 after roughly a decade each in urban Colorado, rural Idaho, and upstate New York. By day a C-level officer of a manufacturing company in

West Valley City, by night he prefers to write contemporary realism, mostly. His novellas and short stories are published in two collections, *The Dad Who Stayed and Other Stories* and *Poor As I Am and Other Stories at Christmas*.

T. Rodriguez is a teacher and advocate for those without a voice. Immigrant children, dogs, and half-dead plants on clearance at her grocery store are a few recipients of her efforts. While the rest of the world sleeps in the early hours of morning, she writes short stories and poetry—pretending that writing is the only thing happening in her life.

M. Rohr enjoys sharing about the hard things in life in hopes it will make the journey just a little easier for someone else. Her creative nonfiction focuses on addiction and her experiences growing up with a Borderline parent.

Maggie Russell is an emerging writer whose works have been published in *Willows Wept Review, Witcraft, BTB Hits* (forthcoming), *Elephant Journal* and *Dark Ink*. She writes nonfiction on financial topics and publishes a semi-regular Substack on the intersection of faith and illness called *Extra-Ordinary*. Raised by the woods in Connecticut, she now lives close to the mountains in Utah with her husband and pets.

Talysa Sainz is a freelance editor and award-winning author who believes life's deepest truths can be found in fiction. She runs her own editing business and spends her time at the library or volunteering with the League of Utah Writers. Always fascinated with the structure of words, she studied English Linguistics and Editing at BYU. She then went on to receive a Master of Science in Management and Leadership, focusing on nonprofit work, from WGU. Talysa is the President of the Utah Freelance Editors.

Michael Shoemaker is a poet, writer and photographer from Magna, Utah where he lives with his wife and son and where he enjoys looking out on the Great Salt Lake every day. He is the author of *Rocky Mountain Reflections* (Poets' Choice, 2023). His writing has appeared in *Blue Lake Review, Literary Revelations Journal, The High Window, Seashores Haiku Journal, The Penwood Review* and in anthologies at *Pure Slush* and *Echoes of the Wild*. One of his poems is on the shortlist for The Letter Review Prize for Poetry and in the anthology of the Rio Grande Valley International Poetry Festival.

Linda F. Smith has focused on creative writing since her retirement from her job as a law professor at the University of Utah S. J. Quinney College of Law. (She also sneaks in some brief writing for good causes.) She lives in Salt Lake City with her husband, Lee Shuster, and their goofy Golden Retriever Chance; has fun watching two local grandkids play sports; and travels to Ohio to manage affairs for her 100-year-old mother Lil.

Marie Tollstrup hails from a Wisconsin potato farm. In 1951 at fourteen, she entered a convent, the School Sisters of St. Francis, in Milwaukee. After graduating from Alverno College with a BA in English, she taught as a nun for ten years in Schiller Park and Wilmette in the Chicago area where she earned an MA in English from Loyola University. At Jordan High School in Long Beach, California, where she taught twenty-nine years, she founded and advised *STYLUS*, a national award-winning literary/arts magazine for twenty-three years. In retirement, Marie focuses on poetry, but branches out to prose where she enters contests, winning awards for speaking her mind and poetic word play. Her poetry has been published in UTSPS's *Panorama* for ten years, in thirteen League of Utah Writers' volumes, and in ASPS's *SAND-CUTTERS*. Read her published poems and prose in LUW's publications.

Debra Birdwell Winkler is a published author who is passionate about sharing her stories. As a former history teacher, Debra weaves historical events into her stories as well as music. Whether creating short stories, essays, novels, or poems, she excitedly devotes full concentration on writing -- her focus, her job, and her joy (second only to her family). Debra's debut novel came out November 2022 and several of her short stories have been published in Anthologies and online. She was nominated for the 2022 Best of the Net NonFiction Award. Debra is an active member of RWA and LUW Romance Chapter. While reading her story, "Finding Write Where I Belong," Debra suggests listening to Rachmaninoff's "Rhapsody on a Theme of Paganini (Variation 18)".

wᵐ**david** is a retired political scientist and park ranger/naturalist who spent a career writing creative nonfiction for museums, visitor centers, and magazines. His writings and photography have been featured in national visitor centers, museum displays & brochures, as well as by the Associated Press and the National Science Center. His current work in poetry and prose combines natural, spiritual & human elements, sometimes aligned but often juxtaposed. His pieces have recently been featured internationally in *Better Than Starbucks* and *Littoral* Magazines, as well as in *The Berkeley Fiction Review, The Writing Disorder, Kennings Literary Review, The Anglican Digest, Christian Ethics Today, Utah's Best Poetry & Prose, Rememberings,* and *Rundelania*. He currently resides on the slopes of Mt. Ogden, Utah with his wife, thirteen guitars, and a well-worn pair of hiking boots.

Daniel Yocom writes about geeky things because people say to write what you know. Their love of the geeky, nerdy community dates to the 1960s through games, books, movies, and stranger things better shared in small groups. They're an award-winning writer and editor of short stories, books, and hundreds of articles published by blogs, magazines, and gaming companies. They enjoy attending conferences, conventions, festivals, sharing on panels, and presentations. They currently serve on the boards of the LTUE Writing Symposium and the League of Utah Writes as the president of the Infinite Monkeys Genre Writers chapter, they want to help others become the writer/author/creatives others desire to be. Join them at www.guildmastergaming.com.

More From the League of Utah Writers

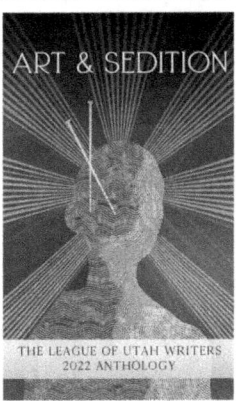

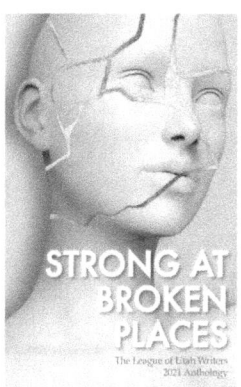

Find all our anthologies at leagueofutahwriters.com

What can the League of Utah Writers do for you?

The League of Utah Writers is a non-profit organization dedicated to offering friendship, education, and encouragement to the writers and poets of Utah. Our organization aids our members in the improvement of their craft and support of their goals.

The League of Utah Writers is a vibrant writing community with chapters throughout the state, as well as online with members across the country. Membership in the League of Utah Writers provides support and opportunities for writers and editors at all levels of their careers.

Join us at www.leagueofutahwriters.com

The Pre-Quill Conference

Pre-Quill is the League of Utah Writers' Spring writing conference - a day long event of classes, workshops, and networking with other wordsmiths.

This event showcases our local Utah writers in classes and courses geared to each unique voice and talent. It is also a great place to start working on stories, poetry, or any of the other categories listed in the Wooley awards - the League's prestigious contest awarded at the annual Quills conference each year.

Pre-Quill helps refresh your creative neurons with the pulse and energy only spring could bring.

Find more about The Pre-Quill Conference at
www.leagueofutahwriters.com

The League of Utah Writers invites you to join us for the Quills Conference, hosted locally in Salt Lake City annually near the end of summer.

The Quills Conference is the League's premium event, bringing in special guest authors, agents, editors, and publishers from around the nation.

This four-day writing conference is for everyone from the fresh voices not yet published to the well-established writers seeking to make a difference in their writing community.

The Quills Conference's annual banquet is also home to The Woolley Awards writing contest and the Quill Awards for published works.

Find out more about Quills at
www.leagueofutahwriters.com